"I've got an idea.

Heather reached across the console to take Zach's hand. "What do you say if we not worry about any of it right now? It's a beautiful, clear night." With her other hand, she turned up the radio. A simple guitar melody filled the air. "And there's a slow song playing in the background. Let's just dance and enjoy it."

"Dance?"

As if he needed any persuasion to wrap her in his arms.

She nodded. "Right here. In the moonlight."

He looked up at the Tennessee sky, the night so clear thousands of stars twinkled brightly overhead. The autumn breeze stirred the leaves in a soft shushing sound, as if nature were telling him to slow down and drink it all in.

Zach switched the car to accessory mode so that only the radio remained on, and then he slid out the driver's door to open hers. The moon hung low on the horizon, slanting gray shadows over them as he held out a hand for her.

Heather stepped across the brick walkway into his embrace as if she was meant to be there...

Dear Reader,

I have long wanted to write about a heroine with a chronic condition. Having battled my own, and seeing others do the same, I know there are many responses to ongoing illness or disease. It's easy to be overwhelmed by pain, fatigue or the frustration of not being able to accomplish things that are simple for others. Some days, I'm overwhelmed, too. But I'm always inspired by the people who battle year in and year out, keeping their doctor appointments and doing whatever they can to manage their condition and maintain the best health possible.

My heroine is a long way from there! But part of managing a chronic condition is figuring out how you will respond to it, and how big a role you will allow those health issues to play in your life. You do have choices and there are elements of chronic conditions you can control. Stay informed. Get lots of opinions. And don't forget to reach around you for a little help sometimes. You will be surprised how many people reach back!

Thank you for spending time with me in Heartache, TN, one of my favorite places. I love to hear from readers online. You can find me on Facebook at facebook.com/joannerockauthor and Twitter, @JoanneRock6.

Happy Reading,

Joanne Rock

JOANNE ROCK

Dances Under
the Harvest Moon

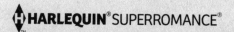

Recycling programs
for this product may
not exist in your area.

ISBN-13: 978-0-373-60930-7

Dances Under the Harvest Moon

Copyright © 2015 by Joanne Rock

Printed in U.S.A.

While working on her master's degree in English literature, **Joanne Rock** took a break to write a romance novel and quickly realized a good book requires as much time as a master's program itself. She became obsessed with writing the best romance possible, and sixty-some novels later, she hopes readers have enjoyed all the "almost there" attempts. Today, Joanne is a frequent workshop speaker and writing instructor at regional and national writer conferences. She credits much of her success to the generosity of her fellow writers, who are always willing to share insights on the process. More important, she credits her readers with their kind notes and warm encouragement over the years for her joy in the writing journey.

Books by Joanne Rock

HARLEQUIN SUPERROMANCE

Heartache, TN

Promises Under the Peach Tree
Nights Under the Tennessee Stars

HARLEQUIN BLAZE

Double Play
Under Wraps

Highly Charged!
Making a Splash
Riding the Storm
One Man Rush
Her Man Advantage
Full Surrender
My Double Life
"Presents Under the Tree" in *A Soldier's Christmas*
My Secret Fantasies

Visit the Author Profile page at Harlequin.com for more titles.

For Dean, the keeper of my heart
along with our three boys.

CHAPTER ONE

STARING INTO HER SUITCASE, Heather Finley wondered what a twenty-eight-year-old should pack to run away from home.

A lifetime "good girl," Heather hadn't tried running away as a ten-year-old, like most kids. As an adult, she knew she needed more than clean underwear and chocolate chip cookies. Although, come to think of it, she definitely wanted both of those. Peeling off her floral headpiece, she tossed aside her last commitment to Heartache, Tennessee.

At least, for a little while.

"Isn't it supposed to be the bride who packs a bag during the wedding reception?"

Heather turned to see her older sister, Erin, in the doorway of the bedroom they'd shared as kids. Swathed in white and incredibly gorgeous, Erin had her caramel-colored hair pulled back in a loose knot with a vintage rhinestone pin secured to the twist.

Outside, the backyard wedding reception was in full swing. Dinner had been served and guests danced, even though it wasn't fully dark yet. Twilight had just fallen and the purple Chinese lanterns around the white canvas tents had turned on a few minutes ago. Heather could see the party from the big bay window overlooking the backyard. She'd always loved this room—including the years she'd shared it with Erin. It had been a retreat from the craziness of the Finley household and their mom's notorious mood swings. Heather and Erin had spent the last two nights before Erin's wedding to Remy Weldon in their childhood bedroom, enjoying girl time and giggling about Erin's future as a married woman.

"Have I told you that you are the most beautiful bride?" Heather got teary just looking at Erin today. Not only because she adored her sister and was happy she'd found a supportive, grounded, hunky Cajun partner for life, but also because Heather wouldn't be seeing her for a while once she left town.

She may have also gotten teary because she was lying about her reasons for leaving Heartache. The guilt was killing her, even if her reasons were excellent.

"You may have mentioned the beautiful-bride thing." Erin grinned as she twirled her way across the hardwood floor of the old farmhouse, watching her floor-length tulle skirt swirl. "But since I'm so in love with this dress, I don't mind another compliment." She stopped beside Heather and clutched her arm to steady herself after the last spin. "That is, of course, unless you're doling out praise to distract me from my question about why you're packing when the party is still going strong?"

Erin pointed out the window where two hundred of their closest friends and family danced to the tunes of a popular country band their brother, Mack, had convinced to play. As the owner of a bar in Nashville, Mack had access to great musicians—lucky for him. For all her love of music, Heather was still stuck in Heartache teaching scales to resistant nine-year-olds.

She squeezed Erin's shoulders, careful of the sheer lace bodice that transformed the dress from fairy tale to sophisticated—and perfect for Erin's eclectic taste. The cut was simple and sleeveless, the lace's pattern dramatic with see-through sections. Paired with the simple fall of straight tulle, the wedding gown was unlike anything Heather had ever seen.

"I'm not trying to distract you. Trying to distract *myself* from my nerves is more like it." She managed a half smile for a half-truth. She definitely would have been happy to sidetrack her sister from this topic. She was jittery enough without justifying her need to leave town.

Or telling more lies.

"You know I'm going to be rooting for you all the way, right?" Erin plunked down onto the chenille bedspread on one of three matching single beds. They used to play Goldilocks and the Three Bears when they were kids, pretending to try out all three beds lined up in a row, headboards tucked under the eaves.

That third bed—their sister Amy's—had been glaringly empty. The youngest Finley sibling hadn't attended the wedding. She hadn't set foot in Tennessee after leaving home at seventeen because of an argument with their mom. Heather had been out of town at the time. She had been devastated to return home to find Amy filing paperwork to become an emancipated minor. Amy had refused all money from their father and accused the family of enabling their mother's behavior.

"I know." Heather was grateful for Erin's support about her new adventure, especially when Erin had so much on her mind with her honeymoon and the transition to being a stepmother with a teenage daughter.

"You're so talented," Erin said. "It's about damn time you let the world see your bright light shine."

Heather had sold her share of the consignment store she owned with Erin back to her sister so she could follow her own dreams—finally. As a part-time music teacher and full-time worker with Last Chance Vintage, Heather had always imagined trying her luck at singing, but up until now, she'd found too many reasons to put off stepping out of her comfort zone. Her family needed her. Her bipolar mother, especially, needed her. But there were other things, too. Heather volunteered at the local parks and recreation department, trying to maintain civic ties to the community, which had been important to her father. She had music students who counted on her. She'd also been a driving force getting Last Chance Vintage off the ground. But now Erin had really made the shop her own, expanding it to double the former size. And after a recent health-scare reality check, Heather was done putting her own life on hold.

"It seemed like the right time to give it a try now that *American Voice* is holding auditions in Charlotte." Heather's gaze wandered the room in an effort to change the subject. While she knew she had Erin's support, she hadn't really talked about how long she would be gone or how *soon* she planned to ditch town. And she didn't want to slide into that particular chat right now.

Heather's friend and former music student, Sylvia, had offered her a place to stay in Nashville for a couple of months if she wanted to knock on some doors in the country-music business. It was a good plan B. "But you didn't come up here to listen to me talk about my plans. Where's your suitcase? Can I help you pack for your honeymoon?"

She moved to Erin's bed—still unmade from the night before when they'd painted each other's toenails and eaten popcorn while watching movies. Plucking at a corner of the spread where it pooled on the floor, she reached for the handle of Erin's train case.

"That's okay. We're not leaving yet. We're thinking about waiting around until after the wedding breakfast tomorrow since there are so many friends from out of town we'd like to visit with." Erin stood and pulled the curtains over the windows, making the room darker. "Right now, I thought I'd change dresses so I can really cut loose on the dance floor."

"Of course." Heather let go of the luggage and hurried toward the closet. "Did you decide what to wear yet?" She pulled out a couple of hotly debated options. "The pink lace halter dress or the blue satin pinup-girl number?"

"Remy warned me not to wear the satin one. He says he won't last ten minutes in public with me in that dress." Erin's smile glowed with that "I'm sexy and I know it" brand of joy a well-satisfied woman tended to get. Not that Heather would know anything about that. Her last relationship had been with a guy she'd chosen because he'd checked all the right boxes.

No wonder they'd had zero chemistry.

"In other words, it comes down to this. Do you want to torment the groom a lot?" She held up the slinky blue one. "Or a little?" She held up the pink one, which was still a stunner.

Then again, everything looked amazing on a woman who had that "I'm sexy and I know it" glow.

"Maybe just a little." Erin slid down the side zipper of her wedding dress and stepped out of it. She handed the gown to Heather and took the pink lace. "I still can't believe I'm a married woman six months after meeting the man of my dreams."

"When it's right, you know it." Heather's heart had hurt for Erin when her private sister had finally opened up about Mr. Not Right, who had come before Remy—a guy who'd been married to someone else and never let on while dating Erin.

The Finley family had precedents for keeping their private lives on the down low since their mother tended to feed off strong emotions and unhappiness, making them her own until her kids ended up comforting *her* over their misfortunes.

"Exactly. Why wait to start your future when you know what you want?" Erin wriggled her way into the slim-fitting lace. "That's why I'm so excited for you to have an adventure of your own. I never knew you were so passionate about singing."

"Still waters run deep." Heather winked at her sister and fixed a few strands of hair that had slid free. "Are you going to keep the brooch in your hair or do you want me to take it out?"

"I'll leave it." Erin patted one side absently.

She'd never been the kind to spend a lot of time on her looks, even though she wore the most interesting clothes of anyone in town. She had an artsy flare that worked for her, whether that meant she had pink streaks in her hair one day or Goth-girl black strands the next. "You ready to come down and dance? You can pack tomorrow, right?"

Heather had told everyone she was leaving after the wedding. But she'd thought she could slip out as soon as Erin and Remy took off for their honeymoon. Leave it to Erin to party half the night.

She swallowed.

"Right. I just wish I was more organized for my trip. You know how I am…always trying to plan ten steps ahead."

That had been true right up until she had an acute onset of rheumatoid arthritis. When she'd been on a buying trip for the store, she'd had a flare-up so bad she literally couldn't move. The pain and stiffness had sent her to the hospital for a battery of tests until a doctor had come up with the diagnosis. The disease wasn't life threatening, but it was a serious immune system disorder with lifelong consequences. Different from regular arthritis that most people experienced as they aged or as a result of old sports injuries, the rheumatoid variety meant a body's immune system attacked its own connective tissue, pretty much just for the hell of it.

Getting ahead of the problem would mean draining bouts of strong medication until the doctors discovered what worked best with her body chemistry. There was no one drug that worked for everyone, and Heather desperately wanted to investigate some homeopathic remedies, too.

Receiving the diagnosis while she'd been on the road—in Austin, Texas, and all alone—had made her realize how much she preferred the quiet of her own thoughts as she sorted through what the diagnosis meant for her. She didn't want the Finley family hubbub around her right now. She wanted to focus on herself. And more important, she wanted to start living her dreams. It didn't matter if she was tired. If she flared up. Or if her new medicines didn't agree with her. The health scare had made her reassess. She'd realized she'd been living a safe, boring life and never taking hold of the reins for herself.

She was so done planning ten steps ahead.

"Well, you can organize once I'm in the Cajun bayous with Remy for my honeymoon." Erin dug in the other side of the closet. "Plus, I think the mayor has his eye on you. You should wear the satin siren-girl dress and see what happens."

Heather did not want to think about the long looks Zach Chance had been giving her lately. She'd hoped it was her imagination, even if he was one of the most sought-after single men in Heartache. Now was definitely not the time to get involved with anyone.

Besides, Zach was…the mayor. She was putting small-town life behind her, not campaigning for it. He seemed to see her as her father's daughter—himself a former mayor of Heartache. But Heather was about to change all that good-girl stuff before her body started wearing out prematurely. Who knew how long her window of good mobility would be?

She smiled. "First of all, my boobs wouldn't hold up that dress in a million years. Second, *you're* going to be the star of the show tonight." She reached for a yellow sundress instead. "How about this for me?"

"Too sweet and not nearly sexy enough. There are hot guys down there, Heather. Come on. Did you see Remy's brothers?" Erin dug deeper into the closet and emerged with a bright pink jersey dress with cutouts at the waist. "Here."

"Redheads don't do fuchsia. And yes, your brothers-in-law are definitely turning heads." Armand and Landry Weldon were as handsome as their brother, Remy, and their Cajun accents had all the women in town swooning.

Erin tugged the dress off the hanger anyway. "It's berry, not fuchsia, and don't argue with the bride."

"Okay, but keep in mind you'll have to see

this eye abomination in your wedding album for the rest of time." Heather slid off the simple lavender maid-of-honor dress, which Erin had let her choose for her big day. Laying it on the bed, Heather slipped the bright jersey over her head and pulled the fabric to cover her hips.

It was surprisingly comfortable, even if the diamond-shaped cutouts bared skin on either side of her waist.

"Hoochie mama." Erin whistled. "Now *that's* a dress." Picking up the discarded daisy floral crown from the bed, she pulled three flowers out of it and tucked the stems behind Heather's ear. "You ready to have some fun?" Her cornflower-blue eyes roamed Heather's face.

"I'm ready." She would have to delay her great escape for a few hours to make her sister happy. She hoped her joints stayed quiet for a little longer. Her right wrist throbbed a little, but she could ice it later. "I'm simply not going to look in any mirrors."

"Would I send you out into the world unless you looked gorgeous? Give me some credit. I'm kind of a professional at dressing people."

True enough. Besides her work at Last Chance Vintage, Erin had single-handedly started a hugely successful Dress for Success initiative to help women in tough economic situations find great outfits for job interviews. So many clothes had been donated to the cause that Erin had enough to sponsor a mobile unit that traveled to remote parts of the state where poverty was the worst.

"I know. I don't always have the same bold aesthetic as you." But she was going to try harder, right? She'd promised herself that when she left town, she would start breaking a few rules. She had a lot of lost time to make up.

"Once you're competing on *American Voice* in front of the whole country, you're going to have to find your boldness." Erin swept Heather's long red curls behind one shoulder. "Why don't you practice tonight by letting your hair down and shaking your moneymaker?"

Erin swatted her on the butt before darting in front of her and rushing down the stairs, cackling the whole way.

"My moneymaker?" Heather called down, following more slowly. "I'm definitely going to tell your groom to cut off your champagne supply," she teased as she spotted Remy in the kitchen at the foot of the staircase.

Surrounded by his brothers, along with Zach Chance, the very man Heather had been avoiding, Remy seemed to be involved in a drinking game. All four guys held shot glasses in hand, a dark bottle resting on the open bar cabinet between them.

"Looks like we've moved beyond champagne,"

Erin noted dryly, pulling her new husband's attention from his empty glass.

Remy's approval of the dress was obvious as he moved toward Erin faster than if magnets pulled them together. He kissed her thoroughly, to the delight of his brothers, who contributed howls and wolf whistles that drew the attention of the catering staff in the kitchen. Zach kept his eyes on Heather, his quiet, focused gaze missing nothing.

"We're taste-testing Harlan Brady's distilling efforts," he informed her, pulling another shot glass out of the bar cabinet while Remy and Erin finally came up for air.

Zach wore khaki pants and a vest, his jacket discarded in deference to the warm evening. The guys in the wedding party were dressed similarly, with gray vests and pants. One of Remy's brothers had lost his tie, his white dress shirt unbuttoned at the collar. But no matter, the group of men in the farmhouse dining room made for a formidable bunch, all thick shouldered and well built.

Still, it was Zach who held her attention. He'd grown up in Heartache, so he was a local guy. Yet even back in high school, he'd exuded a prep-school vibe, which suggested more money and better breeding. The more-money part was true—his father had made a fortune in the stock market. But the better-breeding part? Not so much. Zach's dad went to jail for securities fraud, creating a huge scandal in the small town and far beyond. Zach worked hard to make people forget that, by volunteering at a nursing home as a teen, charming all the teachers and generally doing everything "right."

His light brown hair was perfect, for example. Neither too short nor too long, it always looked as though a woman's fingers had just tousled a few strands. His clothes were well pressed, surprising after a day when everyone else was starting to rumple.

To be honest, he had looked like the mayor when he was a senior in high school. Heather had been a year behind him. He'd left town for college on the West Coast and returned last year wealthier than before. Not that Heather cared about any of that. If anything, it made it tougher to like Zach, as he had the appearance of a man who breezed through life, while others slogged to get ahead. No, the thing that drew her to Zach was simply this: he had a slow, brooding way of looking at her that made her insides tingle. She felt the awareness hum through her now as she closed her eyes to force herself not to look at him.

"Count us in," Erin announced. "Heather?"

She opened her eyes, her cheeks heating. "What?"

Erin waved her closer, but Heather kept her gaze locked to Remy's. "If Harlan brewed it himself, it seems only polite we give it a try."

"I draw the line at moonshine." She edged around the newlyweds to stand closer to the door. How could she drink Harlan Brady's potent brew when she planned on driving tonight?

Not to mention the medications she'd already started taking. Two of them came with the "absolutely no alcohol warning" label.

Zach set a fresh glass for Erin on the counter and followed Heather out of the dining area. "Wise move skipping the home brew." He lowered his voice for her ears only as they passed through the family room toward the glass doors leading to the patio. "Harlan's got a ways to go in his distillery skills."

"You being an expert in moonshine?" She wasn't the sarcastic type, but the words leaped out anyhow.

Something about Zach's polished ease had always ruffled her a little. Maybe she envied his confidence. His perfect sense of belonging at all times. He'd done such a good job separating himself from his father's criminal life, emerging a small-town hero when he took over the mayor's job after Heather's father had passed away. Only a few weeks after he'd arrived back in Heartache, in fact.

"Connoisseur of moonshine is on the list of qualifications for mayor. I thought it best to prepare myself for the job." He paused near the fireplace, not moving any closer to the patio doors.

Country music vibrated the window panes, the tempo of the night kicking up a notch.

"My father must not have been as dedicated," she shot back, reminding him of the Finley family's lock on the mayor's seat for over a decade.

She was jittery and off balance. She told herself it was because she'd already had one foot out the door when Erin had thwarted her plan to take off. It definitely wasn't because of the way Zach Chance wore a shirt. Or the way he smelled like bay rum and sexy male.

Realizing how close they stood, she skittered a step back.

"I'm pretty sure your father just kept the still far from the house." Zach surprised her with a smile.

The easy, lazy, heir-to-the-throne smile that had won him the job after her father died. Not that Zach had campaigned. He was the write-in candidate of choice—a natural leader. His return to town had been front-page news in the local rumor mill.

"He did like a good tailgate party," Heather admitted, even though Zach was teasing. Probably. "I'm pretty sure he chose to entertain far from home to ensure none of us would embarrass him."

"Everyone knew how much your father loved his family." Zach turned serious. "Family first, right?" He quoted her dad's favorite line, which he had often used while assuring the people of Heart-ache that they were all part of his personal clan.

"So he said." However, her father had spent very little time with his flesh and blood and made very little effort to help manage his wife's severe bipolar disorder. All his energy went to building a business and then rebuilding the town. She took another step back, her ankle jamming into an ottoman. "I'd probably better check on my mom."

Yeah, color her lame. She always made excuses to escape from talking to cute guys by running to mama. But she had too much emotional flotsam in her head to sort through whatever was happening between her and Zach.

"Of course." He was so smooth, so socially adept, he never let on that he found her as awkward as a preteen. Straightening, he reached for her. "May I?"

His hand hovered near her cheek.

Her heart rate spiked and she didn't trust herself to speak. Let alone move. She managed a nod.

Gently, he pulled away two of the daisies that Erin had tucked behind her ear. She'd forgotten all about them.

"Two of these are turning the wrong way." He set them aside and adjusted the one remaining flower, giving her plenty of time to absorb the warmth of his fingertips against her scalp.

The silky flutter of her hair along her neck as he moved a few strands.

Her mouth went dry. She stood so close to him, her gaze eye level with his throat and the strong column of his neck above his crisp white collar. Despite the dimly lit room, she could see the bristle of whiskers shadowed there. Imagine the feel of his skin if she were to touch him.

Disconcerted by those thoughts, she risked a glance higher. Only to have her gaze drawn to his square jaw and full, sensual mouth. Quickly, she looked down.

Only to see his broad shoulders and lean torso tapering to narrow hips. Strong thighs.

"There." He stood back to admire his handiwork.

Not—she reminded herself—*her.*

Her face flamed as she mentally finished undressing the mayor. What was wrong with her?

"Thanks," she muttered, cursing herself for noticing Zach.

Fleeing the scene before she did something stupid—like taste the moonshine or possibly even the man—Heather rushed out of the house and away from temptation. Unfortunately, she couldn't escape from the images now burned into her brain after that close encounter. Why the hell had she let her imagination run away and not the rest of her?

She had no idea what he'd been thinking to corner her like that. What did he want from her?

She sighed. Heather had taken a lot of time to sew up loose ends in town so she'd be ready to leave Heartache after Erin's wedding. Now her sister was married and laughing in the kitchen with her new husband. Heather's work here was done. She had a life to get on track and an illness to battle.

The sooner she left, the better. Zach Chance could remain safely in her fantasies and well out of her life.

CHAPTER TWO

RUMOR HAD IT that Heather Finley was leaving Heartache.

Zach just hadn't realized she would be going at a dead sprint.

Now, three hours later, he drove around the outskirts of town in an '87 Mercedes convertible, a relic from his dad's heyday as a car collector. Zach had hoped the night air would blow some sense into his head, but half an hour into the drive and he still stewed over the fact that Heather Finley was moving on.

That sucked for several reasons, not the least of which was that he had his eye on her. She'd fascinated Zach back in high school. The world would be at a fever pitch around her—a pep rally, a football game or a fight in the hall—and she'd be the calm eye of the storm, her long auburn waves always falling in perfect curls along her shoulders. Her clothes were timeless and feminine when every other girl in school decided combat boots were the thing to have. Heather was never part of an in crowd, yet everyone liked her. She championed other Finleys, never showing up at school functions unless she was there to support her drum-majorette sister or her football-playing brothers.

Zach had been curious about her then, but he'd needed to move on after school to put his father's crimes behind him—along with his own guilt at the way his sister had fallen apart afterward.

Pounding a fist on the steering wheel, Zach turned onto the interstate at the last minute, needing to pick up more speed than the roads around Heartache allowed. Sure, he had an aversion to scandal after the media circus of his father's arrest, but that didn't mean he led a perfect life. He just chose his moments to put the gas pedal to the floor and blow the cobwebs out of his head.

He knew Heather would be a perfect mayor for Heartache. She'd grown up there. She clearly cared about the town, what with all the hours she volunteered at the recreation department, spearheading summer volleyball leagues and importing talented coaches to conduct camps for their youth. Plus, she had business sense, evident by her successful storefront with her sister. The fact that she had a thriving sideline as a private music teacher proved how much all the local kids liked her. And of course she juggled all of that and still looked after her widowed mother, taking Diana Finley to doctor's appointments for the bipolar disorder that had crippled her for years, and making sure her mom stayed on her medicine.

Heather was a quiet dynamo.

Cranking up the radio louder, he tucked a finger in the knot of his necktie and loosened it a fraction of an inch, just enough to unfasten the top button of his shirt. He should have made his personal interest in Heather known earlier this year, but he'd been steamrolled by work and then—when he'd planned to see her at a rec-league soccer tournament she'd organized—he'd discovered she'd gone out of town on a buying trip for Last Chance Vintage.

The timing had been crap, as it had been since he'd moved back to Heartache. Shortly after he'd arrived, she lost her father, the town's previous mayor. Definitely not the time to start something with her. Then he'd gotten caught up in small-town politics when the town council had called him to fill the vacancy. He'd gotten the most write-in votes, tying with a country star, a comic-strip dog and Heather Finley herself. The council had talked him into it, slyly suggesting that Heather—a sensible woman with "a good head on her shoulders"—might be persuaded to take over the spot in the future.

So, yeah, Zach hadn't just been interested in Heather personally when he approached her tonight. He'd also wanted to see if there was any chance in hell she'd be done with this itch to audition for a singing show in time for the next election. She'd volunteered with the town's recreation department for years, as civic-minded as the rest of her family. Zach planned to offer his campaign skills himself if it meant quitting the job to make time for personal business he needed to follow up on. Besides, he hated the petty infighting and backstabbing of small-town politics and had little patience for it, whereas he pictured Heather smoothing over it all with one wave of her capable hand.

Too bad Ms. Good Head On Her Shoulders was committed to ditching the town she grew up in.

Frustrated about his failure with Heather, he was distracted by the time he saw a car on the side of the road. A vehicle ahead of him had moved to the passing lane to avoid the blue sedan on the shoulder that looked kind of familiar...

Heather?

Taking his foot off the gas, Zach squinted at the older-model luxury-sized Nissan on the shoulder of the road. A heart-shaped bumper sticker was prominent in the back windshield—the logo for Erin Finley's Dress for Success program. No doubt about it, that was Heather Finley's car on the side of the interstate.

He slammed on the brakes.

He pulled onto the shoulder a few hundred feet in front of her, and checked his rearview mirror to be sure there was no one in front of the car. Slowly, he put it in Reverse.

It was past midnight. Other cars flew by them

at seventy miles an hour, the headlights a blur.
The sedan had been parked with no lights on, not
even the hazards. He couldn't see anyone in the
vehicle. What the hell?

Stepping out of the convertible, he shut the
door and jogged back to the other car.

"Zach?" Heather's voice rose from outside the
car…somewhere near the rear passenger fender
as she straightened from wherever she'd been
crouching. "Is that you?"

She still wore the knockout dress she'd changed
into for dancing at her sister's reception. Bright,
short and clingy, the dress gave him a whole lot
of reasons to like it. He'd bet money her sister had
chosen it for her since Heather was the type to
wear gray flannel pencil skirts with creamy silk
blouses. Both of which now occasionally figured
in his fantasies. But the bright pink showed off a
whole other side of Ms. Proper.

A tractor trailer barreled past them, rattling
his teeth.

He edged between his bumper and her hood.

"Car trouble?" He forced himself to be casual
as he leaned against her car. Friendly. The last
thing he wanted was to send her running again.

What if fate had kept her in town—right where
she belonged?

"So it would seem." She bit her lip, her hesi-
tation illuminated by the single headlight of a
speeding motorcycle. What was it about him that

had her putting up defenses when they barely knew each other? She sighed. "And I was starting to get paranoid that I heard someone in the bushes over there, so it's nice to see a friendly face."

Zach peered into the dark woods off to the side of the highway, his skin chilling with an old memory of those woods. His fists tightened and he forced himself to relax.

"That land backs up to the quarry. There haven't been cougar sightings in town for a long time. Although a black bear could be trouble." Was it wrong to try to terrify her into jumping into his arms?

"Yes. Well." She rolled her eyes. "Lucky for me you're here."

"So what's the trouble with the car?"

"Apparently, you need gas to run these things." She meandered closer and he noticed she'd traded her strappy high heels for a pair of flip-flops. His gaze tracked to the diamond-shaped cutouts in her dress that fell along her narrow waist.

"I've heard as much." He cocked his thumb at the trunk. "Do you keep a spare container back here?"

His gaze dropped to the flat rear tire he hadn't noticed before.

"Er. No. I got nervous when the car stalled, and steered off the road sort of sharply." She frowned at the tire she must have been inspecting when he'd arrived.

"You hit a rock?" The tire was beyond flat.

"A boulder roughly the size of Texas." She had an edge in her voice that he'd never heard before.

Then again, he'd never gotten to know her nearly as well as he would have liked to.

"I'm not much with a car jack," he admitted. "Give me a computer and I'm the man of the hour. But cars?" He shook his head. "I only know how to drive them. And keep the tank filled."

She shot him a sideways glance. He'd hoped for a smile, but nothing doing. Her lips pursed, her jaw jutting.

"Changing the tire won't help when I have no gas," she pointed out, illuminated by the blinding LED fog lights of a pickup truck blasting country tunes out the open windows. "I'd better get a tow."

He waited while she called the only local tow truck service, the Elliot brothers. The Elliots were farmers who had a garage on the side. When she clicked off, he smiled.

"I'll stay with you until they get here. And I can definitely give you a ride wherever you're headed." He offered because he was a good guy like that and not because he had any intention of ogling the smooth skin above her hip.

Much.

"It's a long way to North Carolina," she observed drily. "Especially for a guy who was testing the moonshine a few hours ago."

"First, I swilled about half a teaspoon of that so-called beverage before deciding it tasted like battery acid, so my driving skills are excellent. But what do you mean you're going to Charlotte *now*?" He straightened and stared into her car. Where was her luggage?

Maybe her trip out of town wouldn't be for long.

"Well, not now exactly, since I have an empty tank and a flat tire."

"But you planned on it." He hadn't really believed she'd do it.

"Don't tell me you haven't heard? I've officially lost all my good sense. I sold off my share of Last Chance Vintage to go pursue a singing career." She shoved her hair aside and winced in the middle of the movement as if something hurt.

"Are you okay?" He reached to steady her, his focus quickly shifting. "Did you hit your head when you went off the road? Maybe you should sit down."

Already he was opening up the passenger door of her car with one hand, while keeping the other on her elbow. What other injuries hadn't he noticed while he was thinking about how to keep her in town?

The interior light of her vehicle came on, spilling onto her back, but the front of her remained in shadow.

"I'm fine," she protested. "I didn't—that is,

maybe I bent my wrist funny. But I definitely didn't hit my head."

"You sure? Sometimes when you hit your head you black out and don't remember it."

Frowning, she shook her head, although she did allow him to maneuver her into the passenger seat. "No. I remember it clearly."

"Then how did you hurt your wrist?" He leaned closer to get a better angle on her face. "May I?"

Without waiting for permission, he smoothed a hand over her scalp, checking for bumps. Her pupils were dilated, but not in an unusual way. When he tipped her chin higher, however, she edged back in the seat.

"You have to admit this is an unorthodox way to cop a feel." Her voice was breathless.

"If I were going to cop a feel, don't you think I'd start somewhere more memorable?" Gently, he thumbed a dark patch on her cheek, but it smudged at his touch. Not a bruise. "You've got some grease or something here."

"Okay. Stop." Straightening, she gripped his wrist and lowered his hand. "I'm fine. I merely didn't have a good plan for this adventure of mine."

"That doesn't sound like you." He crouched in front of her, staying still for a minute, enjoying the feel of her fingers on his skin. "How about your wrist? Can I see?"

"You know, you're not a doctor." Relinquishing her hold on him, she tucked her hands under her arms.

Wincing.

"But I *am* the mayor." He reached for her right wrist and cradled it in his palm, inspecting it. "That gives me considerable authority in this town."

"To call a council meeting maybe," she scoffed, but she let him move her fingers around, checking her mobility.

"Although if at any time martial law is declared, I think I'd be declared king or something." The wrist seemed a little swollen in comparison to the other one, but her range of motion didn't suggest a break.

"Really?" She laughed, finally giving him the smile he'd been looking for earlier. "Is that how they conned you into taking the job—the promise of absolute power?"

"Something like that." He didn't want to stop touching her, especially when she smiled at him that way.

She smelled good, like hothouse flowers in spring, enticing him to lean closer. His forearms brushed against her thighs as he kept her wrists in his hand.

Their eyes met in the dim reflection of the dome light. The throb of her pulse spiked against his thumb for one heated moment. Then her smile faded.

"I'd better check up on the tow truck." She licked her lower lip. "I thought it would be here by now."

He didn't want to let her go.

"Your wrist is swollen." He smoothed over the inflamed spot. "You could have sprained it."

"No." She broke out of his grasp, ending the moment. "It's fine. I'm fine. I need to go."

Reluctantly, he rose to his feet, giving her space while she called the towing service again. When she disconnected, he watched her gather her things from inside the car and stuff her phone in her bag.

"So, Heather, you want me to take you home? Or set a course for North Carolina?"

"If you don't mind giving me a ride, I would settle for home." Keys in hand, she backed out of the car.

On instinct, he reached out to steady her again since the road's shoulder dropped off hard. His fingers grazed a bare patch of her waist, his palm landing on her hip. The feel of her teased along his senses like a fuel-injected aphrodisiac.

He let go before she could say "I'm fine" again. But he wouldn't forget that impossibly soft skin anytime soon. And—bonus—he'd just kept her in Heartache another day. How long would it take to convince her to stay? To take over the mayoral job?

Maybe have dinner with him?

"Do you have a suitcase?" He closed the door behind her.

"In the trunk." They crunched through weeds and gravel to the rear of the vehicle. "TJ said he's almost here."

"That's probably him now." He pointed toward a disco-show of flashing yellow lights coming down the road.

"Wow." Heather stood close to him and popped the trunk with her key fob. "Those lights should come with a warning—may induce seizures."

"They're a little distracting." He stared at the huge piece of luggage in her trunk. "I'm going to grab your bag and pull my car forward to give him room."

"Thank you." She was already flagging down the truck.

With a break in traffic, TJ didn't seem to mind slowing down and stopping in the lane. Besides, drivers would see that tow truck from miles away. Still, Zach hefted the giant suitcase and closed the trunk. He dropped it into the rear seat of his convertible, then pulled the car forward. Before he could do the gentlemanly thing and go back to escort Heather to his ride, she was at his passenger door and letting herself in.

"Of all your dad's cars, this one was always my favorite." She tugged on the seat belt. "TJ is set, by the way. I'm going to call him tomorrow about the tire."

"See ya, Mayor!" the younger man called as he hopped down from the truck cab. "Drive safe."

Zach gave a wave before pulling onto the highway. He handed Heather an extra hat that he kept on the floor of the backseat—an old visor from a long-ago golf tournament.

"You might want to wear this." He noticed she held her hair in a death grip as he punched the gas.

"Thank you," she called over the inevitable wind noise. She put the hat on and tightened the strap in the back, but still held the length of her hair in her fist.

"I could put the top up," he offered.

"Are you kidding me?" She grinned. "I wanted to put a thousand miles between me and Heartache tonight. My only consolation is getting to ride in the mayor's supersexy convertible."

"Nice of you to point out the main attraction." He didn't have far to go before he pulled through a no U-turn spot on the highway.

Where he promptly did a U-turn.

"I'm surprised you got to keep your dad's cars," she observed, adjusting the side mirror before perhaps realizing what she'd said. "Actually, I apologize. That's completely none of my business."

"It's a matter of public record." He didn't mind telling her. He'd rather she knew the truth than think he'd hid assets from the government after his father's arrest. "I bought back my favorites from his collection after my business took off. Only two of the cars I own now belonged to my father. This one and a Jaguar that were purchased by one of his friends at the bankruptcy auction."

A friend who became Zach's mentor after his father went to jail.

"How *is* your father?"

"You mean, how does he like federal prison?" He couldn't keep the bitterness from his voice.

"No. I mean, how is his health? His mind-set? I'm sure it was a difficult adjustment for him… and for you." She tilted her head back against the seat rest in a way that made him think she was enjoying the ride. Or maybe she simply wanted to feel the wind on her face.

His gaze shifted to her legs and the expanse of thigh visible under the short hem of her bright dress. He was treated to a whole different side of her tonight, and not just because of the dress. He cleared his throat and tried to focus on her question.

And the road.

"He's always got an appeal in process. That gives him something to focus on besides, say, remorse for what he did." He drummed the steering wheel with his thumbs. "Since he's never bothered to be forthright about anything in his entire life, I don't keep in touch."

She was silent for a long moment.

"Family dynamics are complicated." She glanced at her legs and, gripping the hem of her dress with both hands, tugged it lower.

"That's putting it mildly. You're fortunate your family is so close."

"As in, most of them live within shouting distance from me?" She wrangled her windblown hair back under control. "Because I don't know if I'd call that fortunate, exactly."

He'd turned off the highway onto the county route that led into Heartache. The car quieted as it slowed, the road deserted. The air had turned cool after midnight.

"So much for 'Family First.'" He still saw weathered old campaign signs around Heartache sometimes that put the former mayor's slogan in bright blue letters.

"You must think I'm a total ingrate, taking off right after Erin's wedding and trash-talking my family like they were a bother instead of the people I love most in the world." She repositioned herself on the leather seat, crossing her long legs so her knees pointed away from him.

The view was still mighty fine.

"No one knows how to get under your skin like family. I understand that." But he didn't. Not really.

His family had been a sorry excuse for a nuclear unit from day one. His father was a criminal. His mother an accessory, if only by a case of big-time denial. Both parents had been more concerned about getting ahead—or not getting caught—than they'd been about their kids. Zach had tried to make up for their inattention to his sister, Gabriella, by being a good brother.

He had failed miserably.

He sucked at being a family to her as much as his parents, too caught up in his dad's scandal to see the signs of depression in Gabriella, which had surfaced after being stalked online and lured out of the house to meet the guy who'd tried to...

Zach couldn't think about that, actually. But later, she'd overdosed because of it. Zach had helped her relocate to the West Coast and legally change her name. Thankfully, Ellie wasn't far from Gabriella.

So his family had been a mess. But he'd always looked to the Finleys as a family who got it right. Their dad ran the small town for years and not because he was a crook. He was a genuinely selfless guy who had good business sense and shared that acumen to help Heartache thrive.

"They mean well," Heather said carefully. "I'm just ready for a change."

They passed through the downtown, driving by the pizza shop, the town square and the darkened storefront of Last Chance Vintage.

"I was surprised you sold off your share of the store." He admired the sisters' tenacity with the shop, expanding the storefront by remodeling a property next door and connecting them. "It seemed like a good investment."

"Erin did most of the renovations with her own two hands. She deserved all the profits." She kept her focus on the road. "Looks like one of the streetlights is out." She pointed to a post near the pizza joint.

"The mayor's office is closed. I'm off duty tonight."

"Me, too. Guess we shouldn't talk about work then."

He turned in time to catch her smirk.

"Right. We could always discuss a run to the ER to get your wrist examined."

"In that case, maybe we should put my work life back on the table for conversation."

"Luckily, we're not at a town council meeting and don't need any complicated agendas." He rolled his shoulders to ease away some of the tension of talking to her. "No need to be prickly."

"Excellent. I don't like agendas. Complicated or otherwise." She let go of her hair as he turned down the quiet street where she lived.

There were still lights on at the farmhouse, but Heather's brother Mack's converted apartment in one of the old barns was dark. Across a meadow, the bride's house was quiet and so was her brother Scott's place.

Zach pulled into the parking area behind a converted potting shed that had been their father's home office at one time. Heather had claimed it for herself after—he'd heard—living with her sister, Erin. Now the shed looked like a Craftsman bungalow, complete with a loft window, cedar-shake siding and glowing cast-iron lamps. Her family's construction business ensured all the Finley places looked showroom ready, even this home-in-miniature.

"I don't like agendas, either. Or secrets." He shut off the engine so he could walk her to the door and bring in her suitcase.

She turned sharply toward him. "Excuse me?"

"I was kept in the dark about a lot of things as a kid." His dad lived one lie. Then his sister lived a whole different one, pretending everything was okay until it wasn't. And *she* wasn't. "So I'm a big believer in transparency."

"Okay…sounds like the opening to your next campaign speech." Her gaze darted away and she looked nervous. But then, he was probably sounding way too serious.

"What I mean is, I don't want to keep my goals secret from you. So I want you to know that I plan to lobby for you to stay in town."

Without the dashboard lights, it was tough to get a read on her expression.

"I'm surprised you would have an opinion on it one way or another," she said finally. Carefully. "It's just a talent-show audition."

"Exactly. Yet you're selling off your share of

the business you worked hard to build? Packing up and moving in the middle of the night just a few hours after your sister gets married? It doesn't make sense and it's unlike you." He was worried about her.

Before, he'd simply planned to talk to her about the mayor's job and maybe try to convince her to have dinner with him. But after speaking to her tonight, he sensed that something was off with her whole plan. As if she was leaving to get away from something rather than like a woman running to embrace her dreams.

"How would you know what's 'like' me? We've barely spoken outside the occasional town council meeting." She shook her head. "Besides, it's after one o'clock in the morning. I'm *not* having this conversation with you in my driveway."

He held up both hands. The gesture of surrender and placation had proven useful in small-town politics. Smile and compromise.

"Of course. It's late. I'll see you at the wedding breakfast."

"Wedding breakfast. Right." She smiled, her teeth a flash of white in the darkness. "If my car's not in the driveway, maybe I can sleep through it and they'll think I'm on the road."

"Because this town keeps a secret so well." He levered open his door and walked around the car to get hers, even though she was already halfway out.

But she was moving slowly.

"Tired?" He held out his arm to help her, wondering about that wrist she didn't want examined.

"It's been a long day." She limped a little on the way to the door.

"Your feet—"

"It's fine." She brushed off his concern and picked up her pace. "Not everyone can do four-inch heels."

"Didn't you tell your sister?" He'd always pictured them as having a close relationship.

"You see why I'm so determined to leave Heartache?" she grumbled. "Everyone in your business."

Digging in a small satin purse that matched the dress she'd worn at the wedding, Heather found her keys while Zach went back to the car for her suitcase.

She flipped on her house's interior light as he arrived at the threshold.

"Where should I put it?" It weighed a ton. She must have packed enough stuff for two months.

Or might that be two years? There was a very real chance she might not return if the *American Voice* show executives liked her. He hadn't given that much thought since it seemed like a one-in-a-million kind of thing, even though he knew she could sing if her pregame "Star Spangled Banner" efforts were anything to go by. He knew her music students all thought she was talented.

"By the door is fine." Kicking off her flip-flops, she sank her toes into the living room area rug.

In the lamplight, he spotted the violet shadows around her eyes. She looked so exhausted he couldn't allow himself the luxury of checking her out in that sexy dress again.

"Anything else you need?" He glanced around at her small house, a loft bed visible in a low ceiling over the lower-level living space.

"No. But thanks." She rubbed her hands along her bare arms to warm them. "It was lucky for me you happened along the highway so soon after I ran out of gas."

"Lucky for me, too." He'd wanted to talk her out of leaving town and fate had settled the matter for him.

At least temporarily.

He said good-night and left her to get some sleep. Zach stepped out onto the front porch and stared up at the stars stretching endlessly in this quiet part of town. He'd wanted Heather to stay in Heartache so he could sweet-talk her into the mayor's gig. He didn't have time to run the town. He needed to focus on something more important. Two months ago, someone on the town board mentioned a rash of incidents around the old quarry where his sister had been attacked—the same one close to where Heather had been stranded tonight. And ever since, Zach had been consumed with the need to investigate things quietly.

The mayor's job made that tougher to do, and he'd genuinely thought Heather might be a good fit to take over the role.

But she'd drawn him in tonight more powerfully than he'd expected. And although she gave off the vibe that she didn't need anyone, Zach had the feeling something was wrong. Something she was doing her damnedest to hide. He planned to keep an eye on her in case she needed him.

And not just because there'd been that moment when he'd felt her heart rate speed up as he touched her.

Sliding into his car, he already couldn't wait to see her again.

CHAPTER THREE

"THREE, TWO, ONE, SMILE!" Heather shouted the next morning from her cramped position in the photo booth. Her oldest brother had rented it for the wedding breakfast at the farmhouse. She adjusted a tiara on her head, the only prop remaining after her siblings had taken all the other toys to play dress-up for goofy photo-booth pictures.

The flash lit up the space with an accompanying *pop!*, making it sound like an old-fashioned bulb.

"No fair!" Heather's niece, Ally, protested as she adjusted a blue feather boa on her neck. "Dad did rabbit ears behind my head."

"I had an itch on my nose," Scott argued with his daughter while his wife, Bethany, reset the switch for another series of pictures. "You hit me in the face with that feather duster you're wearing."

Four of the Finley siblings were crammed into the booth along with Scott's family and Mack's fiancée, Nina. Heather had invited their mom for the photo, but she was keeping a low profile today, tired from the strain of holding herself together over the course of the weekend.

Heather understood that feeling more clearly than ever. Her joints were better today, but she was feeling plenty of strain herself. Health issues were exhausting to manage. Thinking and worrying about hers was draining. Mentally, she'd already left Heartache. But since her car wouldn't be fixed until Monday at the earliest—and TJ Elliott said in a text he "wouldn't hold his breath" on that one—Heather was still very much physically present. And that meant being here for Erin today.

"Let's do a funny photo," the new Mrs. Remy Weldon suggested from her seat on the groom's lap.

"Or a 'kiss the bride' picture," Remy returned, his Cajun twang setting him apart from Mack's and Scott's voices as they shouted their own suggestions.

"We can flex." Scott was already showing off his biceps.

"Or stage a brawl." Mack pantomimed hitting Scott in the face.

Heather took an elbow in the shoulder. And wasn't that just a reminder of what it had been like growing up at her house?

"Whoops." Mack quit fighting and steadied her. "Sorry, sis."

"We should do what Aunt Erin says," Ally

ordered as the booth got stuffier by the second. "She's the bride."

Heather took charge. "On the count of three, we all blow kisses at the camera while Remy kisses Erin. Got it?"

The Finleys—thank you, God—fell in line with nods and affirmatives all around.

"Good." Heather got ready to press the button. "Let's do that for the first couple and then just—do whatever on the last two. Ready? Three, two, one…"

She hit the button and the family kissed on command.

For a few seconds at least. Things fell apart after that—more elbows flying as Scott pretended to choke Mack, Ally and her mother did a *Charlie's Angels* pose. Erin and Remy—surprise— kept on kissing. Their obvious attraction made Heather think about Zach and the surprise of his touch the night before.

When the last flash went off, she blinked and tried to shake off the memory.

"Okay! Done!" Heather sidled her way out of the booth none too gently, needing air.

Stumbling out of the curtain and into the daylight, she searched for a spot to regroup on the sprawling lawn outside her mother's house. She needed to leave a message with the doctor's office in North Carolina that she wouldn't be able to make the appointment she'd set up for tomorrow. She only had a little left of the anti-inflammatory medicine the doctor in Austin had given her and she was anxious to try something stronger. Or an alternative that wouldn't be quite as draining as some of the other medications that were available for the disease.

Heather's stomach rumbled as she searched for a quiet spot on the lawn. She'd been too busy greeting guests to eat properly before. The backyard was filled with small tables and chairs, white linen tablecloths fluttering slightly in the warm morning breeze. The caterers had disassembled the majority of the breakfast buffet, but had left the coffee and juice bar along with muffins and fruit. A few kids played underneath a table nearby, heads peeking out now and again to see if anyone would notice them stealing muffins to bring back to their home base.

Obligingly, Heather didn't notice them even when she went to help herself to a bottle of sparkling water from a cooler.

"Ms. Finley?"

Heather turned to see one of her music students dressed in the catering company's black-and-white uniform, her long blond ponytail tied with a gray bow.

"Megan! So nice to see you." Heather had been working with the younger woman for only a few months, but she knew that Megan Bryer was a talented guitarist. "I didn't realize you worked with the catering company."

"I waitress at the Owl's Roost, and sometimes the caterers pick up servers from the restaurant." She shrugged as she refilled a tub of ice with bottled water. "I needed the extra money."

"Saving up for that new acoustic you saw online?" Megan had been excited about the upgraded instrument when they first talked about it last spring. She'd told Heather she was making her homecoming dress herself so she could save money for the guitar.

"I wish." The younger woman's expression clouded, her mouth drawn tight.

Before Heather could ask her if everything was all right, Zach appeared at her side.

"Looks like you have a thief at work here," he announced, staring at the wavering white tablecloth that hid the muffin-stealing boys. "Maybe I should call the sheriff."

Giggles floated from under the table and the tablecloth flapped some more. One scuffed tennis shoe made an appearance.

"I'd better go," Megan muttered, darting away before Heather could introduce her.

Watching her leave, Heather hoped she'd find time to speak to the girl before the breakfast ended. Now she turned toward Heartache's intriguing mayor, her eyes wandering over Zach's perfectly pressed khakis and dark jacket, his white dress shirt with the top button undone—the only nod to the less formal occasion.

"It just so happens the sheriff is right over there." Heather pointed out Sam Reyes.

More giggles and then three small boys shot out from under the table, trailing muffin crumbs and crumpled napkins in their wake.

Zach laughed as they watched them go.

"Score one for the local Neighborhood Watch." He turned his brooding, lazy stare toward Heather, his tawny brown eyes warm with a look that hummed over her skin. "Another thing to love about life in a small town."

Something about his assessing gaze had her mouth going dry. He'd told her last night he wanted her to stay in town and the words had circled around her brain ever since. What she didn't understand was—why now? His response to her seemed sudden. And while she wouldn't take him for the kind of guy who found a no-strings relationship appealing, she had to wonder if his interest had to do with the fact that she'd be gone soon.

All the more reason to be cautious, since she was far too curious about him. She had no business daydreaming about his clean-shaven jaw, the strong column of his throat or the fact that she knew if she leaned close, she would smell the scent of bay rum on his skin. The way he'd touched her the night before had really scattered her thoughts.

"I didn't know we were making a list." She cracked open her bottle of water and took a long sip.

She peered around the wedding breakfast, where everyone seemed content to visit as the waitstaff circulated with trays of mimosas and Bloody Marys. No live music today, just someone's iPod plugged into the speaker system the DJ had rented to them for an extra day.

"We are absolutely making a list. I thought I made that clear last night when I briefed you on my future goal of keeping you in town."

She'd shut down that conversation fast the night before, confused, flustered and not trusting herself to make sense of what he had been saying.

"I think I was a little roadweary from the wedding," she admitted. "I couldn't imagine why it would make a difference to you. Unless you were thinking of taking up piano?"

A cheer erupted nearby, distracting her from a question she really wanted answers to. A bunch of teens—her niece, Ally, and her friends—were all playing a video game projected on a pulldown screen under one of the leftover canopy tents from the reception. A few of them were high-fiving and carrying on. Heather's eye sought Megan, wondering if she would feel sad to miss a chance to hang out with her peers. But the girl was on the other side of the party with her back to the group.

"Do you have a minute to talk, maybe over there where it's quieter?" Zach pointed at a pair of bright red Adirondack chairs between two old pine trees on the far side of the lawn. They were there for decoration more than anything, marking the property line between her mother's house and Scott's place.

"I have a minute." Even though she was wary of wherever this was headed. "But I'll warn you—my own family tried their best to talk me out of leaving town. I feel like I've put off my own dreams for too long."

"I get that." He greeted a few people as they edged away from the crowd. "I felt the same way after school—I needed to leave Heartache. Remove myself from the family drama."

She wasn't about to throw her family under the bus and admit to any problems there. Even now, her mother remained inside, her tolerance for so much company having worn off the night before. In fact, Heather hadn't gotten a goodbye from her when she'd knocked on her door the night before.

Not that she'd ended up getting far out of town anyhow.

"I earned my degree online." She'd been trying to balance helping her mother with helping Erin launch her online business. Since there were no colleges nearby, taking credits online had seemed logical at the time. "I learned a lot, but I missed a chance to see someplace else. Meet other people."

"It's good to see what else is out there." When they reached the chairs in the small clearing, he produced a handkerchief from his pocket and ran it over the wooden slats of one red seat. "But that doesn't mean you need to move permanently."

"It's hard to say that with any certainty when I haven't seen what else is out there. Up until last spring, Erin did all the buying trips for the store." She settled her water bottle on the wide arm of one chair as she sat down.

A scuttling in the bushes nearby caught her attention and she saw her mother's black Lab, Luce, wagging her tail from a spot in the shade. Like a windshield wiper, the tail swiped over dried leaves, clearing a half circle around the dog.

"I'll tell you what's out there." He frowned and ticked off items on his fingers. "Congestion, pollution, noise, corruption and no sense of community. Here you have clean air, hassle-free traffic, easy parking, a short commute to work and your whole family."

She took another long sip of water and then tossed the empty bottle to Luce to play with. The old dog gnawed happily with the bottle pinned under one dark paw.

"You're really good at these campaign speeches." She smiled. "I feel like you could win Heartache some kind of 'best small town in the

US' award, you make it sound so good." She studied Zach's strong profile, his skin deeply tanned above the white collar of his shirt. "But I'm still not sure why you're trying to sell me."

His expression became serious, the flirtatious glances nowhere in sight now.

"You should be running this town."

The words took a moment to sink in.

"Excuse me?" She wondered if it was too late to bolt from this conversation.

"You realize who tied with me for most write-in votes when no one wanted to run for mayor after your dad's death?"

She'd heard, but she'd been hurting at the time. And something about the news had felt like an ironic slap in the face since the Finley patriarch had never wanted his family involved in his public life. For Dad, the town meant everything—including an escape from a home life that overwhelmed him between five kids and a demanding wife with serious health issues.

So many times she'd tried to be a part of his world, to help him with things related to the mayor's duties. But unless he needed a cute kid for a ceremonial ribbon cutting, he kept his family far from his work.

"You can't seriously be suggesting I..." She shook her head. "I can't even guess. You run the town, Zach. And you do a great job at it."

He nodded. "I took the job because the council

didn't want to approach you so soon after your father died. But you've lived here all your life and you know the demands of the job. You have experience building a successful business from the ground up—"

"Whoa." She stiffened in her chair, unable to absorb what he was saying. "I'm going to stop you right there. I'm flattered, and I think this is kind of you—"

"It's not kindness, Heather. It makes sense." He sat forward on his seat, too, his knee brushing hers briefly.

The warmth of that small contact stole through her, reminding her of the confused mix of feelings from the night before. Had he only been nice to her to talk her into this? Taking over the mayor's duties?

She'd suspected him of romancing her for some kind of short-term fling. She sure hadn't expected a political proposal.

"Maybe to *you* it makes sense, but it doesn't to me. And I don't want to be guilted into yet another reason to stay here."

He frowned. "Guilted?"

She swallowed, wishing she'd kept that thought to herself.

"I mean—I've got everything packed. I've put a lot of thought into pursuing my dream. I don't want to feel like I'm letting you down or letting down the whole town by leaving. This decision came with a lot of difficulties, and that's before you threw all this on it, too. I feel bad enough I'm leaving so many of my music students." She remembered one of the articles she'd read online about stress making her condition worse.

She so didn't need another flare-up because of Zach's pressure. If she could just get out of town for a couple of months and get things under control, things would be better.

"I'm not suggesting you take the mayor's seat to pressure you." He laid a hand on her forearm.

It was a social touch—the kind of touch a person used to convey something heartfelt or important. But coming from Zach, it stirred a fresh wave of warmth that rattled her to her toes.

She stared at that connection. Just a hand on an arm. But the feel of it shook something inside her that she hadn't felt in her last relationship. Her pulse pounded.

"Maybe not, but that's the upshot." She shrugged. "You're doing a great job. I can't imagine why you'd want to hand it over. A small-town mayor has lots of perks and prestige."

"It requires far more time than I realized when I first accepted, and I think you're really well suited for the job." His gaze dropped to where he touched her before he slid his hand away. "But I definitely don't want to pressure you. If you truly have dreams to chase, Heather, you should."

She sifted through his words, thinking about

their conversation. The music piping through the speakers shifted to something slow and romantic, and one of the older couples—Daisy Spencer and her boyfriend, Harlan Brady—stood up to shuffle-waltz in a slow circle. Mrs. Spencer was in her eighties and she had knee trouble, but Mr. Brady moved so carefully with her it made Heather's heart squeeze to see them.

Would she still be dancing in her eighties? Her diagnosis terrified her. The disease could cripple joints into almost unrecognizable configurations. No doubt about it—these were her dancing years.

She let out a breath. "I'd really love to create music that makes people happy." She pointed to the older couple swaying on the lawn all by themselves. "You see them? I wish I could write a song that moves people to dance like that."

She turned to find Zach watching her, something inscrutable in his expression.

"What?" Self-conscious, she wondered if he thought she'd never pull it off. "Is that such a crazy dream?"

"Definitely not." His expression cleared. "I couldn't imagine you being happy outside of Heartache, but I guess now I can picture it. I never knew you were so passionate about music."

"It doesn't come up at council meetings or softball games." She paused, thinking about the only places she normally saw him. "The store was more Erin's dream than mine. I just wanted to help her bring that to life, and I had some good ideas, but now that she's off and running, it's time for me to get serious about my own ambitions."

"Away from your family and friends." He nodded, as if he was still trying to piece together her true reasons for leaving town.

For a moment, she wondered if she'd given anything away about her condition last night. He'd examined her wrist. Noticed her limp. Anxious to squash whatever suspicions he might have, she rose to her feet, making sure she stood tall and steady on her achy joints.

"Unfortunately, I can't pursue all my dreams here." She smiled brightly. "Sorry to cut our chat short, Zach, but I didn't realize my brother is giving a toast."

She pointed to a few people gathered around Scott, who lifted a mimosa toward Erin and Remy. The music had been turned down. The moment offered a perfect escape from a conversation growing awkward.

Zach rose. "Of course."

"I don't think we're doing anything formal for a send-off, but I should probably join them." She realized they stood close together.

Eye to eye, she didn't move away. Neither did he.

The moment spun out as they stood a hand's span from one another, Zach's hand wrapped around hers. Her heart pounded—hard and fast—

as she felt the magnetic draw of the man. Then, slowly, he stroked his thumb down the center of her palm, his eyes never leaving hers. The touch made her breath catch, especially when he traced a circle inside her hand.

"We'll miss you, Heather Finley," he said finally, his words breaking the spell. She nodded too fast, stepping back to regain some composure. She didn't understand this chemistry between them, which seemed to have a new edge. Was Zach sticking close to her because of the mayor's job? Or was there more to it?

"Thanks." Sliding her hand free, she wrapped her arms around herself and headed back to the party with Zach at her side.

She swallowed. What might have happened just now if she hadn't been so dead set on leaving Heartache? Would he have given her another reason to stay? Her skin still tingled where he'd touched her.

Heather didn't hurry across the lawn. Her brother's toast had ended. Sheriff Sam Reyes broke away from the group and headed their way, tugging off a pair of aviator shades and jamming them in his jacket pocket. He was an imposing man with a he-man frame. He had worked in a vice squad on the West Coast before returning to Heartache to take the job in local law enforcement. He and Zach hadn't seemed to hang out much in high school, so it had been a surprise when they'd both ended up in San Jose after graduation. Heather had heard Gabriella, Zach's younger sister, had moved there, too.

Zach slowed his steps. "Is it just me or does Sam look like he has something on his mind?"

"Duty calls." She regretted it as soon as she said it, knowing how much he wanted to hand off the job. "Sorry. I didn't mean that to sound... flippant. I wish I could have bailed you out of the mayor's gig."

"I'll figure something out." He stopped walking. "Will you do me a favor and let me know before you leave town?"

"It might be as early as this afternoon if TJ gets my car fixed." Her eyes went to the sheriff, who had joined them. "But sure, I can give you a shout before I head out."

"Sorry to interrupt," Sam said. "Zach, you have a minute?"

Excusing herself, Heather went in search of Megan to see how things were going with her music. She liked the girl and something about her body language had felt off. As if she might be upset. And after Zach's crazy suggestion that she take over the mayor's seat, Heather seriously needed to distract herself until her car was fixed and she could head for the county line.

At least, that's why she told herself she needed the distraction. Because she couldn't think about those heated moments when Zach's thumb had sketched a light touch over her palm. She shivered at the memory. Now was not the time to get moony-eyed over a man. She had dreams to chase and a coveted audition waiting for her a thousand miles away.

"You've got to work on your timing," Zach groused, scrubbing a hand through his hair as he scowled at his so-called friend. "Do I interrupt you when you're with a beautiful woman?"

He turned his back on the wedding breakfast festivities. The music still blasted and there were plenty of teens playing video games under one of the canopy tents, but as it neared lunchtime, the party was definitely breaking up. Only a few guests remained.

Sam Reyes glared right back at him, undeterred. They'd been friends since high school when Sam had rescued his sister from the guy who'd lured her out of the house after stalking her online. Sam had risked a hell of a lot to save her. Zach owed him. Everything. He'd had Sam's back when he'd helped him leave town and start over again on the West Coast in San Jose. They'd roomed together for a year when they left town, with Zach going into Silicon Valley to learn at the feet of computer industry experts and Sam signing up for the police academy while he worked on a criminal justice degree. Theirs was a friendship forged in fire.

"Heather has lived here forever, and you've been back in town for a year," Sam pointed out. "If you can't get your act together to make a move in all that time, maybe you don't deserve a shot."

"And since I'm sure you're not here merely to remind me of my dating shortcomings, why don't you tell me what you found out about police incidents around the quarry over the last few years." He'd called Sam last night after dropping off Heather at her place, his concern renewed after she went off the road so close to the place his sister had been attacked.

Sam was the only person in the sheriff's department he felt comfortable asking since he preferred to keep his interest quiet. Gabriella—Ellie—had never filed a police report about her attack and now that she'd changed her identity, they were all the more cautious about drawing undue attention to her or her whereabouts.

"I need to compare the number of complaints against some other sites in town. But on first glance, the number seems high to me, and too often involving young women alone. A high school girl went off the road in the quarry last year because someone had taken down a sign on a turn." A dark scowl settled on Sam's face. "Luckily, one of Heather's brothers was in town and he found the girl and got her out of there. But she was alone and vulnerable—that might have been by design on the part of whoever took out that sign."

"You think there's a chance someone knowingly preys on people in the quarry?"

What if Ellie's attacker was a local? Someone who'd been in Heartache ever since? The hairs on the back of his neck rose.

Sam shook his head. "We're getting ahead of ourselves. All I'm saying is that my initial search—and it was a quick scan through old files that haven't been digitized—suggests we should dig deeper."

Just one more reason Zach needed to offload this mayor gig. Digging deeper was exactly the kind of work he should be doing. With his computer forensics company, he was in a good place to analyze data for idiosyncrasies. He freelanced for police departments around the country, analyzing computers for deleted files, web searches or old emails that could help criminal cases. It was a job that called to him since his sister had been lured in by an internet predator, someone using a false identity and befriending Gabriella online.

Old frustration simmered. "I'm making this a priority."

"So am I. But the real reason I'm here concerns the Finley family." Sam folded his arms. Even without the aviator shades, he looked as if he could be Secret Service with his linebacker build and dark jacket.

"I hope it's good news, Sam. I don't have time for more problems in this town." Zach didn't like the vibe he picked up. He'd convinced Sam to come back to Heartache and take the sheriff slot after Zach had been appointed mayor.

Not just because they were friends, either. He'd always hoped they'd find Ellie's stalker, who'd escaped Sam that night long ago.

Sam hadn't been tough to convince. Ellie, on the other hand, hadn't been pleased to be left behind in San Jose.

"You asked me last week to look into the rumblings on the town council." Sam shoved his hands in his pants pockets, taking in the wedding breakfast festivities.

"I did." Zach's gut knotted. "I don't like rumors and gossip BS."

"Some of the council members believe there's money missing from the town coffers. Last month, one of the temporary accounting clerks found an error in a ledger when they were transferring the data to digital formats."

Zach swore under his breath. Multiple times. His eye shot to Heather as she moved through the party guests, exchanging words with almost everyone she passed.

She would have been a great mayor. And now—after a few heated touches they'd shared last night and this morning—he knew she would have been an incredible date. Or more. The chemistry there had him buzzing from the other side of the lawn.

But he'd thought she'd been hiding something. What if it was something a whole lot darker than he'd imagined?

"That's not the worst of it." Sam's voice yanked Zach back to the matter at hand.

"Worse than missing money from the town's books and a restless town council secretly looking for answers? Why didn't anyone come to me?" His head throbbed. He hated scandal and secrets. "And how the hell can things go downhill from there?"

"Apparently, the accounting problem dates back to Mayor Finley's term. Two of the older council members hadn't reported it because they feared Mayor Finley knew about the missing money and never reported it."

Zach's head shot up. "What are you implying?"

"Not one damn thing." Sam shook his head. "You know me better than that. I don't deal in implications. I'm reporting the nature of the whispers you've been hearing lately. I spoke to Rodney Baker, the council's oldest member, at length."

"Shit." Zach knew Sam well enough to be one hundred percent sure he had his facts straight. No doubt that's why his gut sank.

"Exactly. That beautiful woman you were just

talking to? Rodney Baker thinks her father knew all about the accounting issues. According to Baker, Mayor Finley was supposed to be 'looking into it' before he died. Baker never reported it after the mayor's death because he never could hunt down any error in the books anyhow."

"Until last month when the clerk discovered it," Zach clarified.

"Correct."

Zach couldn't sit on information like this for more than a day or two. It needed to be made public so the town could figure out what had happened. Zach was willing to bet the Finley family would soon be embroiled in scandal.

As for Heather? It was a hell of a way to get his wish, but he knew for a fact she wouldn't be going anywhere to chase her dreams when her family threatened to become front-page news.

CHAPTER FOUR

MEGAN BRYER TOOK a deep breath and reminded herself of all the good reasons for taking extra work like this catering job on the weekends.

She needed the money. She couldn't afford the kind of college she dreamed about without some cash of her own to put toward it. And a good college would take her far away from Heartache and all the annoying people at her high school.

She hurried past the canopy where her classmates from Crestwood High were playing video games on a giant projection screen. They looked comfortable sprawled out on a ring of pillows.

"Nice shoes, Megan," one of the girls in the circle called as she texted on her phone.

Laughter all around.

Megan ignored them, refusing to look over. Her black off-brand tennis shoes were fairly standard for waitressing, although hers did have a hole in the big toe. When worn with black socks, it hardly seemed noticeable.

"Would you call that a sneaker or a sandal?" another girl whispered just loudly enough to make sure Megan could hear.

More laughter.

Okay, maybe the big toe hole was kinda visible. But who would comment on it besides a drippy teenager with nothing better to do than make fun of people and spend their rich parents' money?

Megan hurried to pick up the tub of ice that had been set at one end of the tent, anxious to be out of there. She *would not look* at the twisted knot of spoiled bitchy girls lounging on the oversize pillows. But when the boys started cheering over a high score on their latest mission, Megan couldn't help a quick peek at the score.

Child's play.

She had a character in the same game about fifty levels higher than those guys. Perversely, she'd played with some of them online and they'd never known her from the screen name she used: Bruiser12—her badass alter ego.

Her moment of pleasure ended abruptly as her gaze landed on the throng of girls. Five glossy heads with hair straightened into look-alike sheets, their expensive skirts spilling onto one another since they sat so close together. Bailey McCord was there. Of course. Her former friend.

Their eyes met for a nanosecond before Bailey frowned and looked back down at her phone screen.

Hypocrite.

Irritated, Megan lifted the ice tub too fast. Half the contents spilled on the grass in a crash-thud, making everyone turn and stare. The boys broke out in a sarcastic cheer.

"Nice one!"

"Real smooth!"

A girl's voice slid underneath the boys' shouts. "Could she be any more hopeless?"

Of course, Megan berated herself with a lot worse than that. Ignoring the mess, she trudged out of the tent with the tub, her face burning.

"Hey, Meg!" a friendly voice shouted from behind her.

She almost didn't turn around, half afraid of being suckered into another insult, but then a flash of recognition hit. She knew that musical soprano tone.

Slowing her step, she willed her heart rate to slow. Attempted to wipe the pissy expression from her face. Then she turned.

"Hi, Ms. Finley."

Her music teacher hurried across the lawn, red curls bouncing on her shoulders. She always dressed with a fashion sense that landed somewhere between preppy and demure—weird, since she used to own Last Chance Vintage with her sister. The store had the coolest stuff in town, but Ms. Finley didn't look as if she shopped there. She had a Southern-lady polish, from her pedicure to her refined pearl jewelry and barely-there makeup. Today, she wore a sheer yellow dress layered over a simple lemon-colored sheath.

On the plus side, Ms. Finley actually had a brain and a huge love of music, both qualities Megan doubted many of her graduating class possessed. Ms. Finley loved Bach, knew all the alternative bands and could launch into a soaring melody from some random piece of medieval liturgical music when the mood struck her. As guitar teachers went, she was extremely cool. In their next lesson, they were supposed to talk about taking guitar solos to the next level. But now Ms. Finley was skipping town.

Leaving Megan alone in a school system that had turned on her for reasons she didn't understand. She couldn't imagine facing her days without the outlet of her music. Without her one friend remaining—even if she was a teacher.

"Let me help you with that," her music instructor offered, grabbing one side of the heavy tub still partially full of ice.

"That's okay." Megan didn't want to spill it again, but she also didn't want to get in trouble with her boss for letting a client do her job. "Please." She tugged the metal bowl back. Gently. "If I want work again next weekend, I'd better do what they ask me to."

"Oh." Ms. Finley frowned, but let go, pink fingernails sliding away. "Okay. Can I walk with you for a minute? I can tell your boss I was giving you special wedding instructions or something."

"That's okay." Megan slowed her pace since

Ms. Finley wore high heels. "I need to bring this to the truck."

The caterer's mobile cooking unit sat off to one side of the massive lawn beside a box trailer full of tables and equipment. Megan headed toward it with Ms. Finley.

"I wanted to see if everything is okay?" her teacher asked, voice full of concern. "You mentioned taking the job for extra money and I worried—I don't know. Are things all right at home?"

"Fine." The last thing she needed was for Ms. Finley to talk to her dad. He worried enough about Megan. "Everything is fine," she lied. "I'm just thinking more about college now with senior year under way. I'm trying to put everything I can into the fund to help out."

That much was true. Her father could barely afford the household budget on his college-teaching salary. He taught online at a school that wouldn't give faculty members a discount for their kids to attend, but according to her dad, it was the best he could do in an overcrowded job market.

So the money created one issue. The fact that she'd become a target for trouble at school was another problem she wasn't about to share. And the person who'd taken to harassing her online brought her problems to a whole other creepy level.

"That's good of you, Megan." Ms. Finley smiled, her perfectly lined lips saying all the right grown-up things. "College is a great goal." She walked in silence for a moment, frowning.

"But?" Arriving at the catering truck, Megan dumped the ice in the spot allotted for excess water runoff then shoved the tub into the trailer.

"But a guitar is always a great goal, too." Ms. Finley stared back at her, perfectly serious.

Wiping her damp hands on her dark apron, Megan laughed. God, it had been a while since she could remember laughing about anything. Today, roaming around the green lawn of a beautiful old farmhouse might actually be kind of fun if she wasn't hated by everyone under eighteen at this particular party.

"I agree." How to put this? She bit her lip, hating to confess the rest of the news about her music. "But actually, even if you weren't leaving town, I'd been planning to talk to you about canceling my lessons to save up for school. So I'm not only going to have to wait on the new guitar, but I won't bother looking for a new teacher." When she'd found out her single-parent father had canceled his health insurance two years ago for Megan's lessons, she'd flipped out.

What if he got sick or had an accident or something?

Ms. Finley sighed. "You know, it's natural to have a certain ebb and flow of interest when you take up an instrument, Megan. Especially when there are so many other things going on in a teen-ager's life—"

"No." She shook her head. Unwilling to let Ms. Finley think she'd just grown bored with playing. "I promise, it's nothing like that. I still practice every day. I *need* to play every day or else—"

Distracted by one of the other servers hurrying past with a tray, she stopped short of confessing how crazy she felt when she didn't have a cre-ative outlet. Guitar seemed a lot more productive than killing mutant zombies in the video game.

"I'm the same way," Ms. Finley surprised her by saying. "If I don't get my time in—even if it's just singing my heart out in the shower—I feel too bottled up inside. I don't know what I'd do without my music."

"Exactly." Relieved she wasn't the only one, Megan ignored the cell phone vibrating in her apron pocket. Her father knew her work schedule and who else called her these days? Ever since she broke up with J.D. and he'd started dating Bailey, she'd become social poison at Crestwood.

Which was so freaking unfair. Bailey was the one who had broken girl code by dating her friend's ex. Why was Megan the one blacklisted? Probably because J. D. Covington was one of the most popular kids in school. And what J.D. wanted, he got. If that meant everyone had to like his girlfriend, that's what people did.

"Well, I understand about the lessons. But if

you have time and you're practicing anyway, maybe we could keep our old lesson times right up until I leave town." Ms. Finley shaded her pale skin from the direct sun as she squinted up at Megan. "My car is in the shop, so I'm not sure how soon I'll be heading out. But it sounds like I'll still be around tomorrow if you want to meet."

"But I can't pay—"

"I need to practice, too. It'll be a way for us both to stay sharp. I don't want to go into my audition flat because I haven't been rehearsing."

She knew Ms. Finley planned to audition for *American Voice*, but somehow Megan doubted her teacher needed to rehearse with a twelfth grader to hone her musical skills.

"Um. Sure. Okay. I should probably get back to work, though." Megan's phone buzzed again, making her antsy. Plus, her boss had already cornered one of the other servers to chew him out about something.

Megan didn't want to be next.

"Of course." Ms. Finley smiled. "We can take it on a day-by-day basis. I'll text you in the morning to confirm tomorrow's time, okay?"

"Sounds good." Megan walked backward toward the party and her job. "And I really appreciate it."

She might have been voted the senior class's Most Antisocial in one of the school paper's "humorous" categories, but she knew enough to thank a talented musician for offering to spend extra time with her.

"It'll be good for us both." Ms. Finley waved and then headed back to the main house.

Megan had no intention of going back under that canopy where all her classmates were hanging out, so she darted toward a row of overgrown honeysuckle bushes and tugged her phone out to see who'd been calling.

Or—as it happened—texting.

She didn't recognize the number, but she'd gotten three messages in the last ten minutes, all from the same account.

You are such a slut. Have you checked your Facebook page?

The first message was nothing she hadn't heard before. She guessed J.D. had started that particular rumor when she hadn't proven as eager to please as his new girlfriend.

Then again, Megan knew better than to trust anything J.D., said so she didn't necessarily believe the rumors going around about him and Bailey, either. As for the Facebook page, that's where she'd received rude private messages. She had deleted her account, so there was nothing left to check.

She scrolled down to the next message.

Don't you have anything better to do on a week-end than ruin everyone else's good time?

Her eyes flicked to the canopy where five girls still draped themselves over throw pillows, their phones in hand. Had one of them sent the texts? It must be someone at the wedding breakfast. Someone who had seen her spill the ice.

A shiver crawled up her spine despite the heat. Was this message from someone at the party? Or from the person who'd harassed her online earlier this summer?

Or…both?

Her mouth went dry.

Finally, she read the third message—all from the same local phone number that didn't show up as one of her contacts.

You should do us all a favor and die.

A stupid joke, right? Her heart pounded harder, slugging her chest in a slow, fierce beat. She knew the text didn't matter, and it was just a dumb thing to say written by an equally dumb person. Still, Megan's finger shook as she pressed the buttons that would clear the messages from her phone.

Delete.
Delete.
Confirm delete.
Gone.

She took a breath again once the messages vanished from her device, but she knew the harassment wouldn't stop. Playing her music wouldn't make the hurt go away from all the lies J.D. had spread. And working every minute outside of school didn't take away the fact that she spent almost forty hours a week inside Crestwood High with a hundred classmates who hated her.

Spring—and college—couldn't come fast enough.

"IT'S AMAZING WHAT you can observe at a party just by watching body language." Heather's mother's voice rose from a tall wingback pulled next to the window in the upstairs den.

"There you are!" Heather strode deeper into the room, her eyes still adjusting to the dimmer house lighting after being outside in the sun. "I wanted to see if you needed anything before I head home."

She'd been out of sorts since talking to Zach and more so after her conversation with Megan. Zach's suggestion she take the mayor's seat was just…craziness. Even if a teeny part of her was flattered that he thought her competent for the job. Even if a tinier part of her was disappointed that he wanted her in town more for political reasons than personal.

Turning her attention from fractured thoughts,

she knelt beside her mom's chair and looped an arm around her shoulders.

"I need my house back," Diana Finley snapped. "But I don't suppose you can manage that any time soon."

She forced a laugh and tried to take the words lightly. Her niece, Ally, always got along so well with her moody grandmother and insisted she didn't mean any harm. It didn't help that Heather suspected her mother was perfectly serious.

"I think the bride and groom will be heading down to Cajun country before we know it, and most of the out-of-town guests will be right behind them." Rising to her feet, Heather stared at the lawn where the catering crew packed up the round breakfast tables.

The canopy would stay up throughout the day, along with a small drinks station and a few tables for guests that lingered. Heather saw Megan hefting one of the tables along with two other workers. Did it bother Megan to work at an event that many of her friends attended for fun?

"Bah," Diana grumbled, waving one hand impatiently, the way she might swat at a mosquito. "I've got about fifty goodbyes to deal with and more loads of laundry than I can catch up with in a week."

Heather peered at her mom, almost seeing the frustrated energy rise from her the way steam might hiss from an overheated car. Or maybe it was simply because her mom shook her crossed leg, the free foot rattling back and forth as if she needed to get something off it.

"Bethany said she'd come over to do the laundry," Heather reminded her, unwilling to feel guilty for leaving. "Although your only company was just us."

Erin, Nina, Bethany and Heather had all spent time at the farmhouse during the prewedding festivities. They'd managed to keep the house humming with activity, though their sister Amy's absence had been a hurt that ricocheted through the whole family. She'd made excuses for not attending their father's funeral and Heather had kind of understood. But Erin's wedding? It hurt her, too.

"Family makes dishes and laundry the same as strangers," her mother pointed out. She looked out the window, distracted by the activity on the lawn. "Do you know that girl? The daughter of the college professor?"

She pointed to Megan, who seemed to be on the receiving end of a lecture from Cecily Alan, owner of a local sandwich shop and in charge of the catering. The family had decided it would be too much trouble for Mack and Nina's new restaurant to tackle the job when they hadn't fully set up the catering branch. Plus, they were both family members and should enjoy the wedding.

"Meg's father is a professor?" She'd met Mr.

Bryer briefly a couple of times after the family had moved to town a few years ago, but it surprised her that Megan would be concerned about college expenses if her dad already worked at a university.

All Heather knew about Dan Bryer was that he was superprotective of his daughter.

"He gives business workshops for an online program," Diana said. "Nervous sort who keeps close tabs on the girl, but a level head on the town council, from what I hear." Her mom's finger thunked against the grid of small panes in the bay window. "I'm going to ask Ally about his daughter. Megan Bryer doesn't seem to have many friends."

"Cecily Alan doesn't like anyone," Heather retorted, feeling defensive and knowing her mother could be a harsh judge of character. "Megan is a nice girl and a very talented guitarist."

Maybe she felt a kinship with another musician. Or maybe she just identified with anyone who failed to impress her mother.

"The body language from this group here…?" Diana slid her purple-polished fingernail along the windowpane across another grid to point at a group of girls inside the canopy. "Very negative whenever the other girl walks by. It's been a soap opera down there." She sat back in her chair. "Although that wasn't nearly as entertaining as seeing the designs of the young mayor on you."

All thoughts of Megan forgotten, Heather drew in a sharp breath.

"Mom, really." She wished she'd done the laundry instead of putting herself in the path of… whatever her mother had on her mind.

"He wasn't the only one giving you the once-over, but I'm not about to count Jeremy Covington's surreptitious looks since he's married."

"*Eeww.* Mom. Stop." She sincerely hoped her mother didn't know what she was talking about. The local quarry owner had been a renegade voter on the town board for a long time, a thorn in her father's side.

"But the mayor's interest in you was fun to watch," her mother continued, unruffled. "Zachary Chance is a more cautious politician than your father ever dreamed of being, and he plays it close to the vest, from what I hear about the town meetings these days. But my bird's-eye view gave me a whole new perspective today, and Mr. Chance followed you with his gaze even when he wasn't scheming to get you into quiet corners of the garden." She paused, a long silence suggesting she waited for an answer to the question she hadn't asked.

"He thinks I'd make a good mayor," Heather found herself saying, revealing more than she meant to just so she didn't have to discuss the possibility of a mutual attraction between her and Zach.

"He's in such a hurry to give up his seat?" Turning in the big wingback, her mother adjusted her heavy glasses on her nose. "Or does he think he can still run things if you take over for him?"

"Am I so weak willed that you think he could?" Miffed, she stared her mother down.

"For heaven's sake, of course not. No daughter of mine is weak willed. But the mayor is *a man*. Who knows *what* he thinks?"

Heather laughed. Maybe she ought to listen harder for her mother's moments of levity, after all.

"Right. Well, I got the impression his job is demanding and he'd like to return to it sooner rather than later." Her other suspicions were too vague to name—that Zach was keeping an eye on her for some reason. "He reminded me that I had the same number of write-in votes as he did when they took the emergency poll after Dad...died."

She watched her mother closely, and waited for signs of darker emotions—darker beyond what one would expect from any widow who'd loved her husband deeply. Diana Finley hadn't had an easy time of it in the months after his fatal heart attack. She knew her dad supported her mother emotionally, even if he checked out on the family a fair amount. But Heather hadn't fully appreciated the depth of her mother's reliance on him until the aftermath. It had taken months to adjust her medicines so she wouldn't feel too numb to grieve, but to also maintain a safety valve where she didn't fall into a deep depression.

Her mother's doctors had done well. Heather wondered if the drug treatments for her own health issues would be half so complicated. Or physically draining on her body. As much as she dreaded the exhaustion and potential side effects of starting treatment, she prayed she made it to that doctor's appointment in Charlotte before she had another flare-up.

"I think I wrote your name in that blank, Heather." Her mother bit her lip in a rare moment of uncertainty. "Of course, we all thought Scott would be a good mayor, but he was in no place back then with his marriage already splintering."

"Thank goodness he and Bethany shored that up." Her eye went to the window again, but she didn't see any of her family on the lawn below. A few cars were pulling away, and someone had turned the music up on the outdoor speakers, the country tune audible inside the house. Thankfully, there were only Finley-family homes on the cul-de-sac.

"Yes. Scott and Bethany are happy. Erin and Remy will be honeymooning soon. Mack and Nina have their new restaurant in town." Diana ticked off her children on her fingers before sizing Heather up with a look. "Now we just need to get you and Amy settled back home."

"Hmm. Don't you mean we need to leave Amy

in peace and get me a dream recording career?" Heather knew her mother had very little faith in her musical ability, but couldn't she even *pretend* to be excited for her *American Voice* audition?

"I mean afterward, dear." Putting her head back on the chair, her mom closed her eyes. "Of course, I want my children to accomplish their personal goals first. But sooner or later, I'd like you all close by."

The five land lots for the five Finley siblings had been laid out since Amy's birth, their father ensuring the land he'd grown up on remained in the family. The old farm still had plenty of unused acreage, but despite a few offers, their father had kept the property.

"After Amy couldn't even get on a plane to come to Erin's wedding?" Heather heard someone coming up the stairs and lowered her voice. "I'd be surprised if she ever makes Heartache her home."

"Bah," Mom grumbled, eyes still closed, her fingers lacing and unlacing in her lap as if she couldn't quite find a comfortable position. "She's a Finley. She'll come home."

The need to argue that point was strong, but the bride's and groom's voices were out in the hallway, making her think the better of it.

"Hey, sis." Erin untwined her arm from Remy's waist as they stepped into the den. "We're just saying our last goodbyes."

Remy leaned a shoulder on the door casing, his eyes hardly leaving his new wife. "I told her if we left last night, we could already be fishing off the dock this morning."

"Which is why every woman goes on a honeymoon, I'm sure." Heather wrapped Erin in a hug as she teased her new brother-in-law. She adored him, wishing she'd been around to see Erin fall hard in love.

But she'd been in Austin, hospitalized with a mystery ailment and scared out of her mind. What would her mother have said if she'd called with the news? That she must be lazing around because she didn't like working?

Mom's comment about Amy made her all the more grateful she'd kept the incident to herself.

Erin playfully tugged on Remy's hair. "He's just kidding me because I'm convinced I'm going to be eaten by an alligator while we're there." Her breakfast wardrobe seemed more in line with her normal clothes—a dreamy white poet's blouse and a blue wraparound skirt with an iron-on transfer of a rococo painting, *The Swing*. "Apparently his mother's dock is frequently visited by large reptiles."

"If you need to leave the swamp, I hear New Orleans is only an hour away." She was so happy for Erin, just as she'd been happy for Mack when he and Nina had gotten engaged. But sometimes seeing that kind of love hurt when it remained so very absent in her own life. She felt that pang now as she moved from Erin to give Remy a hug goodbye.

"Don't you give her ideas, *cher*," Remy warned her, wrapping her in strong arms and planting a kiss on her cheek. "She's not getting far from me for the next two weeks."

Erin hugged their mother and then, when Remy moved to do the same, Erin whispered in Heather's ear.

"Thank you for staying last night." Erin squeezed her hand. "I know you're anxious to get to Charlotte and I'm excited for you, but it was really nice having at least one of my sisters here all weekend."

Guilt pinched at the reminder since she'd been so close to leaving town last night. Would have, if she'd been smart enough to fill the gas tank.

"I had fun." She walked downstairs with Erin while Remy got the last of their suitcases for the trip. "Have you heard from Sarah? Did she and Lucas make it back to school okay?"

Remy's daughter and her boyfriend attended college in Louisiana near where Sarah grew up.

"Yes. But she'll be back for Thanksgiving, so I want to make sure I have her room ready." Erin grabbed two bottled waters from the fridge before they headed out the front door. "And I forgot to tell you goodbye from Zach. He left with

Sam Reyes a few minutes after he talked to you and they both looked superserious."

"Really?" She remembered the sheriff had needed to speak to Zach privately. "Must have been police business."

"Maybe." Erin backed toward the car, where Remy secured the last bag in the trunk. "A cow got out of Harlan's pen again, maybe. Or our one traffic light went out. You can hear about it at the Tastee Freeze, tomorrow, I'm sure." The local ice-cream shop with outdoor picnic tables was a good spot for gossip from spring through fall. "But as for me, I'll be sleeping *late*."

Heather hoped Erin was right and whatever Sheriff Reyes had wanted wasn't a big deal. She'd see Zach tomorrow since she'd told him she would let him know before she left town. And as luck would have it, she'd gotten a text from TJ earlier saying her car would be ready Tuesday morning.

That meant tomorrow would be her last day in Heartache for—she hoped—a long time.

CHAPTER FIVE

LULLED BY THE scroll of data files across his computer screen, Zach was straining to keep his eyes open, when his cell phone rang.

"Ellie?" he answered at the same time he processed his sister's name on the caller ID, brain moving slow after a long night of work. "What are you doing up so late?"

Tipping back in his leather chair, he closed gritty eyes and pushed back from the desk. He'd set up his office in the basement of the house where he'd spent his high school years, another facet of his father's ruined world that Zach had felt compelled to reclaim.

"Late? Zachary, it's seven o'clock in the morning. Do you feel okay?" His sister immediately went into maternal mode even though she lived on the West Coast, almost two thousand miles away.

"I'm fine." He straightened, though, needing to check his agenda for the day. He had a ribbon-cutting ceremony today and he had told Sam he'd check in after he went through the old city computers for any hint of unusual bookkeeping. "Just lost track of time after pulling an all-nighter."

The basement office made a great place to work—he kept it temperature controlled, with high-tech security in place to protect his clients' sensitive information. But the lack of windows made it tough to tell day from night.

"Really?" Her voice shifted, a hint of pleasure chasing away the worry. "Well, I can't thank you enough for helping me put the finishing touches on the victim-support website last week. We're gaining a really strong sense of community on-line already and it's so good to see. Especially for the women who remain at risk from stalkers, Zach. It's scary to think I have friends still living that nightmare."

"It scares the hell out of me every day." Switching off the computer screen, he let the program continue to run on the copy he'd made of the former mayor's hard drive. "And I'm sorry I didn't follow up to see how the launch went, but something came up in town—"

"Heartache." The word was sharp with the animosity she felt for the town, the house they'd once lived in and the world she'd left behind. "I will never understand why you have the need to help out that godforsaken little map-dot."

He couldn't explain what had drawn him back to Heartache, especially after so many things had gone wrong in the little town. Maybe it was the charm of rural Tennessee.

"I sleep better at night listening to crickets instead of the traffic on US 101." He climbed the stairs to the main floor two at a time. Stepping into the kitchen, he opened a cabinet over the coffee bar and pulled down a mug. The stainless-steel coffee machine required no warm-up. He pressed a button and the scent of dark roast wafted in the air.

"If you say so," Ellie said. "But the analytics tracker you gave me shows we're reaching a lot more people than I'd imagined with the website."

Zach smiled. Ellie headed up a large movement online to draw awareness to cyberbullying and cyberstalking, using an anonymous identity, which he'd insisted upon in order to protect her privacy. The site she'd designed gave potential victims tools for protecting themselves from cybercrime. "I can't wait until we launch the portion of the site where users can create an account and document harassment."

In the background, he could hear the wind-flute music she favored for her morning yoga workouts. He pictured her relaxing on the roof of her condo, which had been built to look like a brownstone. She ran a public garden up there, too—or at least, public in that she'd opened it to everyone in the building.

With her legally changed name, Ellie was as

safe as she could be in California on her own. Zach had made sure she lived in the most secure building, fortified with another layer of cybersecurity to keep her protected online.

"We have to ensure the security on your site is rock solid since the criminals we're going up against are naturally tech-savvy consumers." He gulped his coffee too fast, in a hurry to get his brain in gear.

"Right. They are committing digital crimes by using the internet and texting to intimidate their victims. I understand that much."

"So we need to protect the data our users collect as they log it in the systems. Because if we create more tools that a stalker can use to harass and intimidate them…" Zach knew he was being excessively cautious, but he kept imagining some scared teenage girl trying to use the site's tracking system and then having her account hacked. Her stalker would know that she had collected evidence to mount a case against him. What if an incident like that actually propelled a stalker to take action?

He drained his coffee, then left the mug in the kitchen and searched the pantry for something edible.

"I know you want this to be perfect." Ellie spoke softly, reasonably. "I do, too. But maybe you should think about the twenty people your tools could be helping already instead of worry-

ing about that fraction of a percentage that something goes wrong."

Except that in his model, a fraction of a percentage equaled one human being. One anonymous
teenage girl like his sister had once been alone
and vulnerable out in the woods near the quarry.

"It's almost ready." He slammed the pantry
shut, vowing to look at the second stage of his
sister's website tonight. "I've got a meeting with
Sam this morning. I'll call you tomorrow."

"Tell Sam I said hi." Her voice shifted again,
her old crush on their friend obvious. "I hear they
miss him on the force here."

"I'll tell him." Disconnecting the call, Zach
checked his agenda and realized he needed to be
at the ribbon-cutting ceremony in an hour. Tiffany McCord sat on the town council, and she
owned the rod-and-reel store in Heartache with
her husband, Cole, a decorated war veteran. Since
their arrival, the McCords had been a strong force
for getting things done, and Tiffany would be vot-
ing against every motion Zach put in front of the
council for a month if he missed her big grand
opening today.

He had the sense she'd run for mayor in a nanosecond. But as much as Zach wanted out of the
job, he also didn't want the town overrun by a
woman who would have a fast-food chain on either end of Main Street within the year.

Switching on the shower in the master suite,

he set his phone on the vanity just as it buzzed. He read the text from Sam.

You know my background. I can't afford to keep secrets.

Zach closed his eyes. He understood what the terse note meant. Sam had become a cop despite his troubled teen years. There were things Sam wouldn't want to resurface in this town again. Keeping a lid on the missing town funds from the citizens of Heartache could be construed as complicity if Sam knew and didn't say anything.

Corruption in the town or in the sheriff himself. And yeah, Zach knew how it felt to be the kind of man people suspected of wrongdoing. His father had hung that albatross on him before he graduated high school. He wanted no part of digging up more trouble from the past that would only slow down his own efforts to track the incident reports from the quarry.

Give me until the end of the day, he texted back. He'd let his digital programs run and he'd tell Heather what he'd found so she could give her family a warning. Then Sam would have to go to the media with the report.

TEARS FELL ON her guitar.

Normally, Heather would never allow the strings to get wet, let alone any part of her favorite

Gibson acoustic. It was her songwriting guitar. Her comfort instrument.

And this morning, she couldn't play it for crap.

She had grabbed it first thing, not really paying attention to the fact that her hands were stiff. It had happened overnight. She'd swear her fingers were fine yesterday. Today, the universe took perverse pleasure in rattling her to the core. She was finally ready to pursue her dreams of playing music professionally and she couldn't hold down the strings for a freaking F chord.

She dropped her head to rest on the rounded mahogany shoulder and let the tears flow in a way she hadn't since finding out about the rheumatoid arthritis. She'd told herself to use the disease as a wake-up call. A motivating force to live the life she truly wanted and not the one that happened all around her.

Now, still sitting on her unmade bed, her cotton nightgown strap sliding off one shoulder, she fell apart as she clutched the beautiful instrument she couldn't play. Her fingers throbbed. Her knuckles were on fire. Swollen, too. The upper joints were puffy, especially on the ring and middle fingers of her right hand. The index and middle finger pulsated on her left.

The music in her heart—the song that had been teasing the corners of her brain—muted and vanished. She tightened her grip on the neck of the

Gibson, as much as her sore fingers allowed, and experienced the urge to smash it on the floor.

Hard.

Through the haze of hurt and anger, the chime of her cell phone pulled her back to reality. She reached for the device on her nightstand and took a deep breath.

"Hello?" She hadn't checked the caller ID.

"Heather? Are you okay?" Zach's voice, gentle with concern, cut through her hurt until she wanted to curl up against him and sob out all her problems.

A solution that would not be helpful.

"Fine," she lied, trying to keep her voice light. She used the hem of her long nightgown to swipe her face dry. "Just tired from the wedding revelry, I guess."

"I wanted to see if you were coming to the ribbon cutting for Upstream. I'm going by your house, if you'd like a ride."

"A ribbon-cutting ceremony? I didn't take the mayor job, remember?" She hadn't even left Heartache yet. She wouldn't get sucked back into town politics already.

"But you're such an advocate for local business," he reminded her.

"Am I?" She caught a glimpse of herself in her vanity's tiny mirror. She must have had some mascara on when she went to sleep as she had raccoon eyes. "I'm trying to be a musician, Zach."

Maybe a little too much "real" crept into her voice, because he went quiet for an extra beat.

"You will be a success at whatever you do, Heather," he said finally.

The kind words of a friend. The kind of thing her mom never said to her kids. Not that she blamed her mom or anything. It was simply one of those mornings. Her emotions bubbled under the surface.

"You see why you are the better mayor than me? You have a knack for knowing when to say the diplomatic thing. Unless…" She set her guitar in the stand beside the vanity. "You're using that gift for tact to lure me into attending Tiffany McCord's much-hyped store opening."

She had planned to attend. The woman had spent many hours volunteering at the rec department last summer while Heather had been out of town. But she would have gladly missed the commitment if she'd been in Charlotte already.

Unfortunately, she still sat right here in town.

Zach chuckled. "Funny thing about that. I happened to be completely sincere on your probability of success in life. But I also can't face the thought of a McCord event on my own at nine o'clock on a Monday morning."

"You wouldn't suggest this if you could see what I look like right now." She dug in the vanity drawer for cold cream and a cloth, considering his offer. She liked Zach, and talking to him was a welcome distraction from the crushing fear in her chest. She couldn't play her guitar.

If she didn't go, she'd end up crying again and she refused to sit around feeling sorry for herself. She'd figure out what to do about her audition later, when she wasn't an emotional wreck. Later, she'd email her friend Sylvia, the fellow musician and former student from Heartache who'd moved to Nashville a few months ago. But since Sylvia was only available to her online and Zach was here—in person—Heather sure was tempted.

"I already have an extra cup of coffee for you," he said.

"You can't make me feel guilty about a one-dollar expenditure." Gently, she cleaned her face, wincing as she bent a swollen knuckle.

"We're not talking about gas station coffee. I went to Mack and Nina's new restaurant, and Nina hooked me up with some kind of latte that smells nutty. She said it's your favorite."

"You really didn't want to go to that event alone, did you? Their restaurant isn't even open at this hour." She smiled a little, some of the despair in her chest lightening at the unfamiliar sensation of having a supremely attractive, intelligent man woo her.

Even if it was only because he wanted her to take a job.

"I spotted Nina sweeping up out front and she said she had the espresso machine warmed up anyhow. Did I mention being the mayor has its privileges?"

She had to laugh. That in itself seemed kind of amazing, given the way she'd wanted to smash her guitar before he had called. She definitely needed to get out of the house. Stop brooding for a little while.

"I believe you've hit that point a few times." She pulled clean clothes out of the closet and then climbed down the loft's narrow stairs. "If I say yes to this painful suggestion of yours, I feel like I should be rewarded with more than a latte."

"Such as?"

"Well, since you're kind enough to remember that I don't have a car today, maybe the Mercedes would be a good loaner since you have a garage full of vehicles."

"I'll take it under advisement."

"Really?" She slid into a soft, full skirt, which even Erin would approve of. Heather liked it because it was comfortable. Tossing aside her nightgown, she put the phone on speaker so she could wriggle into a bra.

"Of course not."

"The Porsche then." She cursed the back closure as her fingers struggled to fasten the hooks. She vowed to buy all new—less complicated—underwear before her hands became any worse.

"I was thinking more along the lines of dinner."

She stilled, her fingers pulsing with heated

pain. Only now, her heart pulsed harder, too. And *not* in a painful way.

"Hello?"

"I'm here." Why would Zach ask her out after the big fuss she made about leaving town? Although, there *had* been that electric current between them when he'd touched her. Still, she couldn't help thinking he was hiding something from her. Angling her into position like the skilled politician he was—even if he didn't give himself that credit.

"You force me to wonder if the thought of sharing a meal with me is more horrible than a press event with Tiffany McCord."

"Of course not." She tugged a short-sleeved sweater over her head. "There are simply more implications with a shared dinner."

"We can discuss those implications at length, now that I'm in your driveway."

"Already?" She ducked into the bathroom to brush her teeth. "Give me two minutes."

She ran her fingers under hot water while she cleaned her teeth, changing hands halfway through. The warmth eased the pain a little. She took some of the anti-inflammatory medicine the doctor in Austin had given her and checked the calendar on her phone.

Four days until her doctor's appointment in Charlotte.

A week and a half until the audition for *American Voice.*

Getting out of this town would help her condition, she was certain. She knew stress made it worse, and what could be more stressful than all the family events this week? She knotted her hair into a messy twist and left the house. Only to find Zach slumped sideways in the driver's seat of his dark four-wheel-drive SUV.

Sleeping.

She knew for certain he slept since Zach was the kind of guy who stood when a woman walked into a room and who opened doors for females. Yet, right now, his head tipped onto the window, his breath clouding a small patch of the glass with each exhalation. Something was definitely going on with Zach. Instead of climbing into the passenger seat, she tapped lightly on the windshield.

He startled straight.

"Want me to drive?" She should at least offer.

He shook his head and slid out of his seat, coming around to open her door for her.

"Just resting my eyes." His gaze followed her as she slid into the seat. "You look beautiful today."

"Now I know I can't trust a word you say, Mayor." She eyed him, searching for clues about what he might be hiding from her. She flipped her skirt straight and inhaled the scent of hazelnut filling the interior. Her hand went straight for the cup. "I hope you got one of these for you, too. This is elixir of the gods."

Savoring the warmth seeping through the cup and easing her stiff fingers, she noticed him still staring at her.

"I mean it, Heather. You are going to dazzle those judges in Charlotte before you even open your mouth." He tucked a finger into a twisty piece of her hair that hadn't quite made it into the knot. "I like this."

It was merely hair that he touched. Dead cells with no sensation of their own. But the way he moved the curl around his finger tingled along her scalp and sent a burst of pleasure along nerve endings that should not be paying any attention to him. Her breath stuck in her throat as she tried to think of something to say, and in another heartbeat that lack of air made her light-headed.

For a moment, with his gold-and-amber gaze dipping to her mouth and her heartbeat accelerating like a jet engine, she actually thought he might kiss her. Then he broke the spell by letting go and stepping away with a self-deprecating grin.

"Sorry." He shook his head. "I know you're going to let your music do the talking at that audition. But television does love a pretty face, and those judges know that, too."

He shut her door and then loped around to the driver's side of the SUV. He hopped in and buckled the safety belt. Thankfully, that gave her time to shake off the wave of attraction that had hit her like high tide.

"Damn straight my music is going to do the talking." She latched on to the subject with a fierceness that surprised her. Maybe it came from not being able to play this morning. "When I open my mouth, nobody's going to doubt it's my voice that got me on the show."

"Yes, ma'am." He grinned as he put the vehicle in reverse. "I'm going to keep all my commentary focused on talent and skill. No getting distracted by full lips or—" he glanced her way, his gaze taking a slow path from knee to shoulder "—long eyelashes."

Her heart skipped a beat and she ignored it. Mostly.

"I'm going to get the wrong idea about dinner." She sipped her coffee as he pointed the vehicle north, determined to reroute this conversation.

"I'd like to see you get a few more wrong ideas before you go. Maybe make a few bad decisions, too."

"Okay. Care to tell me why you're flirting— badly, I might add—with me this morning?" Actually, the flirting wasn't bad so much as it made her decidedly aware of him. And whereas she wouldn't mind a friend and a distraction today when her hands hurt and she waited for her car to be fixed, she wasn't ready to navigate the mine-field of a very real, very potent attraction.

"Sorry. I'm on no sleep. That's part of it." He steered toward the interstate. "I have less ability to filter thoughts when I haven't slept."

She tucked that bit of information aside. Those thoughts were unfiltered? Not calculated flirta-tion?

"Um…" She cleared her throat as she hit a raspy note. "Why aren't you going to the Up-stream store?" She pointed to the turn toward the main street as he drove past it.

"The ribbon cutting is out at the river. Better photo op. There's a fishing contest, and a rod-and-reel magazine will be there to take pictures."

"Ugh." She tipped her head against the seat rest. "I didn't dress for fishing. And now I'm cap-tive for hours instead of minutes."

"I thought you knew. Tiffany has been adver-tising it nonstop."

"I knew, I just forgot. I've had wedding on the brain." Along with the audition and her disorder that needed the intervention of a good doctor.

She resisted the urge to flex her sore fingers, remembering how observant Zach had been the night she'd run out of gas and her wrist had been bothering her.

"I can take you back if you want." He checked his watch.

"No. I know you're running late. Worst-case

scenario, you can loan me this for the day." She patted the SUV's dashboard in an effort to keep things light. "I just need to be back in town for a lesson with Megan at two o'clock."

"Are you free for dinner later?"

"You were serious about that?" She'd had a crush on him in high school. And the old feelings were definitely in danger of returning if he kept this up.

"I'll be honest, I have a few things to ask you about the town and your dad's work. But mostly I want to thank you for going with me this morning. I was afraid I'd say something really inappropriate since I'm tired and Tiffany McCord is one of my more challenging town council members."

Heather relaxed a bit. A thank-you dinner was not a date. Maybe he didn't have a secret agenda for wanting to see her, after all.

"She's a force to be reckoned with, isn't she?" Out the window, the signs of fall were starting to show as the road became more rural.

A few yellow leaves mixed with the green, and an occasional tree sported a whole branch of red. Normally, autumn ranked as her favorite season, but it had been a while since she'd walked among the falling leaves and truly enjoyed the season.

"Right. We'll call Tiffany that."

"Why didn't you sleep last night?" She had always envisioned his life as perfect.

Back in high school when his family had

experienced the scandal with his father, Zach had seemed untouched by it all. If anything, he'd been more of a presence in the school and had volunteered at a local nursing home. She remembered he'd organized a concert for the retirees, bringing the high school choral group to the rest home during Christmastime.

"Sometimes I need to burn the midnight oil to keep up with the day job and town business, too."

"Anything you want to talk about?"

"Only if you want to talk about what made you so upset this morning when I called." He glanced her way across the enclosed space, the moment far too intimate with his hazel eyes missing nothing. "You sounded like you'd been crying."

So he was not just observant but also frighteningly perceptive. And apparently they both had secrets to keep.

"Must have been my allergies." She wouldn't discuss her health with family, so she sure didn't plan to bring it up with him. "And you're not exactly making your case for dinner if you're on some kind of fact-finding mission."

His attention firmly focused on the road again, he shook his head.

"Just trying to be a friend."

Remembering how kind he'd been on the phone, assuring her she'd be a success at whatever she tried, she regretted shutting him down that way.

"Thank you. And it was nice of you to see if I needed a ride this morning, too. I appreciate it."

"Is that so?" He shot her a sly, sidelong glance, his good humor restored. "I had the distinct impression you would have gladly overslept and missed the Tiffany McCord three-ring circus."

"She's really gotten under your skin, hasn't she?"

He shrugged. "I'm not a stupid man. I run a successful business. I'm experienced in a lot of areas. But I'd like to think I'm also smart enough to listen to people with much different experiences than me at the town meetings. Like, if Harlan Brady speaks up—a lifetime farmer who's never left Heartache—I'm going to pay attention."

"Harlan doesn't speak unless he has something to say." Heather had always liked him. All the more since he'd started dating Nina's octogenarian grandmother. The two of them painted the town.

"Right. But Tiffany has a way of cutting off people like that with a sentence that usually begins 'When I was in charge of a Fortune 500 company budget…'"

Heather laughed. "I've heard that one a few times. Once, when we couldn't find the box of lost-and-found items for the Little League, she brought up her experience managing inventory for a Fortune 500 company. Because of that, she suggested she be in charge of the rec department stockroom. Which also happens to be one of the barns on the farm, by the way."

Zach lifted an eyebrow, his profile incredibly handsome.

"You store the town equipment at your mom's place?"

"Always have. We don't have storage facilities at the fields. The high school shop class built the shed on the property, and they keep school equipment there for team practices."

For a moment, she sensed he was concerned about it. But then they pulled into the fishing and boat launch area along the river just north of town. Cars and trucks filled every space. Country music played through a big pickup truck's speakers, the back window featuring a pink sticker that read Redneck Princess. A small tow-behind trailer had been converted into a concession stand for the day, and it sat parked at the water's edge. A big banner with the Upstream logo was tied between two massive hemlock trees. A van with the McCords' company name stood open and transformed into a minishowroom next to a small canopy sheltering tables and shelves of gear. Fishing poles and colorful lures overflowed from the racks.

"Wow." Heather waved to Trish, one of the stylists at the Strand salon, as the woman hurried from her car toward the concession stand.

She carried her own pole under one arm. "Maybe we should have given Tiffany the rec department inventory, after all. This looks great."

"I'm sure she spent a long time on it, especially after that fishing magazine signed on to send a reporter."

"I'm half expecting to see ESPN." Heather gathered her purse as Zach shut off the SUV and walked around to her side. "There's a tournament?"

He held the door for her as she stepped out, their bodies coming close enough to remind her how much the man affected her.

"It's a small event. I think she said there were twelve boats signed up." He reached for her hand, confusing her. "Take the keys in case you need to leave." He pressed cool metal into her hand.

Her fingers automatically closed around the keys. "I wasn't serious about that. I'm sure we'll be done long before my lesson with Megan."

"Just in case, okay?" He smiled, stroking the back of her hand lightly and making her pulse jump. "Plus, this way, I know you won't disappear on me if you have my keys."

She gave a jerky nod, not trusting herself to speak. If her hand hurt just then, she'd never know it. Pheromones must block pain receptors or something.

"Good. I'm looking forward to dinner."

"Aren't you tired?" she reminded him, pulling her fingers away and depositing the key into her purse. They strolled toward the crowd gathering near the water's edge. The stiffness in her hands had eased, the throbbing pain turned to a dull achiness.

"Depends. I'll probably be yawning on camera during the interview about fishing." He lowered his voice. "But when I look at you? The last thing I'm feeling is tired."

Tiffany McCord called to him then, waving Zach over to the large yellow ribbon near the tournament sign, her neat blond ponytail capped with a crisp white fishing hat. Zach muttered something about getting back to work, but Heather's mind still reeled from his suggestive comment.

He'd made no attempt to hide that he wanted her. Was this merely part of his goal to sweet-talk her into staying and taking over the job he no longer wanted? Or could there be something genuine? With his keys, Heather could stay or go as she chose and make up her own mind. Sure, it would be safer to stick to less intimate places for a conversation. But part of her health scare had been a renewed determination to live a little and take a few more risks.

Why play it safe with Zach, when she went a little breathless every time he came near?

Given the fluttery feeling in her chest and the warm pulse of desire in her veins, she was tempted to see what he had in mind tonight.

CHAPTER SIX

EVEN MORE THAN she hated stupid anonymous texts, Megan Bryer hated upsetting her father.

"I'll be fine, Dad," she said to him for the tenth time since breakfast. She tugged her blankets higher on her hips as she sat up in bed. "It's only a cold. You can still go to your fishing thing."

She couldn't face school today after the crap that had gone down at the wedding breakfast. Not that she thought of herself as a coward or anything. She just needed a break from high school BS for a day. But her father—a nice normal man in so many ways—had always been a hypochondriac by proxy, where she was concerned. Ever since she was a preschooler, he'd been convinced a sneeze would turn into pneumonia if they didn't put her on antibiotics right away. Her aunt had told her he'd gotten worse when her mother left him the year after they'd adopted Megan. That counted as one of many things she held against her "mom," who rated as just a random woman in Meg's mind. What kind of woman stuck around for only twelve months after convincing her husband that adopting a kid would be a good idea?

Thankfully, her adoptive mother had a supercool life in New York now as a set designer on Broadway, and her supercool family kept her too busy to bother Megan more than once a month with an interminable Skype call.

But Meg's dad was awesome, figuring out how to parent on his own. Sure, it had been embarrassing to be the kid who learned how to ride a bike long after her friends because of Dad's nerves. And yeah, it had sucked to be outfitted with every safety device known to man. Elbow pads, rash guard shirt, shin guards under her knee pads, goggles. Yes, goggles.

For killer bugs, maybe.

Still. At least her dad gave a crap about her, unlike her crack-addicted birth mom, unnamed biological father and the runaway adoptive mother who'd enjoyed Megan's baby methadone treatments a little too well.

Normally, Meg would rather go to school and hack up a lung in class rather than stay home and have her dad worry she was at death's door. But nothing about threatening, anonymous texts had been normal. Even for her as Crestwood High's "Most Antisocial" senior. She needed to regroup. Use the time at home to research her options for catching the person trying to scare her. If her ex-boyfriend had done it, she wanted to know. If it was Bailey and her friends, she needed to find out.

"How can I leave my girl when she's not feeling well?" Dad put a hand on his hip, his plain brown belt and brown dress pants the same work uniform he wore every day with little variation. He hardly ever videoconferenced with his students, but he dressed the part just in case.

"You don't even teach today," she reminded him. "Go enjoy the fishing thing, and that way I can keep my germs to myself." She pointed to the over-the-counter medicines she'd placed strategically on her nightstand. "I've got everything I need and I promise it's nothing serious. Just sniffles."

If he worried this much about a cold, how flipped out would he be if he knew that someone at school wanted her to kill herself?

"I could make you a doctor's appointment."

"Dad. I want to go back to sleep." She yawned, hoping she could get the house to herself to research in peace. Back in the summer when the harassment had started online, she'd hoped it would settle down with time.

But nothing had settled. It had gotten worse.

"I'll come back at lunchtime with something for you to eat," he said finally. "Something healthy."

"No. I want fish for dinner. Preferably a freshly caught smallmouth bass." Folding her arms, she stared her father down. He loved to fish, damn it. "I'll even clean it."

"Honey, you're sick. No cleaning fish for you." He frowned. "What if you needed me and I floated out on the water fifteen miles from here?"

"I have the number for the B&B," she reminded him. "Mrs. Whittaker is always telling me to call if I need anything. Remember?"

Dad stared *her* down before coming to sit on the end of the bed.

"You have her number in your phone?"

Excitement thrummed through her, which said a lot about the sorry state of her life. Seriously? Her dad leaving her alone so she could research cyberbullying was the thrill for the day?

"Yes." She clicked on the screen and scrolled through her contacts. "Do you want me to send it to you so you have it?"

Dad laid a hand on her foot through the quilted coverlet, on the obnoxious yellow sunflowers she'd chosen for her tenth birthday and hated ten months later.

"I have Tansy's number." He gave her a level look. "You really think you'd feel up to fish for dinner?"

"Definitely. I'm just run-down today."

He stared at her so long she thought he was ready to call the whole thing off. But then he straightened.

"Okay. Tiffany McCord got a fishing magazine to cover the event and I know she's hoping for a good turnout to help boost tourism." He headed for her door. "Promise me you'll phone if you feel worse?"

She made the X sign across her heart as if she were a five-year-old.

"Promise." For him, she swallowed all the unkind words that came to mind about Bailey's mom, who surely only organized a fishing tournament to sell more equipment and not out of some selfless need to make Heartache a tourist destination.

Then again, what did she know? Maybe Mrs. McCord wasn't a backstabbing liar like her daughter.

Ten minutes later, her father's old sedan backed out of the driveway and Meg had the house to herself. She dragged her laptop from under her bed, and then opened a browser window in "private session." She hoped her dad wouldn't be able to see it in a search history. Not that he seemed supervigilant about checking her internet hours. True, he might have seen some of the crap that had appeared on her social media accounts a few months ago. But she'd closed most of them four weeks ago when school started, hoping to give her anonymous detractors less means to taunt her. However, ever since she'd received that text about checking her Facebook page, she had worried. What if she hadn't deleted it properly? She wanted to make sure it was really gone.

A quick scan of her old friends' accounts

showed links to her closed account. Bailey was even "friends" with her on one popular social networking site. What the hell?

Clicking on her old profile picture to see why her account hadn't been deleted, Megan waited for the page to load. Her icon photo remained the same as the one she'd used in the past—she held her guitar in last year's talent show performance. Her name and her school were accurate, but the rest of the page had nothing in common with her old account.

The page said she'd transferred from Slutsville Academy. That her contact information referred to a 1-900 number with a name so foul there were asterisks in between the letters to get past the social media censors. Her work experience had been "on the local street corner," with more details that were too vile to read.

She slammed the computer shut, heart racing.

"Oh, my God." She hadn't read the page full of comments from her classmates, though she'd seen them out of the corner of her eye. She didn't want to look. But of course she'd have to look.

This morning, she'd had such high hopes of taking control of her life again. Of doing some web surfing to see if she could figure out who would send her those text messages, maybe use a reverse phone directory. The digits were seared into her brain. She'd had visions of reporting the harassment, or at least taking steps to contact her cell-phone carrier in a way that wouldn't involve her father.

But this...

Water drops sprinkled the glossy blue case of her laptop, and she was so rattled it took her a long moment to realize they were tears. She hadn't realized she'd started crying. The proof that her classmates had gotten to her was irrefutable—tears on the fucking laptop—and that caused a fury to build inside her like a ten-foot monster bursting at her skin to escape.

"I—" she screamed the word, rocketing out of her bed to swipe her makeup, hair dryer and papers off the dresser "—hate—" she shrieked, kicking the crap on the floor "—you!"

With the last word, she picked up a bottle of nail polish and hurled it at her closed bedroom door. China Girl Jade smashed in a splatter of green and dripped slowly down the door.

Heart hammering, Megan collapsed on the floor in a pile of discarded blankets and displaced homework. She wanted to twist and writhe and continue the tantrum for hours until she'd somehow screamed out all the fear and anger.

Except, was it possible?

All the crying in the world would not fix this. Her father would die if he saw that page. Oh, God. It would kill him. How could she ever look him in the eye after he saw something like that about her? She glanced at the cold medicine that she'd carefully positioned by her bed to convince her father she couldn't go to school.

Too bad none of those over-the-counter medicines were remotely strong enough to make the pain inside her go away. Nothing that would make her sleep until she was twenty-one and past this shit.

Or maybe something to make her sleep and sleep and sleep.

Her gut burned.

Unable to touch her laptop—which scared her more than if a coiled rattlesnake lay on the bed—Megan stretched her arm over her head to where her cell phone rested. She reached for it underneath a clunky old vanity she'd bought at a garage sale in an effort to make their house prettier.

To make up for the fact that her father's bitch of a wife had left him because Megan wasn't the kind of daughter she must have wanted when she said she'd adopt a child.

Clicking on the phone, Megan didn't care about the mess or the nail polish or the dirt that might be in the carpet fibers where the side of her face lay. Even though she kept seeing that stupid social networking site in her mind's eye, she forced herself to focus on her phone's screen and typed in "how to stop cyberbully."

Stupid, useless crap popped up about school policies to deal with the issue. Bypassing rules for reporting incidents to teachers and useless advice like "ignore them and hold your head up high." She scrolled through page after page until she got to a support group for women who'd been cyberbullied and cyberstalked. The snippet about the site read as if they might be for real, and that's what caught her eye.

When she clicked on their page in a new tab, she spotted a coming soon! header that advertised a feature to help users collect data. Data that could be useful to the police to help stop the harassment. What if she could actually send cops to the houses of all these false-faced, full-of-shit seniors who acted as if they were such great kids in front of their parents?

Eyes racing over the details, she found the name of the webmaster.

Holy crap.

Sitting up, she enlarged the font on the phone to be sure she had read it correctly.

And discovered the mayor of Heartache, Tennessee, was responsible for maintaining the website that could help Megan. She checked her watch, wondering how fast she could clean up her room. Because she couldn't blow off her music lesson with Ms. Finley now. Not when Megan knew damn well her guitar teacher had a friendship with Mayor Chance. Hadn't she seen them together yesterday?

Going to the lesson would be a better solution than downing too much cold medicine and pretending these poisonous people didn't exist. The hope of fixing this would get her through at least one more day.

"WHAT DO YOU mean you don't know how to fish?" Heather stared at him as if he'd stepped off an alien spaceship. This skill deficiency was unheard of in her world, apparently.

They stood on the banks of the Harpeth River, fishing gear in hand, thanks to Tiffany and Cole, who'd encouraged him to stay by giving him loaner equipment rumored to be top of the line. Not that Zach would know.

All around them, residents of Heartache cast their lines and settled in to enjoy the concession-stand snacks and entertainment. At noon, there would be a free barbecue picnic and the winners of the tournament would be announced.

"My father spent all my childhood scamming investors and wooing potential clients with trips on his private plane. We weren't exactly bonding over family outings, let alone father-son time on the local lake." He passed Heather the high-tech fishing pole Tiffany McCord had given him, his hand brushing hers. He lingered against her soft skin until her eyes widened with awareness. "But I'm sure I'll figure it out if you teach me."

He *didn't* try to make it sound like a come-on. But he knew he'd been fairly transparent when it came to Heather Finley. Not that he was purposely flirting with her. He simply wanted to touch her more. And with the time dwindling until he had to come clean about the missing town money and the old rumors surrounding her dad, Zach couldn't help taking advantage of the hours they had together before everything became more complicated.

Would she blame him for those old rumors coming to light? Worse yet, would she blame him for being forced to choose between her dream audition and standing by her family? His gut churned, but it didn't do a damn thing to lessen the attraction he felt for her. An attraction that grew stronger the longer he spent with her.

"No wonder you brought me." She juggled the fishing apparatus with ease, balancing the awkward weight. Even in her knee-length skirt, she looked at home on the riverbank. "Although you don't need a dinner date so much as a press secretary to run interference for you at events like this."

She pointed to a quieter spot around a small hill and he followed her there, watching her pick her way around tree roots and rocks in a pair of pale blue ballet flats.

"I'd take the date over the aide any day." He sat beside her on a grassy patch. "But you'd be an enticement to come to work more often if you were my secretary."

"In your dreams, Mr. Mayor." She smiled,

though. Just a hint of a wicked little grin that turned him inside out.

"Definitely. But I hope they don't remain mere dreams," he whispered while she cast the line, his eye roaming her demurely covered curves that were—he had to be honest—every bit as enticing now as they'd been the night after the wedding when he'd been treated to a peek at her bare waist.

"Were you paying any attention to how I did that?" she asked, turning the crank on the reel to tighten the line, her cheeks pinker than they'd been a minute ago.

"I think it's safe to say you have my undivided attention."

"Then my work here is done." She passed over the fishing pole.

"It's more fun to watch you." He accepted the rod and reel, but jammed the end into the dirt so he didn't have to hold it. It was what other people were doing.

Heather gasped. "Tiffany is going to have a conniption that you used her three-hundred-dollar fishing pole like a twenty-five-dollar beater." She pointed to the ambitious store owner, who seemed to be enjoying her master of ceremonies role. She mingled with guests just long enough to tout the merits of her sporting goods, but she rarely left the side of the reporter attending the event.

"So I'll buy it. That'll make her happy."

"It *is* the Porsche of fishing gear." Heather eyed it dubiously. "I guess that's about right for you."

"But?" He traced a finger along the edge of her skirt where it lay on the grass.

"But if you can't catch a fish on a twenty-five-dollar pole, all the tricked-out gear in the world isn't going to make you a good fisherman."

"I bet I'll find a way." He sighed as he stretched out on his back on the warm grass beside her, pillowing his head with his hands. The music from the tournament registration desk filled the air and Heather swayed ever so slightly to the tune. "How do you know so much about fishing?"

"Besides being a born-and-bred Tennessee girl?"

"Besides that." From his new vantage point, he admired the red curls draped along her back. He wanted to lift one up to feel the silken weight of it.

"My father taught me when I was small. I have good memories of choosing the right lures for him and playing silly games while we waited for the fish to bite." She smiled for a long moment—lost in thought. "But as I got older and Dad became busy with the mayor's job, I went with my siblings. We spent the summers playing in the woods and along the creek behind our farm." She glanced back at him over one shoulder and then leaned forward again, wrapping her arms around her knees to hug them to her chest. "Some days, we'd fish for hours. The best nights were when Scott—he's the oldest—when he'd build a fire and we'd cook whatever we caught right there along the water's edge."

"Your mother didn't mind?" He liked the image of her family hanging out together—it's how he'd always pictured the Finleys. Unlike his train wreck of a household.

"The times we fished from sunup to sundown were usually the days my mother struggled the most from a medical standpoint." Heather tipped her forehead to lay a temple on her knees, her face turned toward him, though he couldn't see her expression. "So, no. She didn't mind. We stayed out as late as we could, hoping she'd be calmer by the time we came home."

"How'd that work out?" A red curl hung within reach and he twined it around his finger.

Silky as he'd imagined.

"Depended. She could be more spun up than when we left. So in that way maybe it didn't work so well. But the creek gave us a place to be. Fishing gave us something to do." One side of her slender back shifted. A shrug, he realized.

"And at least you weren't hungry when you got home." He took the lighter approach, not wanting to chase her off the topic just yet.

"Assuming Erin and Amy pulled their weight," she muttered darkly, giving him a sidelong glance.

"Not all the Finley girls bring the same skill to the table as me when it comes to fishing."

"Is that so?" He liked touching her hair. Liked her smiling at him. He wished he could capture the day and hold on to it longer.

Life seemed simpler sitting next to Heather. As though he could almost forget the vow he'd made to hunt down his sister's stalker. To give her that peace and sense of justice. He needed to follow up with Sam about that, too.

"Absolutely it's so. Check out what your line is doing, Mayor." Straightening, she nodded at the fishing pole he'd jammed into the soft earth.

"Whoa." The thing bent like a willow in the wind. Or like a squirrel had hopped on one end, the tip practically skimming the water's surface. He scrambled to a sitting position. "What do I do?"

"You grab it." She already had it in hand, jumping to her feet as she tugged against whatever pulled on the other end. "Feels like a bass. They're fighters."

A few people fishing along the river's edge turned to watch her. Zach stood back to give them a clear view. She was something to see in her pretty skirt and girlie shoes, calmly shadowing the movements of whatever the hell battled her on the end of the line.

The line jerked hard, tugging her forward. He

reached for her, just to be sure she didn't fall, and his hand cupped her waist automatically.

"I've got it," she whispered, more to herself than him, as if she was talking herself through it as she turned the crank and reeled in the line, all the while walking closer to the river's edge. "Look out."

With a quick tug, she yanked up and hauled a green-brown flopping fish out of the water. A couple of old-timers nodded and smiled their approval.

"Have I been completely emasculated by not helping in some way?" He wasn't about to steal her glory, especially when watching Heather do just about anything was a pleasure.

"Not as long as you do the cooking." She grasped the end of the line and dangled the fish between them. "Guess I saved you from taking me out for dinner tonight."

"You're putting a lot of pressure on my limited culinary skills." His temperature spiked at the idea of having her alone at his place. "I'll just bring this to the fish-cleaning stand." He peered around the tournament hopefully.

Her laughter reminded him how short-lived her happiness with him would be. Damn it. As much as he wanted her to stay in Heartache, he hadn't wanted her to feel trapped the way she would be once she learned about the upcoming investigation of her father's time in the mayor's office.

"I think you're on your own for cleaning the catch." She tugged the hook from the fish's mouth. "We'd better grab a bag and some ice. I'll go ask Tiffany."

"I will." He slid in front of her, not wanting her anywhere near Tiffany in case the town board member asked questions about the missing funds. "That is, I need to tell Tiffany I'm taking the rod and reel, too, then I can bring you home." He took the pole and reel from her. "I know you've got your lesson with Megan soon."

"Okay." Her gaze darted toward the throng of board members in heated discussion near a pickup truck. "Thank you."

"Be right back." He made fast work of his errand while Heather spoke to a woman who owned the hair salon in town.

When he returned, she was alone, watching him with guarded eyes.

"All set." He patted the bag of ice. "Should we weigh your catch?" His step slowed as he saw a sign about weigh-ins.

"That's more for the boaters who are competing." She slid a hand around his elbow and steered him away from the noise and foot traffic near the scales. "Besides, if the universe grants me only one blue ribbon this month, I'd rather hold out for the *American Voice* prize."

"Who knew you were the superstitious type?"

"Not usually. But I've waited a long time for this dream, Zach. I'm not taking any chances."

Guilt had him by the throat, and tonight's dinner loomed even more ominous. He should have just let Sam Reyes give Heather the bad news this morning, but he'd wanted to wait as long as possible, hoping he'd find proof of her dad's innocence in the town computer system. But his data-analysis program had been running for hours with no luck, or he would have received a notification on his phone. So far he had no lead that might signal good news.

It sucked to think the attraction he felt—an attraction he was damn sure went both ways—would come to such an abrupt end. Before he'd even gotten a taste of her. He knew he'd be ten kinds of ass to push things further without her knowing what he needed to tell her.

And still? He'd have to pray for restraint.

CHAPTER SEVEN

"THANKS FOR THE RIDE, Zach," Heather said, unlocking the front door to her house. Her home was an old potting shed that her father had expanded into an office, complete with plumbing, a loft and a front porch. Later, Heather had reworked it into a tiny home so she could stick close to her mom while giving them both some privacy. The bungalow was hidden from view of the main house—no doubt why her father had chosen it for his work space—and the "driveway" was scarcely more than a car's length, and yet Zach had walked her to the door.

A gentleman.

Albeit one who'd cooled off toward her sometime this afternoon. She should be glad he'd reined in the flirting and the touches since she'd be leaving town soon. Besides, she was pretty sure Zach wasn't being completely forthright with her about his reason for spending time with her. But honestly, the man had lit her up inside hotter than some former boyfriends had managed to do with a full range of physical intimacy. To have him withdraw that electric spark now, before they'd even kissed, left her feeling a bit hollow. And more than a little confused.

"I should be thanking you." His amber eyes were serious, the teasing light muted. "Being with you made a ribbon-cutting event fun. Something I would have once said was impossible."

"Glad I could help." She slid the key to her house back in her purse, the front door open, but she didn't move to enter. "And if you want, I can take the fish off your hands and sort out dinner. I didn't really mean to suggest you should cook, when you must be exhausted from not sleeping last night."

She was curious about the work that had kept him awake. He'd been cagey on that point.

He shook his head, sunlight picking up blond strands among the brown. "I'm looking forward to cooking for you."

That intense gaze of his made her feel as if he'd just said something a whole lot more intimate.

I'm looking forward to kissing you, is what her ears heard.

No need to be ridiculous. But her cheeks warmed.

"I might need a ride." The words caught in her dry throat.

"Can I pick you up at seven?"

"Sure." She was ten kinds of idiot to feel as breathless as a teenager on her first date.

Move away from this secretive, handsome man. But did her feet listen? No. She gazed at him and thought about how she never took chances. About how she'd promised herself she would start living in the moment.

Stop being so damn practical.

"Heather." If he meant to warn her away, the deep timbre of his voice didn't exactly get the message across.

If anything, she drew closer. Zach didn't step back. Her heart pounded so hard it made her lightheaded. She had zero experience making moves on a man. But Zach had touched her. Flirted with her. Insinuated he wanted more from her...

Her lips parted, her eyes never leaving his. She knew the exact moment he got on board with the plan. Something shifted in his expression, a subtle softening that served as her only warning before his hands slid around her shoulders and his mouth met hers.

His kiss was warm and soft, the gentleness at odds with all that hard male strength banded around her where he held her against him. She closed her eyes and fell into the sensations, letting the whisper-brush of his lips tantalize her as she melted into his chest.

No thinking. Only feeling. Surely she deserved that after the hellish few weeks she'd had. She could afford to savor the sweep of Zach's tongue along her lower lip, the increasing pressure of the kiss ramping up and reminding her she was a woman and not just a frustrated daughter, wannabe singer and victim of an exhausting disease. Right now, with Zach's hands skimming down her shoulders to land inches above her hips, she was hot. Wild.

Desired.

"Come inside," she whispered against his lips, tugging him forward.

He stopped. Stared down at her, his breathing hard and uneven.

Which mirrored how she felt, too. Until she realized what she'd just said.

"I mean." Her temperature climbed a few more degrees. She bit her lip. "Er. The house. I meant, come inside the house."

She nodded at the open door and Zach followed the motion. Then smiled for the first time since they'd left the riverside.

"Yeah. I knew what you meant." His smile broadened. "And that's tempting on every level." He eased his hands from her waist to trail up her arms. To rest on her shoulders underneath the blanket of her hair. "You don't know how much."

Yes, well. That was the point. She wanted to see for herself how tempted he might be once she got him behind a closed door. Her skin felt too tight, as if she just might crawl out of it. Her breasts ached for his touch after only a few moments being pressed up against him. She'd forgotten how needy sexual hunger could make her feel.

Oh, wait. She'd never experienced this sensation before. No wonder she practically hyperventilated all over the man.

"That doesn't sound like a yes to me." She forced herself to step back, away from the temptation of his hands. His lips.

"We'll talk over dinner." He stroked a thumb down her cheek. "If you still feel the same way then you'll hear the yes loud and clear."

Her cheek tingled from his scant caress, but she couldn't deny it. She'd been rejected. She backed up another step, out of his reach, so that she stood on the threshold of the open doorway.

"See you then." She didn't wait for his goodbye.

Clutching her pride tight, she forced a smile and closed the door.

When she heard a soft rap a few minutes later, she wondered if Zach had changed his mind. She cursed herself for how fast that thought made her hormones cook all over again. Hoping to get control over herself, she took her time opening the door. She breathed deeply.

Only to find Megan on her front porch.

"Hi!" She checked her watch as she opened the door wider. "Come on in. I wasn't expecting you until after school."

"I didn't go today." Dressed in dark sweats and a pink sweatshirt, she had the hoodie pulled up over her head. "I got behind on some schoolwork so I faked a cough, but I'm not sick. I promise. Or I wouldn't have come over."

Megan set her guitar case on the floor by an antique umbrella stand.

Heather noted the girl's puffy eyes. "Everyone needs an occasional personal day," she said carefully.

Shuffling aside her own frustrated feelings, Heather pulled herself together and morphed into professional mode.

Something must be wrong in Megan's life. Heather would bet her savings on it. But drawing out a troubled teen was a task rife with potential land mines. She remembered all too well how she'd tried to talk to her sister Amy before she'd left Heartache for good. All she'd done was push her further away.

"Exactly." Megan looked around Heather's house. "You're all packed up for your trip?"

"Pretty much." She'd forgotten that the place would have looked different since the last time her student had visited. "I used the trip as an excuse to clean out old things I didn't need and get organized."

"You must be so excited to get out of this town." Megan ran a finger along the edge of a postcard on Heather's bulletin board. It was from Sylvia, and one of the few homey details remaining on the walls.

"It will be fun to test my skills against other

performers." She watched as Megan moved her attention from the Nashville postcard to one from Memphis. Graceland.

Megan nodded. "Plus, you get to be anonymous in a big city. No one knows you. No one tracks your every move." She spun around to face her. "I mean, it can get sort of claustrophobic in a small town."

"Definitely." Heather frowned. Was Megan's overprotective father riding her too hard about grades or college plans? Who else would track her every move? "But I don't mind Heartache most days. My younger sister hated it. She hasn't been back since she quit high school."

"She quit school?" Megan's eyes widened.

Crap. Was that the wrong direction to take this conversation? She wondered what mild-mannered Professor Bryer's reaction would be if he found out Megan's music teacher was filling her head with stories about discontented teenagers who emancipated themselves at seventeen and never looked back.

"There were a lot of factors at work there, but yes. She never liked it here." Heather had been thinking about Amy a lot recently. During the past two years, her sister's absence had felt like more than simply a chance to find herself.

Lately, it had seemed more permanent. As if Amy had no love for any of her family. And that hurt. Worse, it made Heather realize how deeply they'd hurt *her*, and that stung a whole lot more.

"I passed the mayor's car on my way here," Megan announced as she flicked open the latches on her guitar case.

Heather blinked, surprised at the conversational turn, though she was glad to move away from the topic of her younger sister.

"He dropped me off after the fishing tournament, since my car is in the shop." Heather picked up her own guitar, a Taylor Dreadnought with a gorgeous rosewood body. Her father had bought it for her twenty-first birthday. Until that gift, her parents hadn't done much to encourage her passion for music. It had moved Heather that her father had not only noticed and understood how much her playing and singing meant to her, but that he'd gone to the trouble to hunt down a truly special six-string for her.

Making herself comfortable on the couch, she sat across from Megan, who'd pulled up a hard-backed dining room chair, which she preferred for playing. Heather's fingers ran over the chords, and they felt much better than they had that morning. She knew that with RA, she could experience morning stiffness that would ease as the day wore on, but the pain she'd had earlier had been much worse than the phrase *morning stiffness* suggested. Was that really what she had to look forward to every day?

"I wondered about trying to interview him for a school project." Megan picked along the strings faster than normal, tightening and tuning while Heather warmed up.

"The mayor?" she clarified. She knew she was distracted—because of the kiss with Zach and because of her hands—but today's conversation with Megan tread strange water. Normally, they discussed tremolos and legatos, grace notes and slides.

Something was definitely off today with her student.

"Yeah." The girl huffed a breath sideways to blow a strand of blond hair from her cheek while she twisted a tuning post hard. "I'm doing a paper on internet safety for teens, and I saw online that he manages a website that will help with that."

"Really?" How little she knew about Zach, yet she'd been quick to kiss him senseless.

Although, if her goal was truly to be less practical, she must be knocking it out of the ballpark.

"You didn't know, either?" Megan stopped messing with her strings and met Heather's gaze.

"No. I do know that he owns a digital-security company and works on special digital forensics cases as a consultant. But I've never heard him talk about the website. How does it work?"

Megan's eyes darted away. "Oh, I don't really know much about it. Just that it's supposed to help people collect data or something if someone is bugging them online." She focused on the tuning post again, twisting hard and fast on the string she'd already tightened. "The beta version is supposed to launch soon."

The string broke at first strum, the discordant note overly loud.

"Megan?" Heather quit strumming while the girl stared at her broken string. "Is everything okay?"

Megan dragged her guitar case closer, clunking and thunking as she dug around the accessories box. She didn't meet Heather's eyes.

"Totally fine. Sorry, I'm just a little late on that research project. I guess I didn't realize I was stressing about it."

"I'm sure it's not easy juggling a job and school." She wondered how much to say. How much to press. "Is there anything I can do to help? I will see Zach later today for a…meeting. Would you like me to ask him about the interview?"

"You'd do that?" Megan straightened, the guitar string forgotten, her eyes bright with emotion that seemed more intense than gratitude.

"Of course. I don't know what his schedule is like, but I can certainly encourage him to get in touch with you as soon as possible. When is your project due?"

Megan shook her head. "Don't worry about that. It's my fault I'm late. As long as it's good when I turn it in, I'll get some credit for it."

Yet another red flag on a day full of them—why did Megan, who'd always been an A student, seem content with a poor grade?

Heather wanted to offer more help than putting her in touch with Zach, but she didn't want to add to Megan's stress. Besides, one of the benefits of music was that it could take a person away from everything else.

Maybe for today that escape would be the best thing she could offer.

"Good. Then let's get you restrung so we can start practicing. I have some pointers for you on getting creative with solos and developing personal style." Megan was a good player. She could handle this level of play. She'd gone beyond intermediate to advanced over the summer. "I know it helps me as I'm writing to play around with chords and motifs to get some new sounds."

While Megan restrung her instrument, Heather talked through the day's lesson, hoping to find creative inspiration for herself, even as she showed Megan ways to tighten her focus on their craft. Soon, they were busy playing with slides and slurring notes, racing each other through progressions and seeing who could play one slowest for the longest sustains. Heather had fun, and she was pretty sure that Megan—for at least a little while—had forgotten what was bothering her.

Maybe that wasn't a good approach to problems. Heather had tried the "bury her head in the sand" method for years, and that hadn't helped her move forward. But for one day? It sure worked like a charm.

She hoped Zach would help Megan with her research. Heather was thankful to have another topic of conversation over dinner to divert them from discussing their kiss. Because no matter how much music she played this afternoon, she couldn't forget the way Zach's kiss had made her feel. Heady. Sexy. Out of control.

And she'd be lying through her teeth to say she didn't want to experience that again.

CHAPTER EIGHT

ZACH KNEW THE sooner he dealt with the rumors brewing on the town council, the better. That's why, as he drove through the small Heartache downtown to Heather's place, he talked through the approach in his head ten different ways.

It's probably just gossip, but I need to look into some missing money during your father's term as mayor.

He winced. Sounded accusatory.

Funds from Harvest Fest disappeared two years in a row, and council members are concerned your father was involved.

He snorted in disgust. Sounded as if he sucked at his job for not looking into the matter when he first took office.

Your dad may have stolen money from the town coffers, but don't worry, it's only a small fraction of how much my dad stole from stock investors.

He pounded a fist against the steering wheel. He knew damn well there was no gentle way to absorb the news your father might be a crook. Truth be told, he was having a tough time contending with the whole idea of Ted Finley as a thief. Zach had always looked up to the guy—the whole family, really. He'd seen the Finleys as having the kind of home he wanted. The type of bonds his family lacked. The kids stuck up for each other and the parents were civic-minded members of the community who ran a thriving business that helped keep the town strong—first Finley Building Supply and later, the construction company.

He was having a hard time wrapping his head around a new view of Mayor Finley.

When he pulled into Heather's driveway, he hadn't found a good way to break the news. She sat on the porch swing, her silhouette made visible by the glow of light emanating through the bungalow's front window. She didn't move as he shut off the SUV, her attention focused on whatever she held in her hand. Her phone, he realized, noting the pale white light shining on her face from the device.

He took a moment to stare. She attracted him in a way no one else had, her sense of honor and loyalty to her family strong even though her own dreams pulled her in other directions. She'd sacrificed her own wants to help her mother, embodying all the things he'd admired in the close-knit families who made Heartache their home.

Zach shook his head. He'd been spending too much time in his office basement if he hadn't tried getting to know her better before now. What the hell was the matter with him? Why had he waited until he knew she was leaving town?

The kiss they'd shared had been in the back of his mind all day. Every minute they'd been apart.

"Nice night for a swing," he called as he opened the door of the SUV and stepped out.

She looked up. She wore a pink denim jacket with a cream-colored silk scarf around her neck.

"Sorry I didn't see you. I got distracted." She pointed to her phone. "I heard a rumor about you this afternoon, Mayor, and had to check it out for myself."

He knew which of his family skeletons were public knowledge and which ones were buried deep, so he didn't worry. He stepped onto the cobblestone landscaping outside the front door. Pumpkins flanked the door, perched on hay bales. He could now see she wore a sundress under the pink denim, and a worn pair of brown leather cowboy boots, which she scuffled on the stones to stop the swing.

"I'll bet you I can tell you more than any search engine." He dropped onto the seat beside her, weary from a day that was only going to get tougher.

"I'll bet you can, too. But little-known fact about me? I'm not terribly patient."

"Is that right?" He reached for her phone. "Little-known fact about me? Neither am I."

He tried to tug the phone out of her hand, but she held on tight, laughing. He breathed in the scent of her hair, remembering the way it had driven him crazy when they'd been fishing and he'd watched the heavy red mass sway along her back as she moved.

"Wait." She gripped his other hand to hold him off until both their hands were brushing. "I have to tell you the whole story first so you can appreciate where I've been hearing rumors."

Mischief danced in her blue eyes.

And yeah, he hated himself for not confessing the news about her dad immediately. But he hadn't expected her to have confessions of her own.

"Out with it, Finley." He gave her a level look, but he relaxed his hold on her phone.

He didn't let go of her other hand. If she wanted that back, she'd have to take it.

She didn't.

"One of my students is Megan Bryer. She worked with the catering company yesterday."

"I know who she is." Playfulness shifted to concern. "Her father just joined the town council last spring when Tiffany McCord did. He's a good guy. Doesn't let Tiffany ruffle him."

Had Heather heard rumors about the missing Harvest Festival money?

"Weird how two council members resigned

their seats at midterm." She raised an auburn eyebrow at him. "Are you scaring people away, Mayor?"

"Consider how terrified I am to attend the McCords' ribbon-cutting ceremony by myself and you'll realize how ludicrous that sounds." He leaned so their shoulders brushed, tilting his head to confide the secret. Also to feel the brush of all that red silky hair against his cheek.

"Right. I forgot how easily intimidated you are by accomplished women." She edged forward to look him in the eye, still playful, but there was an element of awareness, too. A hint of breathlessness in her words.

His heart slugged harder in his chest and he wished things were different between them. Wished...so much.

"Don't try to distract me." He stroked the inside of her palm, saw the way her breath caught as he did. "Tell me about Megan Bryer."

"She hasn't been herself lately. Stressed about school and college and money. Except there's got to be more to it than that." She frowned and stared at the phone on her lap. "I'm not sure exactly. But I do know she's falling behind in some schoolwork, because she mentioned wanting to interview you for a paper."

"No doubt she heard I won the seat in a landslide vote." He continued to stroke Heather's hand, wondering what she'd needed to research about him.

He didn't like revisiting the BS from his father's crimes. And he sure as hell hoped no one had discovered anything about Ellie's problems. He and Sam had worked hard to make certain she stayed relatively hidden, her identity adjusted just enough to keep her off her old stalker's radar.

"Megan said you manage a website." She flipped the phone around so he could see the page she'd loaded—his sister's victim support group.

Not that anyone else would make that connection.

"True enough." His name must be on one of the pages he'd uploaded for Ellie. Or else Megan had found him in the WHOIS search for ownership of the site. Zach hadn't wanted Ellie's contact information on there.

"You are a man of many talents, it seems." She set the phone back on the swing. The wooden slats creaked as she moved, the only sound except for the chirp of night bugs.

"Do you think my advanced tech skills make up for my lack of fishing expertise?" He wanted to change the subject. Still, he needed to tell her about the soon-to-be investigation into the town's missing money.

But he was curious how the hell Megan Bryer had found that link.

"Possibly. The website sounds like it will offer

valuable tools to victims of cyberbullying." Her eyes were full of questions he wasn't ready to answer. He sure couldn't tell her about his sister's connection to the site.

"I try to choose a few gratis projects during the year." That was true enough. "This group needed some help and their mission lines up well with the goals of my digital-security company."

Before she could ask him any more, he gestured toward the car.

"I'll tell you about it on the way back to my place," he offered, tugging her to her feet as he stood.

An hour later, they were putting the finishing touches on the fish in his kitchen. The sun had long set, but the pendant lights over the breakfast bar glowed with warm light. Heather sautéed the filets and he chopped the mushrooms for a sauce she'd come up with based on the ingredients in his refrigerator. The trout would be served over angel-hair pasta with a light cream sauce. His kitchen smelled amazing.

"So I think I get it." She switched the flame off beneath the skillet and moved the fish off the burner. "The site will offer tools to help victims of cyberbullying track incidents of harassment, which ties into your company's interests. But this has your name on it instead of your company's name, Fortress Nine."

Because it was personal. Because his sister was

nearly raped by a stranger in a nylon mask who'd stalked her and hunted her down when he thought she was alone. But Sam Reyes had made sure that didn't happen, a protector to the core, even before his days as a small-town sheriff.

Too bad that story was never told, not even to his mother.

Sam had beaten the guy until he was scared he'd killed him. But after a car drove past the lonely stretch of road where it had happened, Sam had hid. After the car disappeared, the stalker—what Sam had thought had been a lifeless body—was gone. Zach and Sam had many reasons to keep the incident quiet, even if Zach had wanted police help. The cops had never done a damn thing to help Ellie before, and Sam was old enough he could have been tried as an adult if someone thought he was guilty of assault. But most important, his traumatized sister had begged for time to think about what she wanted to do.

Two weeks later, she'd tried to kill herself.

Zach ground his teeth. Forced himself to breathe normally. He wasn't sharing that part. But he needed to tell her a piece of it. Just enough so she'd understand his personal investment in Ellie's efforts.

"Not many people know this, but my sister had a stalker in school."

"Gabriella?" Heather pulled down the plates from the stainless-steel open shelving while he drained the pasta. "Wasn't she in my sister Amy's grade?"

"I think so." He found a bottle of wine and sought her approval.

"Thanks, but I'd better not." She passed him a water glass. "I'll have water."

"Me, too." He slid the wine back into the temperature-controlled drawer and took care of the drinks.

"I'm sorry to hear about the stalker." She touched his arm lightly, her eyes full of sympathy. "That must have been terrifying."

"She reached out for help, thank God." She'd been scared to tell him at first, knowing the rest of the family was consumed with their father's trial. "We handled it. But I like helping other people going through that kind of problem. Which makes me wonder about Megan finding the link to that article about the app, which I know is buried online. You said she seems troubled?"

He gestured at the table. The scent of sautéed pineapple hung fragrant in the air. His dining room was ridiculously formal, and he planned to change the floor plan to use it for something more practical. For tonight, he'd set them up in a corner of the kitchen with a banquette and medium-size table. An informal meal. Like a regular couple, comfortable with each other.

Good, right?

His gut knotted.

"Yes. But she said her school project was on cyberbullying. I think she was just researching the topic and stumbled across your name." Heather slid into her seat while their dishes steamed. "This smells delicious."

"Tell her to call me. I'm happy to do an interview." He'd quiz her himself once he got her on the phone. He knew a thing or two about victim mentality, thanks to his sister's work with her group.

And he knew for a fact that an average internet search about cyberbullying wouldn't bring up his name. The girl would have been knee deep in articles and references to find a site that was just a couple of weeks old. What if a stalker was still at work in Heartache, targeting young girls?

"So, that's my news." Heather twirled her fork in the pasta. "What's yours?"

"Hmm?" He hated to think of a local girl being bullied, maybe even cyberstalked all over again. What if the predator who'd gone after his sister was someone who'd never left Heartache?

"You wanted to talk to me tonight." Her bite of dinner was poised in midair. "What was that all about?"

Right. No more delaying. He forced himself to try the dinner before he lost the rest of his appetite. For all he knew, his evening with Heather could end any moment. From an objective standpoint, he registered that the food was delicious, but he took no pleasure in it.

"A few weeks ago, I started noticing some strange behavior among a few of the old town council members. Conversations that cut short when I entered a room. Meaningful looks exchanged across a table that suggested shared secrets." His gaze dropped to where Heather's left hand rested on the heavy plank table, remembering how she'd held on to him this afternoon, drawing him closer as he kissed her.

"Probably people who don't agree with your politics." She sat back to take a sip of her water, her lips curving in a smile. "No one liked it when you shelved the plans to develop a new bike park."

Any other time, it would have made him grin. The bike park had created quite an uproar in the small town.

"I hoped that's all it was. But I asked one of them last week if anything was going on and the guy—Harlan Brady—got oddly flustered when he denied it. I asked Sam to keep an ear to the ground to see if I was missing something."

Heather's lone gold bangle clanked against the table. He had brought her here hoping she would understand about the investigation. And that by night's end he'd be stripping off that gold bangle along with everything else she wore.

"I can't believe you asked the sheriff to investigate sideways glances." She cut a piece of bread from the minibaguette he'd picked up at the store, and handed him a piece.

He shrugged. "Just keep an ear out for news. That's all. I was curious what I was missing." He should have poured some wine even if she wasn't drinking. Hell, a few shots would have been helpful to steel himself for this.

"And?"

"Sam found out a whole lot more than either of us expected." He set his fork down. Braced himself. "Remember when he approached me at the wedding breakfast?"

"He looked intense." She continued to enjoy the meal, still unaware of the turn the conversation was about to take. "What did he learn?"

"Apparently, the issues arose a few weeks ago when I'd asked for the books on the old harvest festivals. Some of the long-time town council members were going to dig them out of storage so I |could put them into a program that would help us with future budgets."

"No surprise. My dad didn't use Excel. He wasn't much for technology." She pointed to his plate. "Don't let your food get cold."

He forced another few bites into his mouth, wishing his timing had been better so they could have enjoyed this evening together.

"Small towns are often slow to update because they don't have budgets that afford big changes." That much he understood. Yet, there was no good explanation for what the books showed. "But apparently, the council members took a look at the accounts instead of just handing them over to me."

"They're certainly all very invested in Harvest Fest."

Right. Unless one of them was trying to protect himself or doctor the books.

"I realize that. But they'd been exchanging sideways glances at meetings because they'd discovered funds had gone missing from the festival two years in a row."

"Really? That would have been during my dad's term." She paled, her cheeks losing color as her lips parted with surprise.

He didn't bother confirming what she already knew. As much as he wanted to offer comfort, he knew that touching her now would only complicate things. The last thing he wanted was to drive a wedge between them forever.

"Sam got the books and we went over them last night. I started running a program to analyze the brief bits of digital data we have on file."

"That's why you didn't sleep. You were trying to figure out where the missing money went." She tucked a strand of hair behind one ear, watching him intently, her meal forgotten. "Any luck? A bookkeeping oversight?"

"No. That's why I wanted to talk to you." He traced the condensation on the outside of his water glass while he considered how to tell her. "I'm going to have to call for an official investigation."

HEATHER TRIED TO process the words, willing herself to stay calm, even if worry simmered beneath the surface.

"I don't understand." She cleared her throat, her voice not quite there. "That's a good thing, right? You need to figure out what happened."

She hugged herself, feeling a sudden chill.

"Of course."

"Are you concerned that one of your council members stole town money?" She knew that Zach felt as if the mayor role took up a great deal of his time. Since he'd found out this news, he must be regretting his decision to step into office even more.

"I'm concerned about missing money, yes." He met her gaze straight on, shifting in his seat. "I'm also concerned about a cover-up, a scandal and the possible taint to the mayor's office."

She knew small-town politics could be ugly, but she hoped he was worrying too much.

"Seriously? But you aren't responsible for this—" She stopped, all at once understanding what he'd been telling her tonight, and it chilled her to the core. "You think *my father* had something to do with the missing money?"

Anger surged through her. Just what the hell was Zach saying?

"I would never jump to conclusions."

"He ran this town for a decade," she reminded him, her heart beating faster. "He revived Heartache during a recession and brought back the harvest festival. Finley Building Supply donated all the lumber in the stands and stalls in the fairgrounds—"

"I know that." He tried to lay a hand on hers, but she edged back, curling her fists in her lap, still in disbelief that he'd invited her over for dinner only to accuse her father of corruption.

She'd been envisioning hot kisses. Maybe a little more than that. And all the time, he'd been planning what? A political sneak attack?

"No. You don't. Because if you had any idea how much my father sacrificed for this town..." She didn't want to finish that thought. She stood, too shaky and upset to sit still. "I can't believe you would accuse him of something like this."

"You must be aware that I haven't made any accusations whatsoever." He remained in his seat, one strong hand slowly mutilating a linen napkin. "I hoped my research last night would pinpoint a discrepancy in the books so an investigation wouldn't be necessary, but it didn't, and I can't sit on the knowledge any longer. Sam is not pleased that I asked him to wait until tomorrow to announce it so I could speak to you privately."

Heather stalked into the big kitchen, where she'd so recently had had fun making dinner with

Zach. How could she have come here with ridiculous romantic notions when he'd been planning to drop this bombshell? A bombshell that would destroy all her plans.

"I can't believe you didn't say something earlier." How would she break this news to her mother? She paced, her shoes slapping a fast beat on the hardwood floor.

She didn't know how much money was missing, but in a small town like Heartache, it wouldn't take much to upset the local residents. And rightfully so. Yet, she hated the thought that her father could be implicated when he couldn't even defend himself.

Zach spread his hands. "When could I tell you? At the wedding breakfast, when your family was hosting the most important Finley event of the year? Or this morning at the fishing tournament, when I was on the clock performing my duties as mayor?"

"How about before?" She remembered talking to him on the phone. Hell, he could have called her with this news so she would have had more time to think up a strategy for her family's formal response. "Or how about *after* the tournament? You could have talked to me then instead of letting me kiss you." She paced faster, but damn it, she couldn't outrun the truth that he'd betrayed her. "No wonder you didn't want to... take things further."

Zach rose. One second he was seated and the next he stood in her path.

She'd been in those arms just a few hours ago, her fingers twining through his hair to bring him closer. Even now, the awareness was un-freak-ing-deniable. Only now she knew better. There would be no more out-of-control kisses tonight. No more risk-taking with him.

"Heather. Please." He grasped her shoulders in his hands, his touch confusing things. "I wanted to fix it myself so it wouldn't come to this. I was tired this morning and not thinking clearly. I'm still tired and not thinking clearly. But I promise you, the only thing holding me back this afternoon was the knowledge that I had to tell you about this first."

She eased out of his reach, not wanting to be swayed by the distraction of his strong hands.

"Fine. You should have told me sooner, but at least I know now." She searched the kitchen for her handbag and found it sitting on the counter. "I've got to get home and talk with my brothers. Figure out what to do." She'd probably have to interrupt Erin on her honeymoon, too. And she hated that. "I think I'd like a ride home. Please."

He stared at her in the warm light of the kitchen, his crisp gray button-down as perfect as the rest of him. Too bad that polished exterior had deceived her. Or, at the very least, misled her.

"I can help you think through a response. You

know as well as I that your family's reaction will frame the way the townspeople view the investigation. We could bounce around ideas. Come up with a planned media strategy—"

"No." She didn't need any more of the mayor's charismatic charm mixing up the issue. "I would prefer to discuss it with my family myself." She slung the shoulder strap for her bag on one shoulder. "I appreciate the warning about the investigation, but it looks like it's my turn to pull an all-nighter."

She headed toward the door, not waiting to see if he followed.

Except his house was so big she realized she'd wandered into the wrong room.

"It's this way," he called.

When she turned, she saw he pointed at an open archway, which led to the breezeway attached to the garages.

She hurried to join him as he lifted the keys off a wrought-iron hook on the wall. So much for her plans to leave town tomorrow. No surprise that her dreams were being put on hold again. She'd never be able to leave her family in the middle of a crisis. This wasn't some mood swing of her mother's or a manufactured problem that her mom used to create drama.

At best, missing funds from Harvest Fest during her dad's time in office would be a scandal and an embarrassment for all the Finleys. And at worst? It was the kind of thing that could send her mother into a dark, dark place emotionally.

As Heather slid into the passenger seat of Zach's SUV, she found it ironic that she'd been leaving town—in part—to avoid stress and protect her health. Now she had to stay for incredibly stressful reasons. She hoped she could keep the effects of her RA at bay long enough to help her mother weather the latest storm. With her one sister on her honeymoon and the other sister incommunicado, Heather turned to her phone to email her friend Sylvia in Nashville. Better to have a cyberconnection than none at all.

But as she started typing out her frustrations, she erased them, unwilling to share the depths of her hurt with a friend she hadn't seen in two months. Tucking her phone back in her purse, she stared out the window, feeling utterly alone.

CHAPTER NINE

"I'm SORRY, Ms. FINLEY," the nurse on the phone chirped early the next morning. "I double-checked your records and we haven't seen you yet at our facility. Dr. Moab won't write a pre-scription for medication without an evaluation."

Heather closed her eyes and took a deep breath. No medicine if she didn't get to Charlotte this week. She sat on her front-porch swing with a cup of tea and a blanket covering her lap and legs, keeping an eye on the time. Sam Reyes had invited her and the rest of the family to a press conference at town hall, set to take place in a few hours and—although Scott insisted she attend to present a united front—her stomach was in knots simply thinking about it.

She toed the swing into motion. The morning breeze blew cool and crisp, but the sun shone and the scent of autumn hung in the air. Too bad she felt like death warmed over on such a beautiful morning. She'd hardly slept last night after spend-ing two hours at Scott's house trying to figure out a way to break the news to their mother. In the end, her oldest brother offered to do it, and she'd been more grateful than she could say. By the time she'd gone to bed, she'd been emotionally drained and—she understood this morning—physically taxed. She was like a helium balloon with a slow leak.

She'd read online that autoimmune diseases depleted a person as their immune systems were continually engaged, providing sufferers with a constant "I'm coming down with something" kind of exhaustion.

Heather sighed. The nurse was waiting for her to speak. "I had my medical history released to your office. I thought since I was supposed to see Dr. Moab later this week, I'd be able to get a temporary prescription until I can reschedule."

Not that she was taking much medicine anyhow. She'd had cortisone shots in Austin to tide her over, but the effects were wearing off. She didn't know how much the anti-inflammatory drugs were helping, but she didn't want to stop taking them in case she had another incident like the one that had sent her to the hospital in the first place.

Just as well that things hadn't worked out with Zach, right? She wasn't at a good place in her life right now.

Except that her time with him had been a bright spot in an exhausting string of days. It hurt that it had been tainted, first by his maneuvering to convince her to run for mayor and later, by hiding the truth of the missing funds.

"Have you tried calling your former doctor? Someone who treated you in the past would be in a better position to help, since we've never seen you at our office."

Of course she'd tried that first and gotten nowhere. Doctors didn't just prescribe medicines and leave you to your own devices. She needed follow-up care, blood work and a lot stronger treatment program.

"Hello? Ms. Finley?"

"Sorry. I'm still here." Heather gripped the phone tighter and then winced when her knuckles throbbed in protest. She'd awoken in more pain today than yesterday. "I'll try contacting my former doctor. Thanks."

Disconnecting the call, she lifted her tea and stared at the table beside her. She eyed the green bottles containing her daily meds, each with five pills remaining. She hurt more every day despite her taking the steroid and anti-inflammatory doses. How would she feel when she ran out? She'd considered making a trip into the nearest town with a rheumatologist, but the two she'd tried were scheduling appointments months in advance.

She took another sip of cinnamon tea, then set the cup down, and debated closing her eyes for ten minutes. Maybe she could shake the exhaustion before she needed to get ready for the press conference. Ten more minutes and she'd call Erin to let her know about the new family scandal. Would her younger sister, Amy, care? She could call her, but things hadn't gone well the last time Erin reached out to her.

Adjusting a pillow on the arm of the swing, Heather lay down just as the phone rang.

"Hello?" She sat back up.

"Heather, you'd better get over here." Scott sounded tense. In the background, she heard the low wail of a woman crying. "Mom needs you."

CAN'T MEET TODAY.

Megan pulled on a cap with a red Owl's Roost diner logo. She rechecked the last message she'd received on her phone earlier that day. The text from Ms. Finley, saying she couldn't make their guitar lesson, had been the only one to come through the phone in twenty-four hours.

No new suggestions that she kill herself.

Awesome.

She shoved her phone into her backpack and then stuffed the bag in an empty employee locker. The scent of fried fish hung in the air despite the slow-moving ceiling fan. For today, she would take the small victory of no text messages. However, she didn't dare go on any social media sites after yesterday's nightmare. She was terrified someone was going to find that page. She'd complained to the internet host site yesterday, advice she'd found online about stopping cyberbullying. But she hadn't checked to see if the page had been taken down. She didn't have the heart to look. Besides, once something had been online, it lurked somewhere on the internet forever.

"You ditched me this weekend." A guy's voice behind her made her jump.

"Wade!" She straightened her ponytail underneath the Owl's Roost cap and snagged a clean apron off a hook on the wall of the back room. "I didn't hear you come in."

Wade Sanderson towered over her, a gangly but cute guy who'd been in Megan's grade at Crestwood last year. His father worked construction and had fallen off a roof while on a job last summer, giving him extensive injuries that required long-term rehabilitation. Wade had quit school to earn extra money to help out his family. He had at least two jobs, including waiting tables at the Owl's Roost.

"I would have made more noise if I knew you were gonna be so jumpy." He flicked the brim of the cap she'd just straightened and then moved past her to get to another locker. "Then again, maybe I wouldn't have." He narrowed his gaze as he looked back at her. "I told myself I would hold a grudge against you for not being here for Sunday's brunch crowd. I had to work with Gina."

He rolled his eyes. They'd both agreed the

hostess who doubled duty as a waitress was the most difficult person to work with on staff. When she welcomed people and assigned them to a table, she put all the families with small children and all the cheapest residents of Heartache in one section, and then assigned herself to another.

"So you got all the town's worst tippers?" Megan liked Wade. He was honest, fair and funny. She wished she'd dated someone like him when she'd moved to town instead of that back-stabbing J.D.

Not that she thought about Wade like that. But it would have helped if she did.

"I got to serve a birthday party for a three-year-old thrown by the grandparents. I'm pretty sure there was a food fight." He hauled his T-shirt off so that he sat bare chested while he dug in the locker for a shirt that had fallen into the metal depths.

Had she thought he was gangly?

Wade Sanderson actually had a very nice back. He was just…tall.

When he came up with the shirt, he pulled it over his head and stared at her.

"A food fight. Hello? I was scrubbing frosting off booths for half an hour after they left." He smoothed the wrinkles out of his shirt and she followed the movement of his hands like a total dolt.

Blinking fast, she tried to forget what she'd

seen. She definitely didn't need images of Wade's back in her mind when her life was falling apart.

"Sounds about right for the Sunday-brunch crowd." She looped her apron over her head and tied it in the back.

"So, how was the wedding breakfast? Did you make big bucks over there while I was fending off French fry missiles from insane preschoolers?"

"I pulled in a little more than I make here," she admitted, leaning back on a locked supply closet while she waited for him. "But if I'd known Bailey and her crew would be there, I would have taken your place as target practice for the munchkins."

"She's still being weird?" He grabbed a cap and apron from his locker.

She'd told him how Bailey had decided to hate her guts once Megan had broken up with J.D. and Bailey had started dating him. A watered-down version of the story had come out one day at work when she'd begged Wade to take the Mc-Cord family's table after Gina had seated them in Megan's section.

"You could say that." Straightening, she headed toward the kitchen and Wade followed.

Before she could shove open the door, Wade's long arm reached over her head and levered it wide, clearing a path to their workstation and the daily grind of refilling ketchup bottles, napkin holders and other table amenities before the dinner rush began. For a second, Wade stood all of an inch away from her as he held the door.

"She didn't hassle you while you were working?" He grabbed a stack of menus and a damp cloth to wipe them down, a job Megan hated.

It was cool that he always took it since he knew that.

She sat across from him and started unscrewing ketchup bottles.

"She ignored me." The temptation to confide something—just the text messages even—was strong. She'd hoped so hard that the torment would end, but she guessed that was naive.

"But?" He kept wiping menus.

She stopped what she was doing.

"What?" He stopped, too. "You think I couldn't hear the 'but' in that comment?" He wiped the cloth across another menu. "I quit school because I wanted to. Not because I'm a total dumb-ass."

"Whoa." She snatched the cloth out of his hands. "I know you're nowhere close to dumb." She whacked the towel against his arm and then slapped it back on the table. "You caught me off guard."

"I hate not going to school," he admitted, a rare thing for him to say.

Wade hardly ever said anything negative about anything or anybody.

"I'm sorry you can't be there. How's your dad doing?" She tried to focus on him. It took an effort. She was interested, but she'd gotten really good at letting her problems eat away at her night and day.

"Same." He shrugged. "No closer to going back to work."

"It's good of you to help out." She couldn't imagine if something happened to her dad.

"I still think it was the right thing to do." He scrubbed harder, making her realize how slowly she'd been working. "I just didn't have a good sense of how little money I'd make compared to what my dad brought in. Which maybe does make me a total dumb-ass, after all."

She didn't know quite what to say to that.

"Can I ask you a question?" She finished the ketchups and wiped off the last bottle. "And don't bring up the dumb thing again. My grandmother never finished high school and my dad said she was the smartest woman he ever knew. And he teaches college and has a lot of friends who do, too, so—you know. What does that say about professors?"

Wade looked up, grinning.

"Your granny could have beaten their asses on *Jeopardy*?"

"Um, no." She smiled. "I think Dad meant that my grandmother was wise. You know? She didn't need to know dates in history or how to solve for X. She raised five kids by herself on a waitress's salary and could make her budget go a long way."

"I get it. I was teasing anyway." He finished his menus and started on the napkin holders. "So what was your question?"

"Do you think Bailey is the type of person who would text me mean messages months after I broke up with J.D.?"

"Mean messages like what?" Wade pushed his hat brim back as he propped his elbows on the table. His gray eyes were serious. Concerned.

"Asking me why I had to be at the wedding breakfast and ruin everyone's fun. Stuff like that." She hadn't meant to confide in him.

Hadn't meant to spill her problems on him when he had more than enough of his own.

Before he could say anything, one of the waitresses edged through with a big tray of fried fish, still steaming.

"Hey, kids." Isabel Fielding balanced the tray with two hands, keeping her eyes on it to be sure she didn't lose any pieces. "I've got a big order to wrap for a school group that's doing a fish-fry fund-raiser, and the Bakers had to leave for a press conference this morning, so I'm on my own. Come help me out front when you finish?"

Rodney Baker, their boss and the owner of the place, was on the town council with Megan's dad. Her dad hadn't said anything to her about a press conference, but then, he never talked to her much about his work with the town.

"Sure, Izzy." Wade jumped to get the door for her. "We're almost done."

"Thanks." Isabel disappeared into the dining area, her red miniskirt a popular attraction at the Owl's Roost.

Not that Megan was jealous or anything. Izzy was sweet and fun, and that was half the reason she received great tips. But Megan had seen male eyes follow her more often than not. It made her like Wade all the more that his eyes stayed on Megan.

"Meg, why would anyone send you something like that?" He went right back to their conversation, as if Isabel had never passed through the room.

Megan kept filling another napkin holder. It was tempting to tell him everything. She'd been scared and holding it in for so long. But what would Wade think of her if he saw that awful, awful social media site? No way could she tell him everything.

"Meg?" He moved to sit on her side of the table.

He sat so close she could have cried on his shoulder, if she was the kind of girl to do that type of thing.

"I got some ugly texts that day. Anonymous, ugly texts." She hardly recognized her own voice. Gruff. Quiet.

Embarrassed.

Which made her mad. Why should she be embarrassed by someone else being stupid?

"And they said you shouldn't be at the wedding event?" He leaned down to get in her line of vision, tipping his head sideways so she was forced to see him.

"There were three texts." Giving in, she set down the napkins and looked at him, the concern in his eyes making her need to share something. To offload some little piece of all the stuff that hurt her. "Anonymous texts."

"What did they say?"

"The first one said, 'You are such a slut.'"

He startled backward, as if she'd hit him.

"You're kidding."

"Of course not." Still, she felt a little like the *Scarlet Letter* lady that she'd shocked him. "You know how high school girls can be."

"Uh. No. I don't." He shook his head. "I hang out with guys in shop class and we rebuild car engines for fun. No one is calling anyone a—*that*."

"Well, it's not that uncommon." She definitely wasn't ever letting Wade find out about the social media page. If he thought "slut" was a big deal, he'd die if he saw the kind of crap written there. "Then I got a note that said, 'Don't you have anything better to do on a weekend than ruin everyone else's good time?' That one came after I spilled an ice tub, and a bunch of kids were laughing at me. That's why I figured one of them—at the wedding breakfast—sent the text."

"I wish I'd been there." Wade's face became fierce.

It made her want to hug him. Or maybe tuck herself under his arm. She didn't quite know what she felt. It was nice to hear someone else say she didn't deserve those mean notes.

"I ignored them." She knew it wasn't cool to let other people fight your battles. Especially people like Wade, who had bigger, real-world problems than dumb high school crap. "But the last text said that I should do everyone a favor *and die*, which really put the icing on the cake."

"That's bullshit." The anger in his voice rocked her.

She'd never heard him angry.

"It's just kid stuff—"

"No. It isn't. That's a threat, Meg." His jaw worked, a muscle in his cheek twitching. "You need to report that."

"To who? And what would anyone even do about it when—"

"Guys?" The swinging door from the dining room slammed open, Izzy's red face framed in the opening. "Seriously, I need help getting this order out."

Megan stood, glad to end the conversation.

Wade got up, too, but he blocked her exit from the booth.

"You have to tell somebody."

"I'll think about it. Come on." She nudged him backward. "We have to go."

"Don't let this person get away with scaring you like that."

"I'm not scared—"

"*Anyone* would be scared." He lifted a hand, reaching toward her, then hesitated. When his palm clamped around her shoulder, the touch was awkward, but nice, too. Warm.

"Well, I don't want to be." She shrugged, totally out of her depth but oddly comforted.

Finally, his hand fell away and he moved toward the door so they could help Isabel with the fish-fry order.

"We'll figure out who sent them." His words were close to her ear as he opened the door for her. "Even if I have to go back to school myself to do it."

He gave her ponytail a light tug as they walked through the door into the dining room filled with people. Isabel glared at them from a cloud of steaming fish.

Megan's scalp tingled as her heart squeezed tight. Hard to believe only a few hours ago she thought of him as the sweet, gangly kid she worked with. Now? He sort of seemed like the nicest guy on earth. One of the cuter ones, too.

She didn't want to bring any more trouble his way, though. So no matter how nice it felt to have him offer to help, she needed to figure her way out of this mess herself. First, she'd interview the mayor and see how close he was to launching his app for catching cyberbullies. If that didn't work…?

She'd go straight to the source: J. D. Covington. She'd never wanted to speak to him again after breaking up with him, but if that's what it took to make him call off his dogs, then she had to try.

CHAPTER TEN

LIGHTS FROM TEN different cameras flashed in Zach's face as he fielded questions about the state of Heartache's finances, the town's infrastructure and why it took so long for an "accounting error" to come to light.

Sam was at his side. Most of the town council members were in attendance, although from the shocked expressions on their faces, Zach knew he'd caught them off guard. Only Harlan Brady and Rodney Baker, two of Mayor Finley's closest advisers, seemed to have known about the missing funds.

Sam pinch-hit for Zach on some of the questions, answering anything that might benefit from the point of view of law enforcement. Zach tried to focus and do his job, but his thoughts constantly returned to Heather and what she must be thinking. She sat with her two brothers and her sister-in-law Bethany in the back of the room. Sam had invited the Finleys in case they wanted to make a statement, and Scott Finley had read a terse "we stand behind our father" paragraph, but did not take questions.

Heather had not met his eyes once, her expression fixed as a mask. Calm, neutral. And it stung to know she blamed him for not giving her more warning. Hell, maybe she blamed him for the investigation in the first place. He didn't know, since she'd shut down on him last night on the tense ride back to her house.

"We need to hire an outside accounting firm," Tiffany McCord interjected, her strident voice grating along Zach's every nerve as she rose to repeat a point she'd already made.

All the camera lenses focused on her. The only benefit of hearing her shrill demand for a fourth time was that—with the cameras off him for a moment—he could swear beneath his breath and roll his eyes while he pretended to look at the floor.

"How can we trust the current administration to investigate something that has been willfully overlooked for over a year?"

Wasn't she a part of the current administration? He hadn't expected to be flayed by the town council, especially when he'd lent Tiffany his support for her grand opening just the day before.

"Ma'am..." Sam cut her off. "If you'll take a seat, we have time for a few more questions from media members only."

Tiffany did not sit.

"This question is for the *mayor*." She tossed Sam an even look. "When I was running a Fortune 500 company, we would have considered it a conflict of interest to allow a town sheriff to investigate the books for the mayor who is his friend."

Sam tensed. He was probably the only guy in town who hated this kind of drama more than him.

"Heartache is a small town, Mrs. McCord. I'd like to think we're all friends."

"Family first." She repeated Mayor Finley's slogan with a mocking air. "But at what cost to the rest of the town?"

"Sam and I aren't related," Zach reminded her, standing. "If there are no more questions…"

"I have one." A staffer from the local radio station raised his pen in the air, the only guy in the room taking notes on paper while everyone else thumbed a record button on their electronics. "Mayor, a more pertinent conflict of interest might be your relationship with Mayor Finley's daughter. Can you tell us the nature of your relationship with Heather Finley?"

Heads swiveled as people turned to look at Heather. Zach carefully did not.

He cleared his throat. "I value Ms. Finley's volunteer work with the town's recreation department. I consider her a friend."

Sam reached in front of Zach to yank his microphone away.

"No more questions," the sheriff said. "Thank

you for attending and we'll keep you updated as new details come to light."

More camera flashes. A few observations from around the room that Zach couldn't help overhearing.

"They looked like more than friends yesterday—"

"It was a mighty friendly fishing outing—"

Zach stepped out of the conference room into his office, Sam close on his heels, while a deputy took care of clearing the town hall and shutting things down.

Damned if Zach's first instinct wasn't to go to Heather and see how she was holding up, but he knew that would only add to the flap about their "relationship."

"I hate this." He dropped into the huge leather chair he'd inherited as part of the mayor's office.

"The quicker we find the money, the quicker we'll put this situation behind us." Sam checked his phone and scrolled through messages. "At least it's public knowledge now."

"No need to worry about my relationship with the former mayor's daughter, by the way."

"I wasn't." Sam didn't look up.

"Thanks for that vote of confidence. But if you had been worried, you could stop, because she's no longer speaking to me."

"I noticed she's also no longer looking at you."

Sam glanced his way. "But what did you expect, when you launched an investigation of her old man?"

"When someone investigated my old man, I applauded." Zach had always been uneasy at the way his father conducted business. It had seemed shady to him even as a preteen.

"Ellie didn't." Sam set down his phone and slid aside the window blinds. He peered out.

Zach tried not to flinch from words that shouldn't still hurt so damn much.

"Heather is not an emotional teenager." He spun a polished wooden award from the local Lions Club. He had helped them with their computer system. "She's stronger than that."

"Right. I'm simply saying, people handle things differently. You were glad for your old man to get caught. Your sister was devastated. There's no accounting for how people feel about their parents—whether they deserve it or not."

Zach let that sink in, knowing the words came from Sam's own shadows and—hence—hadn't come easily.

"True enough. I guess I'm used to thinking of Heather as the practical one in her family, so I wasn't prepared for her to react so emotionally." He'd known she would be upset. He'd understood that she'd want to protect her mother.

But he hadn't been prepared for her to feel so betrayed by him. Maybe he should have made it a higher priority to let her know about the possibility of an investigation. He'd just been so sure he could avoid it if he could find the right piece of evidence.

"You see why I'm not worried about your relationship with her?" Sam stood, shoving his phone into the back pocket of his uniform. He picked up the hat he'd left in Zach's office earlier and plopped it on his head. "Tough to get to know someone when you only see what you want to see."

"You're full of smart-ass brilliance today, aren't you?"

"You think so?" He pulled a pair of aviator shades out of his shirt pocket. "Because I was thinking about going over to the Owl's Roost and seeing if Isabel's working. I could use a little extra smart-ass in my game."

"Haven't you got an investigation to start?" Zach banged the wooden award on the desk like a gavel pounding out order in the court.

"A man's gotta eat." Sam stalked for the door. "I'd lie low for a little longer. The deputy will let you know when the media has cleared out."

He nodded, his chest squeezing with an unfamiliar ache that might have been guilt. Even Sam knew he'd screwed up with Heather, and Sam had about as much knowledge about women as Zach had about fishing. The guy had never noticed that Zach's sister had been in love with him since they were teens.

"You could try stopping by her place later," Sam offered on the way out. "Update her on the investigation or something."

"It would help if I had something to report." He stared meaningfully at his friend.

"Or you could apologize for whatever you did to tick her off. It would be helpful to have her family's cooperation." Sam didn't wait for an answer before he slipped out of the office, closing the door behind him.

Apologize? For doing his job? For trying like hell to exonerate her father by running data analysis all night?

Clearly, Sam didn't know what he was talking about, his brain preoccupied with the new waitress at the Owl's Roost. Zach hadn't done anything wrong.

Still, it bothered him that Sam had brought up Ellie and how his sister had reacted to their father's indictment. What if Heather grappled with that kind of emotion—the kind Zach had sworn he wanted his sister to share with him and not keep inside?

Sure, Heather was an adult, and a practical one, at that. But then again, she was used to being the outlet for everyone in her family. Who was *her* outlet? Where did she go to vent and be upset?

Dragging his feet off his desk, he rose. Maybe he could catch her in the parking lot if she had stayed behind to talk to her family.

He gripped the doorknob at the same time the phone rang. He paused to check the screen, but the caller was unknown.

Frustrated, he swiped the key to answer the call.

"Hello?"

"Mayor Chance?" a young woman's voice asked on the other end.

"Yes. This is the mayor." Not for much longer, if he had anything to do about it. He needed to be done with this job and let other people fix small-town dramas.

"Hi. Er. It's Megan Bryer. My dad is on the town council?" She sounded tentative.

Because she was a high school kid nervous about calling the local mayor's office? Or because she faced a lot bigger problem than that?

Zach's thoughts shifted from Heather to the young woman on the phone. A young woman he was worried about, even though he wasn't even sure he remembered what she looked like.

He lowered himself to sit on the edge of his desk, ready to give her his full attention. If she were in trouble, he would be there for her the way he hadn't been for his sister.

"Yes, Megan. Of course I know who you are. I've been looking forward to talking to you."

"YOU CAN'T GIVE up your audition spot because of this."

Heather held the phone away from her ear slightly. Erin had raised her voice over the din of live accordion music at the Gumbo Fest, where she and Remy had been taking in the sights. Heather had disrupted her sister's day with the news about the town's investigation.

"I won't," she replied automatically, even though she had no idea if it would come to that or not. "At least, I hope this will all be taken care of before I have to leave for Charlotte."

She sat in her newly fixed car outside the town's baseball field. She had a front-row view of the game currently in progress between the fire department and the local teachers' association. New lights flooded the field, an addition she'd lobbied hard for last spring. They'd been expensive, but a government matching fund had helped. And despite the griping about the increased costs passed onto various leagues who played on the field, they sure did pack the stands now that they had a better place to play. Concessions alone would make a serious dent in paying down the money the town had borrowed for them.

Heather planned to help out in the concession stand tonight as sitting at home and brooding wasn't doing her a damn bit of good. Besides, Finleys didn't hang their heads and worry about idle talk. Better to be in the thick of things and prove she had nothing to hide.

"You hope it's taken care of? Heather, that's my whole point." Erin must have taken the call somewhere more private since the zydeco music in the background had faded a bit. "You can't afford to wait and hope the situation gets taken care of. You know the family runs on drama. Even if the new sheriff figured it all out and Dad's name was cleared, Mom will be too distracted to take her meds and she'll go in a tailspin. Or she'll overcompensate with meds and she'll need help leveling out again."

"She can't help that—"

"I know. I understand her better than I used to, so I'm not suggesting she uses the drama for attention. But we've weathered enough episodes where we should realize that any implication of Dad's involvement in the scandal is going to wreak havoc with her emotions and her health."

"I asked her to make a doctor's appointment so we can get on top of that." Heather tipped her head back against the upholstery seat, watching as Quinton Lee, the owner of Lucky's Grocer and a fire department volunteer, tapped his bat on home plate. "I want to be with her when she goes. I want to hear what the doctor says firsthand."

"Let Mack or Scott go with her," Erin urged. "You've waited too long for this chance to follow a dream, Heather. You have to go for it."

Right. Except with her own appointment now canceled, she didn't feel quite as motivated to sing her heart out in front of strangers. What if her fingers were stiff that day and she couldn't play her guitar? She really needed medical help and she'd feel better if she could get on a treatment program before her audition.

"I can catch up with the program when they do auditions in New Orleans next month." She'd already checked to see where else *American Voice* would be scouting talent. "The invitation doesn't expire."

Out on the baseball diamond, Quinton Lee connected with a pitch, sending the ball over the fence and into the parking lot nearby.

"Next month?" Erin must have moved again, because the sounds of a fiddle grew louder. "And then you'll be saying 'next year.' Don't do this to yourself. I'll come home before I let you miss out on the audition."

"Absolutely not." A couple of kids scampered down from the stands to retrieve the baseball. "You're on your honeymoon."

"Yes. And that's how important it is to me that you get to your audition. I would leave my honeymoon early."

"I won't let you do that."

"Well, *I* won't let *you* stick around Heartache to be Mom's keeper anymore. It's as simple as that." A low voice with a Cajun twang spoke in the background on Erin's end. Remy must have joined her. "You know, you could always call Amy and see if she wants to take a turn overseeing Mom."

The hometown crowd cheered while Quinton ran the bases. Heather used to play on the teachers' team, but she hadn't signed up for the fall league once *American Voice* had invited her to audition for the show. She had counted on being gone by now.

"If she didn't want to come home for a fun thing like a wedding, she's sure not going to run home to cart Mom to doctor's appointments." Heather checked her watch to make sure she wasn't missing her shift at the concession stand. She'd volunteered to take over for Trish, her hairdresser, who'd wanted a chance to watch the fire department guys in action.

"You should stop in Atlanta on the way to Charlotte and see Amy." Erin's voice went quiet. Thoughtful.

"I thought we were mad at her for not coming to the wedding." Heather hadn't been mad. But she knew Erin had been hurt.

Her gaze flicked to a couple pushing a stroller, who walked in front of her car, their baby covered with a fuzzy blue blanket to keep out the autumn breeze. That could be Erin soon. Would Amy come home for a new baby in the family?

"We *are* mad at her. We can be mad at one another and still love each other. It's a sister thing."

Family first.

Heather remembered how resentful she'd felt toward Tiffany McCord today when she'd used her dad's slogan to try to make him sound like a crooked politician scheming to line Finley pockets. She'd censored details like that from Erin, knowing they'd only fire her up.

And, of course, she wasn't mentioning that the whole town now thought she had a relationship with Zach. Obviously, the "more than friends" vibe she'd gotten from him at the fishing tournament hadn't been the product of an overactive imagination. The rest of Heartache had thought the same thing.

"So, are you mad at me for delaying my trip?" She toyed with her necklace, a vintage Wedgwood cameo of two girls jumping rope, a gift from Erin long ago.

"Possibly." Erin didn't sound mad.

Heather smiled. Relieved.

"But since you love me dearly, and you're on your honeymoon with a supercute new husband, you can hardly let this ruin your trip, right?"

"Right. In fact, I owe that cute new husband a dance, so…"

"Go have fun." Heather dropped her keys in her leather satchel. "Don't worry about us."

Disconnecting the call, she grabbed her sweater

from the backseat and stepped outside. The chill of the evening hit her, a brisk breeze that made her pause to pull on the heavy sweater over her old baseball jersey.

She wrapped her arms around herself and jogged to the back of the infield behind the fence, dodging a few teens who were working on a car in the parking lot. When she arrived at the concession stand, she slipped in the back door.

"Heather!" Startled, Trish dropped the paperback she'd been reading. "You surprised me."

She scooped her book off the floor and held down a few T-shirts on hangers to keep them from blowing in the breeze while the back door was open.

"Sorry." Heather closed them inside the negligible warmth of the building. With one window always open to the outdoors, the concession stand was never temperature controlled. "I just pulled into the parking lot and I thought it would be faster to come around the back way than to bypass friends in the stands."

"Are you sure you're not just avoiding questions about the hunky mayor?" Trish shoved her book into a pink, leopard-print shopping tote and straightened to leave. "I heard a reporter called you out in the press conference today."

"News travels fast in this town. But he had no idea what he was talking about." Heather lowered herself onto the stool that Trish vacated. "All conjecture."

"Is it? Because the day before, Daisy Spencer told us she saw you and Zach fishing together by the river and there were sparks flying all over the place." Trish did a fair impression of Mrs. Spencer's country drawl.

"Trish, you know I adore Mrs. Spencer. We all do. But she's a romantic with a capital *R*."

Trish grinned. "And that journalist from the local radio station? I suppose he's a romantic, too?"

"You're determined to give me a hard time, aren't you?" Heather rose as a throng of dirt-smudged preteen boys approached the stand.

"Not at all." The woman shuffled back a step to give Heather a one-armed hug. "But I work at the Strand, honey, so I like to think I'm better at sniffing out a good news story than any member of the media. And I'm telling you that—true or not—this town is going to eat up a story about our handsome mayor falling for the next superstar on *American Voice*."

"He's not falling for me." She remembered how much it had hurt when he'd pulled away after their kiss. "But I understand what you're saying. If I don't want rumors circulating, I shouldn't be teaching eligible bachelors how to fish in my spare time."

Live and learn.

Heather turned to take five orders at once as the boys chose drinks from a cooler and pawed over the candy bars. Trish had slipped out the back door during the hubbub, so that by the time the boys had spent their last nickel, Heather had nothing to do but watch the game in progress. The fire department led by three runs, but then teenage J. D. Covington came up to bat for the teachers. He was one of the best athletes in town. His mother taught social studies, but his father owned the quarry and was the wealthiest man in Heartache. Heather knew who J.D. was because Megan had dated him briefly last year.

J.D. dug in at the plate, his long legs spider-like as he crouched to assume his hitting stance.

"Go, J.D.!" the small crowd cheered him on while the pitcher checked out the sign from his catcher.

Behind Heather, the door to the concession stand opened, a cool breeze blowing the hanging T-shirts on the walls and chilling her legs. She thought Trish must have forgotten something until Zach Chance stepped into the small space and shut the door behind him.

"Zach." Her heart sped a little just seeing him, even though she was upset with him. "This isn't a good idea—"

"No one will see us." He cut her off, his expression unreadable. "We need to talk."

She glanced through the front window again. No one was headed this way. Yet.

"But what if someone wants a drink or something? My family doesn't need any more fodder for the rumor mill, and I know you don't want that, either." She remembered something he said to her the night he'd rescued her from the side of the road—how much he hated secrets and agendas.

"I'll stand over here, and no one will see me." He backed into the corner, half hidden between the popcorn popper and a broken refrigerator.

It wasn't a bad spot. It would keep his presence secret.

Although, that left her alone in a very close space with a man who set butterflies off inside her.

A bat cracked outside the concession stand, and the crowd roared. Heather turned to watch as J.D. rounded first base. Tiffany McCord and her daughter, Bailey, jumped up and down in the stands. Tiffany high-fived Jeremy Covington, who stood in the bleachers behind them.

"Is that the Covington kid who hit that?" Zach asked, folding his arms over the same suit he'd worn to the press conference.

Her heart ached for him. True, she blamed Zach for not telling her about the missing money, but she felt bad he'd been working all day without a break to go home and change. Faint lines surrounded his eyes. He looked exhausted. Appealing, yes. But tired, too.

"Yes. He drove in two runs and made it to third base." She tugged her sweater tighter around her, wondering if it was just her imagination or if Jeremy Covington and Tiffany McCord looked particularly friendly. "But I'm sure you didn't sneak in the concession stand to discuss J.D.'s batting average."

Zach shook his head. "I want your family's permission to review your dad's home computer or laptop, if you still have it. If you're concerned about conflict of interest, hire another digital forensics firm. But you should review his files."

Everything inside her stilled.

"You don't ask for much, do you?"

"Your family lawyer will advise the same thing. I'm sure Sam will approach your family about giving the police access. But I wanted to talk to you first." He rubbed a hand over his face. "I don't know, Heather. I thought I owed it to you to speak to you directly. To tell you I'm sorry I screwed up by not talking to you sooner. It might look like I didn't have your family's best interests at heart, but I only did what I thought was going to be best for everyone."

"And you want to run tests on his computer like you did on the town computers?" She recalled him saying that's what he'd been doing the night before the fishing tournament—scanning documents for something that would show where the missing money had gone.

"Yes. We could find information that would clear your dad and it will bring the investigation to a quick close."

Right. Or they could find something that would incriminate her father. She didn't think her dad had done anything wrong. But what if he had secrets that he didn't want made public? She wouldn't want *her* recent computer searches documented for the world to see.

"I should ask my brothers first. Or call a lawyer." Voices approached the concession stand and pulled her attention back to the window. Outside, Bailey McCord and another girl that Heather didn't recognize had their heads together, laughing and whispering over something on Bailey's phone.

Heather didn't need reports of Zach in the concession stand getting back to Bailey's mother. The news reporter in the press conference had made an excellent point about close association between the mayor and the Finley family. It didn't look good for either of them.

"Hi, girls." Heather smiled, hoping Zach was flattening himself to one wall so he wouldn't be seen. "What can I get you?"

"Do you have any bandages?" Bailey asked. "My boyfriend took the skin off his elbow sliding into home."

The words elicited a fresh round of giggles from the girls.

Heather checked the scoreboard and noticed the teachers' team had one more run. The fire department was up now, so she must have missed an at-bat.

"Sure." She had stocked the first-aid kit herself at the start of the spring season. Digging it out now, she handed them bandages and disinfectant wipes. "Be careful using those wipes around the cut skin. They will sting if they touch an open wound, but you might want to clean around it."

"Thanks." Bailey stuffed the paper packets in the pocket of her sweatshirt. "Good luck with *American Voice*. My friend Megan says you're supertalented."

"Thank you." Heather would have said more, but she didn't want anyone lingering around the stand with Zach inside. "I really appreciate that."

"I'm dying to get out of this town, too." The girl smiled shyly before the two of them turned to leave.

When they were out of hearing range, Heather finally turned back to Zach. He looked different today—rougher, tense, the five-o'clock shadow on his jaw a rarity.

"So can I get back to you about handing over the computers after I consult my brothers? I'm not sure yet."

"Of course." He gave a clipped nod as he leaned

a shoulder into the popcorn machine. "I spoke to Megan Bryer today after the press conference."

"Really?" His words drew her in when she needed to keep boundaries in place. But she wanted to know what he'd found out. For Megan's sake. "How did that go?"

"She said all the right things. That she was doing the research for a project. That she found my app after researching the steps teens can take to protect themselves." He shrugged. "I should feel reassured, maybe. But I don't."

"She's a very intelligent young woman," Heather mused. "If she was hiding something, I have no doubt she'd be good at it."

A prickle of unease tripped down her spine as it occurred to Heather how much alike they were. They both loved music. They both used it as an escape. They both dreamed of leaving Heartache—Heather with *American Voice*, Megan with college.

What if they were both hiding a secret?

"You're not telling me something." Zach straightened, his focus intense as he looked at her. "What is it?"

Caught off guard, Heather was relieved when the crowd roared again. She glanced up in time to see a ball fly over the fence.

"Heather? What aren't you telling me?" Zach persisted, taking a step closer.

"Nothing." She swallowed hard, unwilling to

let him get too close for myriad reasons. "I was just going through recent conversations with her to try to remember anything significant." She narrowed her gaze. "I'm not as fast with my data analysis as your computer programs."

"And? Anything come to mind?"

"Her goals shifted over the summer from wanting desperately to buy a new guitar to putting every penny toward a college fund. Which I guess shouldn't be a surprise for a forward-thinking high school senior, but I was surprised by how much she seemed to want to get out of town."

"Most kids feel that way at some point during high school." Idly, he picked through a box of giveaway items with old peewee-team names and the logo for the Heartache baseball league. A flashlight. A key ring. Some toddler-size T-shirts. "When my father was indicted, I would have given anything to leave Tennessee. Hell, leave the whole country. Because that's about how far I'd have to go to get out from under his shadow."

A chant for the pitcher began. No doubt the game neared the final outs.

"I never would have guessed back in school." She remembered well the image she'd always had of Zach in her mind "You seemed completely untouchable. Like nothing about the scandal could taint all the good works you did. All the ways the teachers liked you."

When she realized he was staring at her curiously, her face heated. Had she just revealed paying way too much attention to him? Not that it mattered. High school was a long time ago. Still...

"I did all the good works because I couldn't stand being around my father. And once he was in jail, I resented being around my mom since she stuck up for him like he'd been wrongly accused or something. So, yeah, I practically lived at the senior center, but it wasn't because I was such an altruistic guy. It was just that life at home sucked."

The rawness of that admission hinted at a hurt that had never healed.

She nodded. "A lot of teenage kids choose much less healthy outlets during tough times," she offered quietly, sensing she should tread with caution. Her own niece had battled a problem with cutting herself last year, an issue that had terrified their whole family until the girl started seeing a therapist and got herself under control.

Leaning over the candy counter, Heather reached for the handle to pull down the metal door that would lock up the concession stand for the night. The slide and clang of the metal ended with a soft thud as it fell into place, sealing them in total privacy.

An intensified quiet.

"You're right about that." Zach's eyes revealed

nothing, yet she sensed he spoke from experience. "It's a good thing Megan has her music. I want to make sure we don't miss the signs if she's struggling with issues she's not telling anyone about. I'm going to talk to her father."

Zach stepped closer now that they didn't need to hide from any concession stand patrons. Heather heard fans' excited chatter as they filed out of the bleachers and headed to their cars. Engines revved. A few tires squealed. The raucous bunch seemed hyped up on the fun of a good game.

She tried to keep one ear on the sounds outside to prevent herself from focusing too much on Zach. His eyes on her warmed her from the inside out. Her own gaze flitted lower, noticing the shape of his mouth that she'd once kissed with total abandon...

"Don't do that," she blurted, forcing her attention back to the conversation. Away from kissing a guy who had only approached her in the first place to convince her to take over his job.

"Don't do what?" His hand lowered.

Had he been reaching toward her?

She was mixed up inside, and it was because of him. She didn't understand what he wanted, didn't know why he'd sought her out again. Had it really just been about seizing her father's old computers?

"Don't..." She struggled to hold a thought. "Don't talk to Meg's father. At least not yet."

"What if she's in danger?" The concern in his voice was obvious, making Heather wonder if part of his protective streak was rooted in his role as a big brother.

He'd been a stable force in his sister's life, anchoring her during tumultuous teen years.

"Her father's one of the most overprotective parents I've ever met." Heather frowned. "He must have spent forty-five minutes on the phone with me once to discuss the blisters on Megan's fingers from playing." She tipped up her own hands to show him the calluses. "But everyone gets them. You can't play without them."

He brushed a thumb along the tips of her fingers, testing the calluses and causing a shiver to trip through her.

Heather swallowed. "A year ago, she wanted to play soccer in the rec league with some friends, and her dad wouldn't sign off on the permission form after reading the concussion stats." She stuffed her hands in the pockets of her sweater, unwilling to get caught in the spell of Zach Chance again.

"Concussions and sports is a combination that makes plenty of parents nervous," he reminded her.

"This was after he let her come to the first practice with headgear. The kind a professional wrestler wears." She outlined the shape of it with her hands, including the extra padding around the forehead. "She was mortified. She didn't think anyone would see her when he dropped her off and she could ditch it afterward, but he stayed to watch for the first ten minutes."

"Really?"

"It was a community team, so it wasn't all high school kids, thank goodness. There were some good-natured guys from the sheriff's department who tried to help her have fun with it, but I could tell she was…"

"Miserable." Zach seemed to understand at last.

"Right." Heather hated to be the kind of person who pointed fingers at a good parent, especially one who obviously loved his kid as much as Mr. Bryer seemed to. But there was such a thing as overdoing it. "Why don't you let me talk to Megan first? See if I can get anything more out of her. I'll ask some more pointed questions about the research she's been doing and why the sudden interest in cyberbullying."

His jaw flexed as he stared at the ground, seeming to think it over. When he glanced up, his eyes fixed on hers in a dark stare.

"If I keep a lid on this for another day, will you do something for me in return?"

A shiver leaped from one shoulder blade to the other. Still, she felt damn defensive, considering the way he'd kept quiet about the investigation of her family.

"I don't think I owe you any favors. If anything—"

He laid a hand on her shoulder and cupped it, the touch releasing a pent-up sigh she'd been unaware of.

"Let's get out of town tonight. Far from Heartache."

She was already shaking her head, despite her love of driving at night and the rush of the wind from the open windows. Especially in that convertible of his.

But that was foolishness talking.

"I don't think so."

"Just for a few hours. You can sing, even." His lips curled up on one side. A half smile. "Come to karaoke night with me."

CHAPTER ELEVEN

"THANKS FOR COMING TONIGHT," Zach said. Music from the honky-tonk rib shack vibrated the wooden floor beneath his feet as he sat across from Heather in their booth. He still couldn't believe he'd talked her into it.

She'd hemmed. She'd hawed. She'd been rightfully worried about how a relationship—or being perceived as having a relationship—might have implications for the investigation. But he could tell she was ready for a night out. Zach had won her over by describing the little hole-in-the wall bar in Franklin, Tennessee, where they'd never run into anyone from Heartache. He'd hidden out here plenty of times when he needed to be anonymous.

Charlie Ray's Rib Shack was a backwoods place on the town line. Live music played on weekends. Tonight, the crowd was small as the karaoke singing got under way. An older couple crooned a country duet to one another, while the smokehouse scent of cooking meats and burning hickory chips filled the air.

"I've needed a change of scenery ever since

Erin's wedding," Heather admitted. "You remember how fast I ditched town after my sister's reception."

"You didn't even bother changing out of your dancing dress," he teased. He had fond memories of that dress, but he tried to be careful about flirting with her tonight. A careful, measured approach was more likely to win him a second chance with her.

She might be sitting at the small table across from him, but there wasn't a chance she'd forgotten about the investigation he'd ordered, implicating her dad. Would she be able to get past that? The possibility she wouldn't bothered him more than it should.

"I had hoped if I timed it right, I'd be able to catch the sunrise while I was crossing the Smoky Mountains." She pulled a saucy rib free from the basket they shared while the duet onstage reached a crescendo. "Not one of my better-laid plans."

"Selfishly, I'm glad you stayed in town. Because no matter what you think about my motives for this investigation, I genuinely wanted to get to know you better." He hated that she seemed wary of him. Hated that he'd given her any reason for the mistrust in her eyes. "But for your sake, I'm sorry you didn't get to see that sunrise."

She set her rib aside to applaud the older couple as they finished their song. Then she put her fingers between her lips and whistled. The couple grinned and a few heads turned toward their table.

As the clapping died down, Heather took a sip of her water.

"I know it sounds cliché—leave town and watch the sunrise to start my new life. But some things are cliché because people enjoy doing them. You know? Like singing in the shower. Or taking a family photo at the Grand Canyon."

"Or a kiss to seal a deal," he offered.

Her eyes narrowed and she shoved a fried corn nugget in his mouth. "This is all you're getting from me tonight."

He shrugged, chewing through the crispy batter to the cheesy corn center, then answered, "It's the first one that came to mind. But this will do for now."

He picked up another and brought it to her lips, but slower, feeding it to her with a precision and, hell yes, seduction that couldn't be missed. Her pupils dilated in response, but she didn't tell him no. Her blue eyes filled with confusion and a hint of arousal before she plastered on an overbright smile. But that was okay for now. He knew what he'd seen. She was far from indifferent to the attraction they shared.

A young guy took the planked stage to sing a country-rock tune from the seventies, and a group of his friends howled their approval, lifting long-neck bottles in salute. A few girls shimmied up to dance on the hardwood floor near the stage.

"Anyway, there are some clichés I've never experienced," Heather continued, keeping time to the music with a subtle tap of her finger against the table. "Like loading up the car as a teenager and driving to a faraway college. Or hunting for my first apartment with a friend." She stopped drumming her fingers. Her gaze fell away and she toyed with a corn popper. "Falling in love."

She tacked the last one on like an afterthought and pushed away the appetizer basket.

"You've never been in love?" He hadn't expected that. She had been a year behind him in school, which made her twenty-eight.

"I thought I was a couple of times, but I knew later..." She shook her head. "It hadn't really been love. I'd just felt a combination of affection and *wanting* to be in love."

Her words rolled around inside his head, and he tried to understand what they meant. Her admission had been unexpected, for sure. But he was more surprised she'd shared something so personal with him. He hoped like hell it meant she was thinking about forgiving him and getting back to where they'd been before the investigation news broke.

"I know how it sounds," she said quickly, her hands fidgety as she tore off a paper towel from the roll by the row of different barbecue sauces.

"How does it sound?" He wanted her. Badly. It was the only damn thought in his head at the moment, but it didn't seem like the time to share it.

"Like I'm a loser. Or hard-hearted and unfeeling."

Those were untrue statements. Unfeeling? Hell, the kiss she'd given him torched that theory. He remembered exactly what she'd looked like before their lips had touched. The flare of awareness in her eyes. Merely thinking about it made him ease back in his chair to give himself a little space.

"I think it makes you sound like a woman of taste and discretion."

"Picky, you mean?" Her gaze followed an elderly couple holding hands as they walked past with the hostess.

"I don't believe in compromising my standards, either." He flagged down a waitress, needing another drink to cool him off. They were only throwing back colas tonight, but his mouth had gone dry right about the time he'd watched Heather whistle.

"I guess I truly am picky." She clinked her glass to his. "Sounds like you suffer from the same affliction."

"Caution is a good thing." He was trying to be cautious tonight, for example. He hadn't leaned over the table to kiss her. Hadn't slid around to sit beside her so he could stroke her hair or slide an arm around her waist and feel the warmth of her skin through the baseball jersey she wore.

"I'm so tired of being cautious. And practical. And organized. And picky about *everything* in my life." She set her drink down hard, the fierceness in her voice surprising him. "I keep thinking if I can get out on my own, away from the family, I'll take more risks. Live my dreams like my former student Sylvia. She just packed up her guitar one day and went to Nashville. She's playing with three different bands and doing everything she can to take her career to the next level. I want to do that. Or at least be the musician I was meant to be."

"You will be." He clapped as the kid onstage finished his song, drawing out the last note while his friends lifted their cell phones overhead to signal an encore.

"What if I'm not? What if my family is just an excuse for the fact I haven't risked my heart in love or life?"

"That won't happen." He paused as the waitress arrived with refills. He took a sip of his drink before he continued. "Don't *let* it happen. Take the risks. Starting now."

"What do you mean?" She arched an eyebrow at him, all wariness again as she twisted the paper towel around her fingers.

Did she think he meant with him? A romantic risk?

"Go sing." He jerked a thumb at the stage. "You're a performer. Let's see you perform."

Her shoulders relaxed, her blue gaze turning to the small stage with an unmistakable longing.

"You wouldn't think it was rude of me to leave you sitting all alone?" She bit her lip, although he'd hazard a guess she wasn't all that concerned about leaving his side.

"Why do you think I brought you to a karaoke bar? To listen to a bunch of hacks belt out tunes after they've had too many drinks?"

She grinned, her eyes back on him, where he liked them. Hell yes he did. Especially when she smiled like that, and he was the one who made it happen.

"If you wanted a personal performance, you could have just told me so."

His breath caught in his chest. Hard.

"I wasn't sure how willing you'd be after I messed up with you." His throat remained dry. Didn't matter how much he drank.

There was only one thing that was going to quench his thirst tonight.

"You're right." Her smile faded. "I felt betrayed. But I don't believe you set out to deceive me."

Hope sparked. That sounded like an opening to make things right.

"Never. I had wanted to fix it before things came to a head. I really thought there must be an accounting error or information that I was missing. Or something." It bugged him that he couldn't figure out where the money had gone, and it bothered him more that it made Mayor Finley look guilty.

"I understand."

"Really?" His breath whooshed out of his lungs as if a ton of bricks had eased off his chest.

"I think I do. I'm frustrated that this investigation is going to hurt my family and my father's reputation, but I know you *had* to look into it. I wish you'd told me sooner, but I can see why you didn't." She slumped in the booth and studied him. "You really thought you might be able to solve the problem and it would never see the light of day."

"Exactly. I've had my family's name dragged through the mud and I can tell you, it's painful. If I could spare you that kind of public scrutiny, I would."

"Do you always try to fix things by yourself, Zach?"

"The curse of the competent person." He tucked around the booth table to slide in beside her. "Thank you for trying to understand. Your opinion is important to me."

He twined a silky red wave around his finger and watched her eyes shift from cornflower blue to a darker shade.

"Your opinion matters to me, too." She laid her

hand along his forearm and squeezed softly, lingering. "Which is why I hope you like the song I'm about to sing."

It took a minute for the words to sink in. He'd been looking for a kiss, but he would take whatever she offered. Song included.

He cupped her elbow and backed out of the booth, bringing her with him. "Knock 'em dead, Heather Finley."

"Just for you, Mr. Mayor." She nodded once and headed for the stage, her hips twitching with just a touch more swagger.

He hoped like hell that only he noticed, but heads turned as she walked by. Whether or not she could sing, she would definitely attract more than a little attention.

Zach hoped that her forgiveness meant they could salvage some time together before she left. Because no matter how much he wanted to finish his app and get it to market, no matter how much he wanted to clear her father's name and find the missing town funds, his goal for tonight was a whole lot simpler.

Now that there were no more secrets between them, he wanted to kiss Heather again.

"THIS IS CRAZY." Megan stood under the bleachers in the dark with Wade long after the power to the overhead lights had been cut and most of the parking lot had cleared out.

The baseball game had finished an hour ago. A few people remained near their cars talking, but most had gone home for the night or met up at a local bar for a celebratory drink. But Megan and Wade remained because J. D. Covington had lingered in the dugout with a friend. When Wade had stalked closer to them a few minutes ago, they were still debating the best size for a bat barrel.

"It's not crazy." Wade had convinced her to attend the game after they'd finished their shift at the Owl's Roost. "This is the perfect time to have a little talk with J.D. and find out if he's the one harassing you."

"I have homework," she'd argued, thinking about the undone math problems and how much she didn't want to face J.D.

The sounds of night were amplified as the parking lot cleared out. Frogs and night bugs turned up the volume, making their own brand of music. She and Wade leaned against the metal framework under the bleachers. Shadows slanted over Wade's face.

"Don't rub it in. Obviously, I don't have any homework," he grumbled, then pointed to another car still in the parking lot. "Isn't that Bailey's mom?"

Megan followed his gaze, regretting that she'd made him feel bad about school again. But those thoughts crumbled to ash when she spotted Mrs.

McCord. She stood beside J.D.'s dad. The next throng of townspeople talked and laughed around their cars at least seventy yards away from them.

Mrs. McCord and Mr. Covington stood very, very close together on the darkened perimeter of the lot.

"Yes. But they serve on the town council together, the same as my dad. So they're probably just—" She paused as J.D.'s dad peered over one shoulder, toward the only other figures in the parking lot. At least, the only other people visible in the dimness of the night. Then, as if satisfied no one could see them, he reached for Mrs. McCord.

And kissed her. Not a friend's kiss, either. This was an all-out face suck complete with groping. Megan hadn't particularly cared for either of J.D.'s parents when she'd met them briefly last spring. They paid zero attention to their son. But she still felt bad for Mrs. Covington, who headed the girls' track team at school.

"Do you believe that?" Wade shook his head. "Pretty ballsy move right out in public."

"They're hidden by his truck." She didn't want to see any more. "I'm sure they don't expect anyone is hiding under the bleachers. Come on." She might have reason to dislike J.D., but she didn't know for sure he was the one who'd built that stupid website about her, and she didn't like the idea of him seeing his father being such a prick.

She tugged on Wade's arm as she turned away from the parking-lot soap opera and led him out from under the bleachers toward the field.

"You think the guy has any idea his kid is still in the dugout?"

"I don't know." But she thanked her lucky stars Wade was with her for this. Ever since she'd told him about the text messages she had felt less alone.

"Like father like son," he grumbled, shoving open the fence that led to the baseball field.

"What does that mean?" She stopped in her tracks, her tennis shoes scuffing into the dirt.

Wade paused. Turned. She couldn't read his expression in the dark as he stared down at her.

"I thought you knew."

A chill clutched her stomach and squeezed.

"He started dating Bailey before you two broke up."

"Of course he did," she muttered, since she should have known. Except she hadn't. And she wasn't sure who she felt more betrayed by—Bailey, who'd been her friend, or J.D., who shouldn't have the power to hurt her anymore. "I'm just late to the party realizing how stupid I've been."

Part of her had held out hope that somebody else must be trying to ruin her life. Someone besides two people she'd once really cared about. Tears burned her eyes, so she stared up at the night sky to try to make them drain back into her head. She would not shed idiotic tears for idiots.

Overhead, a plane's lights winked so far above, it didn't make a sound. She wished she could trade places with someone on that flight so she could be headed anywhere but here.

"Hey." Wade leaned over her, his face suddenly blocking her view. "He's the stupid one, Meg. No one but a total dimwit would waste his chance with you."

The teary feeling stopped stinging. She blinked, realizing how close Wade was. Her heart tripped over itself, the beats out of sync.

She didn't know what to say. But she was saved from thinking of something when Wade eased back a step onto the trampled field.

"Let's go find him." He laid a hand on the center of her back and she forced her feet to move in the direction of the metal dugout.

J.D. appeared, stepping onto the infield's grass. He was tall, too, but not even J.D. was as tall as Wade. Megan froze.

"What the hell are you doing here?" her ex-boyfriend asked.

"Looking for you." Wade stopped on the grass a few feet away from him.

Megan fought the urge to tuck herself under Wade's arm. And though she hated J.D.'s aggressive tone and his jutting chin, she turned to make sure he couldn't see the parking lot from here. The bleachers helped block the view.

J.D.'s gaze went from Megan to Wade and back again.

"You don't need my permission to date her, big guy." J.D. hitched his baseball bag higher on his shoulder. "We've been done for a long time."

"Longer than I realized," she muttered, but Wade's voice rose over hers.

"Someone's hassling Megan. Sending ugly texts. Is that you, J.D.? Or one of your boys?"

"Someone's sending texts?" J.D. rolled his eyes, an expression she could see, thanks to the moonlight. "That's girl shit, man."

"You think Bailey would do that?" Wade pressed.

"Hold up. I don't like hearing you say her name. And I definitely don't want some high school dropout talking smack about my girl." J.D. stepped closer, his shoulders squaring.

"Don't be such an ass, J.D." Megan found her voice, anger surging that he'd try to intimidate Wade. "Whoever is harassing me sure sounds a lot like you online." The whole business about her attending "Slutsville Academy" was the exact same thing he'd said to her in the cafeteria one day. "Or are you going to say you never put up a stupid website about me?"

She could feel Wade's surprise as he faced her. But her focus remained on J.D., trying to gauge his reaction. His shoulders fell. The heavy baseball bag he'd been carrying thunked to the ground.

"What are you talking about?" J.D.'s voice cracked.

"Are you going to deny you wrote that smut about me?" The fury she'd felt on seeing all those rude words burned like bile up the back of her throat. Later, she'd figure out what to say to Wade. How to make him keep it a secret.

Right now it was all she could do not to fling herself at her ex-boyfriend and pummel him with both fists.

J.D. held up both hands. "I don't know what you're talking about." He hauled his bag off the ground and looped the strap on his shoulder. "Get out of my way."

"You're going to get caught," she yelled at his retreating back. "It's illegal!"

Wade dropped an arm around her shoulders, the warm weight taking some of the fight out of her.

"Let him go, Meg. We'll get it sorted out another time."

She sucked in a deep breath, the cool night air easing her fury and leaving her wrung out. Exhausted. Confused.

"Did he look guilty to you?" she asked, startled when Wade jogged a few steps ahead to peer around the bleachers.

"He's gone and so are all the rest of the cars in the lot." Wade dropped onto one of the bleacher seats, the metal bench clanging dully. "Sit for a minute."

"I. Um." She stared at the empty space beside him and her throat went dry. "I really need to get home."

"What website?" He rested his elbows on his knees.

Swallowing hard, she shook her head, her face hot. If Wade saw what was on there, she would die.

"It's too embarrassing. I don't want to talk about it." Her voice rasped, a barely-there whisper. Just thinking about what it said made her close her eyes tight. She hated seeing it even in her mind.

She didn't want anyone else to look at it. Ever. Especially Wade.

"I can't help if you don't talk to me. And for what it's worth, I don't think J.D. is sending those texts, but he looked freaked out about the website. Whatever that is."

"It means a lot to me that you helped me confront him." She kicked herself for saying anything about the stupid website. "Please don't ask me to talk about the…the other stuff you heard. I can't do it."

She wrapped her arms around herself, trying

to stay warm. Too bad most of the chill came from inside her.

"Keeping this stuff secret only helps the person who is harassing you. You know that, right?" Wade pushed to his feet and slid off his sweatshirt.

He dropped it across her shoulders, a warm welcome weight.

"You should keep it," she argued, reaching to take it off.

He gripped one of her hands to hold it still.

"Let me fix one thing for you tonight. Okay?" He sounded so exasperated that she nodded.

"Thank you." Gripping the lapels with her hands, she tugged the fleece cotton tighter around her. "I hope you're not mad at me."

He paused, staring at her intensely. "God no. I could never be mad at you." Swallowing hard, he looked away but kept an arm around her shoulders.

Together, they headed for his truck parked on the street at the far side of the field. The damp grass soaked through her canvas tennis shoes.

He squeezed her shoulder once. "Don't worry so much about how other people feel. You need to look out for you."

"I can't help it." She glanced up at him through her eyelashes. "I care a lot what you think."

He slowed his step as they reached his pickup, a vehicle he'd salvaged with his friends from shop class. Her dad would have called it "souped-up" since it combined parts from different kinds of trucks, but somehow worked together.

"I'm glad. Because I care how you feel." He didn't touch her, but as they stood under one of the streetlights, she could see his face.

The way he looked at her made her toes curl inside her shoes.

Butterflies fluttered in her belly. She didn't know what to say as she stared at him and hoped he did.

He shuffled closer, his eyes never leaving hers. Even so, it surprised her when he touched her cheek, tilting her jaw as he bent over her. Covered her lips with his in the softest kiss imaginable.

Vaguely, she registered the warmth of his body—close to hers, but not touching other than where he brushed her mouth with his. He didn't grope and devour her like Mr. Covington had tried with Bailey's mom. Wade took his time, as though the only thing he wanted from her—or maybe for her—was one perfect kiss.

When he broke the kiss, he didn't move away. Eyes closed, he rested his forehead to hers as if he needed a moment to catch his breath. Or maybe that was just how she felt.

"I wish you trusted me more." He spoke softly, but she didn't miss the frustration threaded through the words.

She forced her eyes open and backed up a step,

unwilling to argue about the website with him. It was hard to trust anybody anymore.

He drove her home with the same quiet, thoughtful competence he did everything. She felt safe with him. Happy, even. That kiss played over and over in her mind, the light bubbly way it made her feel, an almost magical sensation after the crappy few days she'd had.

However, she couldn't escape the fact that he was disappointed with her. And that disappointment hung between them in the silence, a dull pressure that wouldn't go away and made her feel guilty for keeping secrets.

It was the only thing that prevented the kiss from being absolutely perfect.

CHAPTER TWELVE

HEATHER LOVED A STAGE.

Didn't matter if it was the old auditorium in the high school where she'd sang the heck out of her role in *Into the Woods* or on the beer-sticky floor of Charlie Ray's Rib Shack. She felt stronger, smarter, prettier and just plain better when she stepped into the spotlight. Even among musicians who did it for a living, that love of the stage ranked as a rare thing.

Rock 'n' roll icons regularly drank themselves numb before standing in front of an audience because stage fright was as common for most people as a fear of public speaking. Yet Heather never suffered from that particular issue. Maybe because she so rarely got the chance to perform. Now, thumbing through her music options near the karaoke machine, she chose a country tune that she knew backward, forward and sideways. The piece was a good fit for her vocal range and had a hook that would, with any luck, pump up the crowd.

It might only be the Tuesday-night regulars at Charlie Ray's, but they still deserved a good show.

And for Zach? She wanted to knock his socks off in more ways than one tonight. She needed to show him why her dreams were worth pursuing. Why she needed to get out of Heartache.

"You all set, honey?" a thin blonde with frizzy hair called over to her, her voice as raspy as if she'd smoked a couple packs a day since birth. Or maybe she just had vocal cord problems.

"Yes." Heather gave her a thumbs-up and handed her the slip of paper with her choice written on it. "I'm ready when you are."

"Sugar, I was born ready," the older woman retorted with a wink. "How about you find your spot up front and adjust the mic stand while I cue it up?"

"Do you have a mic back there?" Heather asked on a whim.

"Sure do, sweetie. Just in case the crowd gets too rowdy, I can set 'em all straight."

"Would you mind giving me an intro? My name's Heather."

"Heather, huh?" The blonde chewed her gum for two snaps before she nodded. "You bet. Go get 'em."

"Yes, ma'am." She planned to. Not just because she took pride in a good performance, but because Zachary Chance sat at a table watching her every move with moody, broody eyes, which made her aware of every nerve ending in her body.

Setting aside the mic stand, Heather scuffed along the stage and found the stickiest spots. She's seen performers take a header when they'd gotten a little too dance happy and landed a foot in beer—wet or dried.

Behind her, the piped-in music quieted.

"Folks, we have a treat for you tonight, courtesy of Charlie Ray and me—Dee Ray, your Queen of the Karaoke Machine." She cackled so hard that Heather feared a coughing fit, but the crowd pitched in a few hoots and hollers for Dee until she returned to the mic. The lights lowered a little more. A pink spotlight swirled near Heather. "Ladies and gentleman, give it up for Heather."

The small crowd cheered, practically drowning out the intro to her music. She knew the shouts and hollers were for Dee Ray and not her, but she'd made a wise decision bringing the woman into the act, however briefly. Excitement buzzed in her veins, a warm pulse under her skin, better than a caffeine jolt.

Draping herself across a table in a pinup girl pose, she let the pink lights swirl around her while the early melody rose. When the drumbeat kicked in, she shifted her shoulders, shot to her feet and launched into a fiery Carrie Underwood song.

Before she hit the first chorus, Charlie Ray's had gone silent except for her voice and her background music. Patrons set their ribs down. A cook wearing a sweaty T-shirt and apron shoved through a door at the back of the restaurant to see what was going on. A waitress tucked her tray under her arm and leaned a hip into the bar to watch the show. On the little stage, Heather shook, shimmied, but most of all, she sang.

And not until the second chorus did she allow herself to look at Zach.

He straddled the chair backward, arms draped along the back with his chin resting on his forearms. He gave her his full undivided attention when she strutted through the small crowd as far as the microphone cord would allow her. Then, her eyes locked on him, and the performance wasn't just for fun anymore.

It was all for him.

Every breathy note. Every heartfelt high. She felt it from the bottom of her soul as she reached deep to deliver lyrics about a woman done wrong but ready to move on with a new lover. The moving-on part at least was true. And as she planted one foot on a chair to lean into a gritty hook line before the outro, she knew the part about wanting a lover was about her, too. She wanted Zach.

Tonight.

And she didn't give a damn about the risks.

Maybe that's why she lifted her arm and pointed toward him with the song's ending words. It wasn't like the rest of her moves—part of the showman-ship. That bit was unscripted. Unpracticed. And didn't feel nearly as smooth as the rest of her de-livery. Her voice vibrated with an extended note and her eyes closed as she held it for as long as she could, letting the moment last. Even with her eyes shut, she could feel the connection between them as he stared at her from forty feet away.

When she finally ripped off the note and straightened to stand, the guitars on the kara-oke machine strummed through the last notes. But once again, she could hardly hear them from the applause. Every person responded in some way—applauded, whistled, stomped or shouted. The praise humbled and gladdened her. It had been a pure pleasure to entertain the small room with a talent that had been a fortunate gift of her genes and not something for which she could take credit.

Still, it felt nice.

Even if there was only one man's response she was interested in. And with so many people on their feet, she lost sight of him as Dee Ray swirled more lights around Heather—blue this time.

"Nice job, darlin'," the woman called to her from behind the table where she operated the sound system. "Although I'd be surprised if we get anyone else to take the stage after that. You're gonna be a tough act to follow."

The applause died down, and Heather stepped off the stage to accept a few congratulations. The older couple who'd sung earlier in the evening was the first in line, standing shoulder to shoulder as if they moved as one.

"That was beautiful, honey," the woman told her. She wore a plaid Western shirt with silver snaps in contrasting colors to her husband's. Silver pins from a square-dancing association flashed on their collars.

"You must be one of those Nashville acts polishing the moves before you take to the road," the gray-haired gentleman inserted, his bolo tie slightly askew as he put an arm around his wife. "I sure hope we hear more from you, Heather." He winked.

"Me, too." She shook both their hands. "Thank you so much."

After a few more kind words from some of the patrons—including Charlie Ray's insistence that dinner was on him anytime she wanted to come to karaoke night—Heather finally saw Zach standing in front of her.

"No wonder they think you're a Nashville singer." He shook his head slowly. Disbelieving. "That was…" He shrugged "The word *fantastic* doesn't do it justice, but I can't think up anything else that would sum up your performance."

"You liked it." She smiled like a girl in a toothpaste ad. Her grin that wouldn't stop.

"My God, Heather. Your voice."

"Are we set with dinner?" she asked, peering toward their table.

"The waitress refused to let me pay for dinner, but I did leave a fat tip."

"Good. Let's get out of here." She grabbed his hand, pulling her sweater off the table.

"Are you sure? There's still some food left. I don't want to rush you out the door."

"No." She hooked her arm through his, the adrenaline still singing in her veins. "Remember we talked about a private performance?"

She felt the change in him. An alert tension in every muscle.

"Yes, ma'am. I do." He lowered his voice and picked up his pace as they headed for the exit.

She smiled. "I think I'm ready to deliver."

HE COULD BE sitting beside country music's next superstar.

Zach weighed the idea as they sped back into Heartache that night, the top down on the convertible despite the chill in the air. He hadn't understood the level of Heather's talent until tonight. Until he'd seen her take command of the backwoods restaurant with her jaw-dropping voice and natural stage presence. He would have never guessed the local music teacher who volunteered for the rec department hid so much talent.

And while that was exciting for her and the career she seemed to want on a bigger stage than rural Tennessee could offer, it became all the more real to him that once she left, she might not come back.

Glancing over at her in his passenger seat, strands of red hair whipping in the wind—despite her hand clamped around the bulk of the thick mane—he memorized the way she looked right now. She sang along with the radio as they cruised to a stop sign outside town. Lit by the soft glow of dashboard lights, she crooned with her eyes closed, her chin tilted up as if to catch the breeze. Maybe he'd been stopped at the sign too long, because she opened her eyes, catching him staring.

"I'm making a spectacle of myself, aren't I?" She readjusted her hold on her hair, scraping more loose pieces into one closed fist. "Sometimes I can't stop singing once I start. Or put down my guitar after a few minutes of playing. It's a sickness."

His eye drifted to the exposed length of her neck where one stubborn red wave still clung to her creamy skin. He wanted to trace the trail of hair with his finger down to where it disappeared in the collar of her shirt.

"It's a damned entertaining one." He reached across the console to tug the strand free, his knuckle skimming her throat. "But I wouldn't say you're making a spectacle of yourself. It's a fairly common condition that I can't take my eyes off you." Zach stepped on the accelerator, more than ready to have her all to himself.

He wanted to think about that—being with Heather—and not whatever tomorrow might bring. He wasn't wasting this chance to be with a woman who fascinated him the way she did.

"You do have a way with words, Mayor Finley." She shifted in the leather seat, her thin bangle bracelets jingling as she moved.

"I've tried to step up my game since I took office." He turned down the long private driveway leading to his house. "Although the part about me watching you isn't flattery. That's the truth."

Had he surprised her with his honesty? His gut told him she was wary about getting too close too soon, no matter what she'd told him back at Charlie Ray's. Part of him wondered if her singing came from nervousness.

He pulled up to his house and left the car engine running. "Heather." He turned in the seat to face her. "I'm sure performing kind of supercharges emotions when you have to bring so much energy to the stage. So I understand if what you said at the bar was a result of that energy rush. We don't have to take this further—"

"No." She shook her head, letting go of her hair so it fell around her in a wild tangle. "What I said back at the bar came from the heart. That wasn't the performance talking. I want to be here."

Just hearing her say it made his blood run hotter. Made his hands itch to touch her. But he knew once he started, he wouldn't be able to stop. So he wanted to be very, very sure.

"I tried to do this the right way. Get to know you first. Go easy."

"I know." A sweet, slow smile curved her lips. "It's my fault we're running out of time together."

"And my fault for starting an investigation that's keeping you here when you want to be long gone." He hated that there would be talk in town about the ethics of him being with her if they went out together. He hated it for her sake as much as his.

She was one of the most ethical people he knew, a fact he'd gleaned from the times she'd shown up at town council meetings to discuss the needs of the recreation department or suggesting ways the rec department could give back to the community. It was one of the reasons he'd thought she would make a great mayor. One of many reasons he gravitated toward her.

"I've got an idea." She took his hand. "What do you say we not worry about any of it right now. It's a beautiful, clear night." With her other hand, she turned up the radio. A simple guitar melody filled the air. "And there's a slow song playing in the background. Let's just dance and enjoy it."

"Dance?"

As if he needed any persuasion to wrap her in his arms.

She nodded "Right here. In the moonlight."

He looked up at the Tennessee sky, the night so clear thousands of stars twinkled brightly overhead. The autumn breeze stirred the leaves in a soft shushing sound, as if nature were telling him to slow down and drink it all in.

Zach switched the car to accessory mode so that only the radio remained on, and then he slid out the driver's door to open hers. The moon hung low on the horizon, slanting gray shadows over them as he held out a hand for her. Heather stepped across the brick walkway into his embrace as if she was meant to be there, her hands slipping around his neck, her breasts against his chest in a way that robbed him of speech.

Folding his arms around her, a slow shudder went through him. He'd been waiting for this—imagining this—for a while. The reality was much better than the fantasy. She tucked her head into his shoulder, her windblown riot of waves a soft place for him to rest his cheek. Breathe in her scent. Just be.

He knew that ignoring tomorrow wasn't going to make the inevitable problems go away. But Heather had a point about simply enjoying the moment while they could.

"This was a good idea," he whispered into her

hair, hands stroking her back through the soft knit of her sweater.

Straightening, she tipped her face up to his. "Lots of country bars hang a big neon moon over the dance floor to try to simulate this, but nothing comes close to the real thing."

She arched her neck to peer at the sky, giving him access to taste the skin along her jaw. Down the smooth column of her throat. She shivered when he kissed beneath her ear, a place he vowed to return to once they were inside and she was in his bed.

"I think it's the woman I'm holding that is making it fun. Doesn't matter if we were dancing at Charlie Ray's or at your sister's wedding."

"Maybe you just think that because you're moonstruck." She slowed her step, not that they'd been moving at much more than a shuffle anyhow.

"Maybe you don't give me enough credit for knowing what I want." His hands grew restless, eager to cover more of her.

Or would that be uncover?

A little of both, maybe.

"Really?" She stood still as the song ended and a new tune played. "I think we both know what you want, Mayor."

"If you knew, you'd be calling me by my first name." He leaned away from her just long enough to reach over the car and switch off the ignition. He pocketed the keys.

"Maybe it turns me on to remember your position of power and authority," she whispered in his ear when he returned to her.

Knowing she was teasing him didn't begin to dull his body's response.

"In that case, you can forget about using my first name." He backed her toward the house, keeping a tight grip on her waist just in case she stumbled in the dark.

Also, because she felt so incredible against him.

"I have to let go for a minute." He eased away from her slightly to pull out his cell phone and disarm the home alarm system.

"You are high-tech." She twined an arm through his, her cheek pressed against his shoulder as she watched him key in the codes.

"I called my digital security company Fortress Nine. With a name like that, I can't afford to get hacked or have any break-ins. Too much bad PR."

"I'll let the local crooks know to stay away." She followed him in as he opened the front door and switched on lights in the small foyer.

"You're on a first-name basis with Heartache's criminal element?" He locked the heavy double doors and used the commands on his phone to lower blinds all over his house while she tugged off her sweater.

"Actually, yes. A lot of them come to the rec department to do their community-service hours." She peered around the corner into the living room. "Most of them are young guys, though. I'm sure they'll sort themselves out."

He guessed that nerves were setting in, no matter how much she wanted this night. In the darkened living room, she stood in front of the fireplace, staring at a photograph of his sister on the mantel.

He definitely didn't want to think about Ellie right now. So, right when Heather opened her mouth to say something, he covered her lips with a kiss.

Thankfully, she seemed to agree with that, her body sinking into his as if she'd been waiting for him. He reached behind her to flip the switch on the fireplace, starting the flame to warm up the room.

And so he could see her.

She was lovely in the firelight, a handful of pale freckles dotting her nose and cheeks. Her baseball jersey had twisted to one side, the neck-line gaping wide. He could see the light pink strap of her bra, right down to where it met the satin cupping one full, beautiful breast.

His whole body caught flame faster than the blaze in the hearth.

He pulled away from her just enough to notice

her blue eyes were bright and unfocused. Her lips bee-stung and damp from his kiss.

"I might have used up all my restraint that time at your house when you kissed me." His heart slugged so hard he thought she must hear it, echoing the truth of the words.

"I didn't want any restraint then," she said slowly. Clearly. "And I don't want it now."

The brakes were off with him and Heather Finley.

It was the only coherent thought in his head.

He pulled her to him, his mouth dropping to the pink satin strap to feast on her skin. She gripped his shoulders hard, her nails digging into the fabric of his jacket. He hadn't guessed how much passion lurked beneath her organized, capable surface. Not until she'd started singing tonight. But now he knew. He sensed it in her hungry kisses and heard it in her throaty sighs as she tugged at his clothes, pulling the jacket down his shoulders and off.

His fingers worked on the buttons of her jersey, sliding them free one by one until she stood in front of him in nothing but her jeans and a few scraps of pink satin. She trembled everywhere he touched her, her whole body vibrating with a need he couldn't wait to fulfill. He peeled the bra straps down her shoulders.

And not just for himself. Hell, he thought she

might burst into flame if he didn't touch her soon. Her skin flamed hot. Her fingers quivered as she unfastened his belt and splayed a hand along his abdomen. His muscles twitched in answer, more than ready to give her what she wanted.

Lifting her up, he carried her to the leather sofa closest to the fireplace. Her legs wrapped around him, bringing all her feminine warmth against the throbbing length of him. Every step he took told him just how damn perfect it would feel to be deep inside her.

When he tried to set her down, she wouldn't let go, her legs locked tight around his waist while she worked the buttons of his shirt.

"Let go," he urged, needing her naked as soon as possible. The heat between them had been a long, slow build. But it was consuming him now, singeing the edges of his brain and taking on a life of its own. Shrugging out of his shirt, he flicked open the clasp on her bra. Savored the sight of her high, perfect breasts.

"Heather." He wanted her eyes on him one last time before they became totally lost in this. Needed that connection with her so she understood what this meant to him.

"Mmm?" She said it between kisses, her lips barely pausing as they molded to his chest, her tongue sneaking out to stroke lightly.

He cupped her cheeks in his hands, holding her

delicate, perfect features. He studied her in the firelight until she opened her eyes and looked at him. Really looked at him.

Of course, she couldn't see all the things he was feeling. All the ways he wanted this moment to mean something. Hell, he barely understood it himself. He'd been on the periphery of her world for so long he hadn't realized how much he wanted inside. But since he couldn't stand to think about losing her, he would focus all his effort on making sure this would be a night she'd never, ever forget.

Laying her down on the sofa, he tugged her jeans down long, slender legs. Stripped off the pink satin that clung to her hips.

His brain burned with the image of her body glowing in the firelight. Blue eyes locked on his. Unwavering. His heart quickened with the need to take her. Have her. Keep her. He discarded his pants and boxers, remembering belatedly to retrieve a condom before he set the pants aside.

Staring into her beautiful eyes, he made room for himself between her thighs. Steadied her hips. And slid deep inside her.

Finally.

HEATHER GAZED AT ZACH, mesmerized by what was happening between them. It wasn't merely the amazing feel of all that male strength over her, around her, inside her. No, it was more than that. A soul-deep fire that she would have been just as happy not to acknowledge.

Zach had made her look in his eyes though, so she could see it. Whatever was happening between them burned away all her good sense. All her cares about anything but him. This.

Right now.

When at last he moved, she realized he'd been holding still, waiting for her to adjust. To relax. To be ready for what was happening. That movement turned her inside out, sent her arms around his neck to hold on tight.

The slick, heated glide of his body with hers undid her. She couldn't think, couldn't respond so much as simply *feel*. The hard plane of his chest against her sensitive breasts. The warmth of his breath on her neck as he lowered a kiss to a spot beneath her ear. The sensation of his tongue circling an erogenous zone she'd never known existed. She couldn't catch her breath.

She wasn't sure she wanted to.

Her hands streaked down his back, savoring the feel of all that male muscle. Staring up at him through her lashes, she admired all that taut, lean strength his well-cut suits had only hinted at. She wanted to slow down. To take her time and make this night last and last, but her body didn't want any part of slow.

Her heart thrummed at its own pace, caught up in the way Zach moved inside her. The way he kissed her neck. Cradled her hips in strong hands.

Then he rolled her on top of him, sitting up so she straddled him. Her hair blanketed her shoulders, her only covering as his eyes roamed over her. Devoured her like a starving man.

All it took was a few encouraging words in her ear, words whispered in a seductive breath along her damp, overheated neck. He told her she was beautiful. Sexy. That she drove him out of his mind…a litany of sweet words that were a teasing touch compared to the hard, relentless thrust of his body inside hers. It drove her higher and higher, pushing her over the sensual ledge until she flew apart in his arms in a haze of endless, lush sensation.

He joined her soon after, her body still pulsing around his when she felt the surge of his hips. The double time of his heart rate when he clutched her to his chest and held her as if he'd never let go.

It was perfect.

Absolutely freaking perfect.

But she couldn't catch her breath to tell him. Couldn't make her brain function beyond the soft cloud of thoughts in her head.

Yet, as he lay beside her on the sofa, both of them fighting to slow their breathing, Zach tucked a strand of hair behind her ear.

"You want to know the best part?" he asked.

"It gets better?" she asked, proud of herself for making her tongue work.

"This was just the first time."

CHAPTER THIRTEEN

HEATHER WASN'T SURE how much time had passed when she felt a warm blanket sliding over her hip. She lay on the leather sofa, half wrapped in Zach's arms, her cheek pillowed by one hard biceps. His other arm slid around her waist now that he had the blanket in place.

The light of the fire remained the only illumination, so she guessed they'd only been lying together for an hour or two. She should feel happy to have so much male warmth around her and the promise of more sensual touches throughout the night.

Instead, panic gnawed her gut as she became more fully awake. Because for a moment, she wasn't sure if she could move.

"Zach." His name burst from her lips in a fearful moment.

"I'm here." He tugged her closer.

Pain shot through her hips as he moved her stiff, unyielding body.

"Wait." Heart rate spiking, she gripped the couch cushion to steady herself in the wake of the pain.

She immediately regretted it, her knuckles protesting in a fiery scream.

"What is it?" He must have heard the worry in her voice. He levered himself up on one hip to peer into her face. "Are you okay?"

"Yes," she replied automatically, though she couldn't begin to school her features in a reasonable semblance of okay.

Nearly every joint had locked into place. Worse, absolutely every joint burned with pain. Mentally, she went through them all. Toes. Ankles. Knees. Hips. Fingers. Wrists. Elbows. Shoulders. Even her jaw. God, how could talking hurt? The panic in her gut gnawed harder. What the hell had happened to her?

"You're not okay." Zach stared at her, concerned amber eyes unblinking. "What's the matter?"

She closed her eyes. She couldn't deal with his questions and all this hurt, too. And fear. It was too much.

"I must have fallen asleep wrong. I have a really bad crick in my neck." While technically not a lie, the admission neglected to mention the hundred other places that hurt.

And not just a little, either.

The pain was so intense, a wave of nausea rocked her.

In the meantime, Zach was speaking. She didn't know what he said because she was too busy battling the sick feeling in her stomach. But vaguely, she sensed him sliding off the couch to pull on his pants and crouch in front of her.

She opened her eyes and met his intense, assessing stare.

"I need a few minutes." She forced her hand to move. Fingers to clench around the heavy fleece blanket he'd given her. She tugged it up to her face and hid inside it.

Not from him really. Just from the pain inflicted on her with every movement.

"You're scaring the hell out of me, Heather." Zach's voice knifed straight through the fleecy folds to pierce her ears with a tone she'd never heard him use. "Start talking to me now or I'm calling an ambulance."

She yanked down the blanket.

"No. My God, no." Fear warred with pain, battling all her fiery hurt into submission so she could prop up on an elbow. "It's happened before. I'll be okay."

His palm covered her forehead.

"You're pale. You're burning up." He reached for his cell phone. "You're getting medical treatment."

"No." She clawed the phone awkwardly from his hand. "Please, Zach. My family can't know about this."

"Can't know about what?" The concern she'd seen in his eyes earlier had been replaced by frustration. Anger, even.

Damn it, she was the one in pain. Why did she have to justify her reasons for keeping it to herself? Finally, she let herself say the words.

"I was recently diagnosed with a chronic condition. I was supposed to see a doctor in Charlotte, but I had to cancel my appointment when—"

"What condition?" His hand lingered near the phone she still held captive.

Logically, she knew it shouldn't matter that she had decided to keep her health issues quiet. But her family was unique. Her mother's tendency to see crisis in every situation had taught her to keep upheaval to a minimum. And damn it, this problem was *hers*. It was not about her mom.

"An autoimmune issue. But I've got some medicine at home, Zach. I just need more rest."

"Your fever is way too high." He cut her off. He grabbed his phone and jammed it in his pocket. "I'm bringing you to the ER because whatever you're doing to take care of yourself, it's not working."

"Not in town." She wouldn't cave on that. No way in hell did she want the news of this getting back to her family—her mother—and adding to the Finley drama. "I can't drive myself. But I won't go somewhere local."

Damn it. She hated relying on other people. Hated being in this position where she felt weak and hurt and couldn't stand up for herself. This was why she wanted to get out of town.

But right now she hurt too much to be a good advocate for herself. Something had to be really wrong, something more than arthritis. Virtually everything she did was colored by waves of pain that churned nausea and forced her to lie back down. And that's exactly what she did now. Gently, she placed her head back on the leather sofa and listened to Zach rummage around the room to find her clothes.

He dressed her gently. Thoughtfully. Even so, she could feel his anger and frustration in the tense way he moved. The cool divide between them. She wanted to tell him this wasn't a big deal, but the fatigue of so much pain kept her from doing anything that wasn't necessary. Besides, she remembered how much he hated secrets and agendas.

Her body had given up. It killed her to think that an hour ago she'd been enjoying the sensual nature of her body—and his—in a way she never had before.

Sex had been beautiful. Profound. And she'd been looking forward to more with him all night long. Except she didn't have that kind of physical stamina anymore. In fact, when the time came to leave the house and head to a medical facility, Zach didn't bother trying to help her to her feet.

Instead, he scooped her up in his arms, cradling her as if she weighed nothing, juggling her in his arms as he slid her into the passenger seat of the SUV, already warmed and ready with blankets inside.

He was such a good man. A good, angry man. She didn't quite know why he was so upset about a health secret that was hers to keep. But the cold set to his jaw as he drove her north—out of town—toward Franklin, told her everything she needed to know.

He'd treated her with tenderness and made her body come alive under his touch, but in exchange for a beautiful time together, he felt betrayed. Too exhausted to figure out why, let alone explain or apologize, Heather closed her eyes and fell asleep to escape the hurt.

Not only the physical kind, either. There was a new ache in her heart that had Zach Chance's name on it.

THE MORNING AFTER confronting J.D. on the baseball field, Megan waited in line at her study hall teacher's desk to get a pass to the physics lab. The class was quiet, the room unnaturally dark with a rainstorm raging outside. The girl in line in front of her wore headphones despite the teacher's strict rules against it. Her head whipped back and forth to music only she could hear, her spiky blue Mohawk immobile, shellacked into place.

Sure enough, the teacher gave Mohawk Girl a pass to the principal's office.

"Can I go to the physics lab?" Megan asked. "I have a makeup to complete."

"I don't know. Can you?" Mrs. Markowitz, an old-school English teacher, already scribbled the information on a scrap of blue paper.

Seriously?

Megan tried to smile as she corrected herself. "May I?"

Mrs. Markowitz winked at her as she handed over the pass and Megan scurried out the door. She'd dressed in sweats and a hoodie today, so tired from the night before she hadn't even showered. But she needed to take the lab she'd missed the day before. She knew the science teacher— Ms. Leister—had a free period and would let Megan make it up.

As much as she hated being stuck in the halls of Crestwood High every day, she felt guiltier hating it when she knew how much Wade would give to trade places with her.

Wade.

His name circled her mind as she hurried past the full classrooms and down toward the science wing. She'd thought about him way too much since his unexpected kiss. What was she doing mooning over a boy when she needed to leave Heartache as soon as school was done? It wouldn't be fair to let him think otherwise. And yet...

The kiss had been the nicest thing to happen to her in a long, long time.

Turning a corner at the end of a row of red lockers, Heather hurried into Ms. Leister's room. A handful of underclassmen were already working in the back of the lab. Up front, she spotted the teacher speaking with Bailey McCord.

Crap. Crap. Crap.

She spun on her heel, causing her tennis shoe to squeak on the hard floor.

Everyone stared. At least, it seemed that way. Her face burned.

"Your timing is perfect, Megan!" Ms. Leister called with a seemingly never-ending supply of good cheer. No other teacher embraced their subject matter with as much insane enthusiasm. "Bailey missed yesterday, too. You can be lab partners for the makeup."

Bailey made eye contact for the first time in months. With her perfect makeup and flawless blond hair held off her face by a black lace headband, Bailey looked about as different as possible from Megan in her ratty sweats. Yet their expressions matched perfectly—both their mouths hung open in disbelief.

Megan's brain worked fast to think of an excuse. She was deathly ill. She just got her period. She could fake a fainting spell like the women in all those Ann Radcliffe novels she'd been obsessed with last summer.

Then again, why should she?

She needed to complete her work. If Bailey hated her so much, she could come up with the excuse.

"Here you go, ladies. Follow me." Ms. Leister waved them toward a lab table off to one side of the room. "I left out a few sets of the beakers and cylinders for student makeups today. Just find the instructions in the book for the density lab. If you work quickly, you should be able to finish before the period ends."

Any moment, Bailey would think of somewhere else she needed to be. Beg off for one reason or another. Yet when Ms. Leister walked away, Megan's former friend didn't speak.

Megan flipped open a spare textbook. Each turned page made a snapping sound that echoed her annoyance.

"You know, you don't *have* to do the experiment with me." Bailey withdrew a bookmark from the page she'd already flagged in her text. Columns neatly drawn, she had the paper all prepped for the work.

Megan rolled her eyes. She might steal boyfriends and lie to her friends, but the girl was seriously organized.

"And let you get the A while I take an F for not completing an assignment? You'd like that, wouldn't you?"

"Since when do I root for people to fail?" Bailey frowned at the text, one manicured hand smoothing over the bookmark with glossy ultra-pink nails.

Megan recognized the bookmark and the book it advertised—a romantic trilogy with a hot hero from an alien planet. They'd both read the series in between the Ann Radcliffe stuff last summer when they'd been friends.

"Oh, I don't know. Maybe ever since you started stealing boyfriends and trash-talking your friends behind their backs." Keeping her voice low, Megan yanked graph paper and a ruler from her bag.

She didn't know what had gotten into her this week—this need to confront people. Maybe it had been eating away her insides for so long that the toxic poison was starting to leak out.

"That's bullshit," Bailey whispered furiously. "I never trash-talked you."

Bailey walked to the sink and measured the necessary water so they could start taking their mass and volume measurements. Megan opened the isopropyl alcohol and filled another cylinder, two steps ahead so they could finish faster and get the hell away from each other.

"So you'll admit to stealing J.D.—not that he was any great loss—but you won't admit you tried turning the whole school against me?" Megan noticed Ms. Leister looking their way, so she made an effort to pull her mouth into a smile that felt more like baring her teeth.

"Girls," Ms. Leister called. "Do we remember the first law of thermodynamics?"

Bailey straightened from her work on her graph. "The total energy of an isolated system is constant despite internal changes," she retorted, never missing a beat.

"Show-off," Megan muttered between her teeth.

"Exactly!" Ms. Leister beamed. "And if you add heat to a system, there are only two things that can be done—change the internal energy of the system or cause the system to do work to use that energy." She peered at them over her glasses. "And since you have quite a bit of heated energy over there, let's use it for *more work* instead of distracting chatter. Okay?"

"Yes, ma'am," both of them answered at once.

For the next thirty minutes, Megan worked next to Bailey in silence, the lab going faster and—she had to admit—better than it would have with Jennie, her usual lab partner. She and Bailey had been friends once, after all. Despite everything that had happened between them and Bailey's decision to be a backstabbing liar, they still had some things in common. Intelligence, for one thing. No surprise Bailey had known her thermodynamic laws.

Commitment to good grades was another.

Megan knew plenty of smart kids at Crestwood,

but not all of them bothered to—as her father would say—"apply themselves."

Bailey did.

That was probably why Wade had discounted her as the sender of the mean texts. Wade hadn't believed that a smart girl with her eye on the future would be involved in the kind of bullying Megan was experiencing. And considering how fast Bailey had denied the trash-talking accusation, it made Megan wonder about it, too. What if Bailey wasn't the reason behind all the evil at school?

What if she hadn't sent the texts? And if J.D. hadn't, either... Yes, that amounted to a lot of ifs. But she felt less sure about what the hell was going on. And as much as she hated the idea that Bailey and J.D.—or their friends—were harassing her, it freaked her out even more to think that a total stranger had targeted her.

"Time to finish working," Ms. Leister announced, glancing around the room at the few people still using lab equipment. "Let's get things packed up and put away before the bell."

Crap. They really hadn't worked fast enough, because Megan hadn't gotten all the data written down for Bailey's portion of the lab. Normally, they would have had a double period to work on their measurements and copy all the notes.

"Switch notebooks?" Bailey thrust her composition book full of neatly written columns in front of her. "We can take pictures on our phones. Ms. Leister won't care. I've done it before."

Megan glanced toward the front desk, where the teacher worked on her laptop.

"Either that, or you can call me later." Never had words been spoken with more sarcasm.

"Good point," Megan muttered, passing over her notes while she withdrew her phone to take a picture of Bailey's data.

When the bell rang, Bailey practically sprinted out of her seat, leaving Megan to put away the last of the equipment. At least the work was done. Honors physics was tough enough without taking late grades, too. Besides, Megan didn't need to rush since her next period was her regular physics class anyhow.

She didn't know what made her look up at Bailey again as her ex-friend reached the door, but she was just in time to catch sight of J.D. in the hall, waiting for her. He had such a pissed-off look on his face that Megan wondered if he'd seen her. But from where she stood, it sure seemed as if he glared at Bailey instead.

And although she couldn't see Bailey's face, she could sure tell that she darted right past him. Ignoring him?

Maybe she was just in a hurry or had a class on the far side of campus. Still, Megan didn't like the vicious expression on J.D.'s face. What had gotten into that kid to make him act like such a complete waste of space all the time? He didn't use to be that way.

Packing up her papers, Megan slid them into her bag before she noticed a pink sticky note on the back page of her composition book.

You stopped talking to me, remember? I've never said one bad thing about you, no matter what you think.

The note wasn't signed. But—unlike the mystery texts—Megan knew exactly who'd written this.

Was it true?

Had she concocted the whole rift between her and Bailey? She sure hadn't dreamed the way the kids had made fun of her at the wedding breakfast. Or the mean texts and website. But when she thought about the way her friendship with Bailey had dissolved, she had to admit that there'd never been a big blowup or confrontation. Had Megan imagined that Bailey was talking and whispering about her with her friends?

Peering around the physics class, Megan could find at least three pairs of girls who were talking and whispering right now. Some of them even looked her way as they did it. As if they were talking about her.

But what if they were simply looking around to see who was watching them? To see if they were overheard? To see if any boys noticed them, since that seemed of inordinate importance to most high school girls.

Maybe Megan could imagine a scenario where she'd dreamed up the idea that Bailey hated her. But she sure hadn't imagined that Bailey had set out to steal J.D. Even Wade knew the two of them had been hanging out before Megan broke up with her former boyfriend.

As the bell rang to signal the start of class, Megan settled deeper in her seat and shoved aside Bailey's note. She could ask Wade what he thought. He'd said he wished that Megan trusted him more, so she would trust him with this new piece of a puzzle she didn't understand. If nothing else, it helped to know she had someone to talk to.

And if there was another kiss in their future…? Megan couldn't wait.

CHAPTER FOURTEEN

"ARE YOU RELATED to the patient?" an emergency room nurse asked Zach three hours after he'd brought Heather to the hospital.

He'd been by her side for the first hour, waiting for one kind of doctor and then another, watching over her as she snagged snippets of sleep that didn't look all that restful, based on the pained expression pinching her mouth and furrowing her forehead. But he'd been there when she'd spoken to the first doctor. Heard her confess she'd been diagnosed with rheumatoid arthritis over the summer. Heard the doctor discount that RA could be causing her such sudden acute pain. But when they'd wheeled her down to the imaging department for some X-rays, Zach had been left behind and he hadn't managed to find her since, after a staff change at dawn.

Frustrated, he was in the general waiting area searching the hell out of rheumatoid arthritis on his phone. He wanted to be with Heather, and instead, he was surrounded by assorted coughs, broken bones and one old man who couldn't stop wailing despite no visible injury. Zach's nerves were stretched thin, and the scent of antiseptic air was giving him serious flashbacks to the worst night of his life—when he'd brought Ellie to this hospital. He just wanted to find Heather. Make sure she was okay.

Unable to stand it any longer, he shot to his feet. He tucked his phone away and strode to the nurses' station.

"I brought Heather Finley in last night." Too tired to apply any charm to the situation, he stared down the nurse, the woman who was now in charge of the registration desk. "I have her personal belongings," he lied. "I know she'll want them. Can you just point me in the right direction?"

"Unless you're related, sir, I can't allow you into the restricted section." Unimpressed, the woman lowered her attention back to her computer screen. "But I can print a label with Ms. Finley's name and give you a bag for her personal items. I will make sure she gets them."

"I don't want a label." He covered his face with one hand, squeezing his temples to ward off the ache in his head. "I want to see my…girlfriend." What else came close to describing their relationship? "We are not related. But I'm not some stranger off the street asking about her. I'm worried about her. She's seriously ill."

Pulling her hands off the computer keyboard, the nurse swiveled her chair to face him. One long ponytail trailed over her shoulder, not quite covering a name badge that read Lorena.

"Sir, I realize you want to be with Ms. Finley. But this is a hospital, and there are strict privacy laws in place to protect our patients. Those laws are there for a very good reason, even if they feel inconvenient to you this morning."

Right. They were there to protect people like Heather, who didn't want to share jack shit about herself with him. Who hadn't told him or anyone else in her life that she was suffering from a serious condition, which he'd only learned about thanks to scanning the internet. Clearly, in Heather's mind, it didn't matter that they'd slept together. That he was falling for her fast. He had been for months.

Heather Finley had one foot out of Heartache before she'd ever kissed him, and nothing—not him, and not a debilitating disease—was going to slow her down.

Zach debated storming the doors behind the admitting desk. As he stared at them, the first doctor who'd seen Heather shoved through them, his attention on his phone.

Thanking Lorena for her help and leaving her to her work, he jogged to catch up with Dr. Watts. The resident hadn't been much on bedside manner, bleary-eyed and spending half the exam time talking about growing up on the West

Coast once he'd found out Zach had attended college in San Jose.

"Doctor." Zach matched his step to the older man's, noticing the guy checked out ESPN highlights on his phone. "I've been waiting for Heather to return from her X-rays. Do you know where they would send her afterward?"

"Sure, sure…" The guy nodded, never taking his eyes off his screen as he pivoted the device so Zach could see it. "Look at number 33 tomahawk this one down."

A one-handed dunk followed, and Zach faked interest, figuring he hadn't gotten anywhere with Nurse Lorena by being demanding.

"Nice," he commented, fresh out of sports enthusiasm at the moment.

But the bland remark must have been enough, because Dr. Watts clapped him on the shoulder to turn him around, then marched him right past Lorena through the restricted-access doors.

"This way." Dr. Watts nodded to a colleague as they passed a nurse escorting a shuffling older woman down the busy hall. Most of the doors were open to treatment rooms where patients waited to be admitted or see different doctors. "I ordered some fluids for her and called for a rheumatologist to take a look before we send her home."

"Even with the fever?" Zach dodged a janitor's

cart and then skirted a group of interns following a nurse around the unit.

"It's holding steady at 102." Turning another corner, Dr. Watts pointed to a quieter hallway. "She's in the last room on the right."

Zach wanted to question him further, to shake out more answers about what the hell was going on with Heather's health. Two things stopped him. First, that Heather had made it clear she wanted to be in charge of sharing those details. Second, he guessed Dr. Watts knew more about college hoop than whatever was wrong with Heather.

"Thanks, Doc. Much appreciated." Zach nodded and headed down the hall.

The long walk gave him too much time to think about Ellie's time here. Too many medical professionals had kept him away from his sister then, too. He'd been stuck in some outer waiting room when he'd heard the code call over the speakers. Knew it was an emergency by the way nurses and doctors took off running.

And he'd known in his bones who the code was for. Whose life hung in the balance that night. All because she'd kept her damn secrets, too. And because Zach had been too focused on getting out of Heartache—away from his family—to notice how depressed she'd been.

"Hey, Zach."

The soft sound of his name called him out of the past, making him realize he'd reached Heather's room and stood framed in the doorway. Staring at her but not seeing her. At least, not at first. His brain cleared, the present shoving aside the past, even if it left him ice cold inside. Heather lay in a bed with a bleached-white blanket tucked around her. Her pink tennis sneakers stuck out of the bottom of the thermal cotton, the same shoes she'd worn to dance in less than twelve hours ago. Her cheeks were flushed, the fever evident no matter that Dr. Watts hadn't seemed concerned. She looked more alert, though, her blue eyes clear and not as pain-fogged as before.

"Hey, yourself, superstar." He said it to make her smile. But maybe he had already stuck his foot in his mouth.

Would her health prevent her from the dreams she so desperately wanted to pursue?

"I feel bad you're still here." She moved over on the bed and tugged the blanket closer. "Want a seat? You must be exhausted."

"I'm guessing I feel better than you." Stepping deeper into the small room, he tried to pull his head together as he closed the door. Focus on Heather and not think about the sound of Ellie's heart-rate monitor when she'd flatlined for interminable seconds.

His mother had been visiting his father at the county jail that day, leaving a seventeen-year-old kid in charge of his sister.

"I'm not sure how long they are going to keep me here. You definitely don't need to stay."

"I'm not leaving." He lowered himself to sit on the side of her bed. He was still mad that she'd drawn a line in the sand with him, hadn't wanted to share anything with him. But hell, he wanted to be close to her.

"Yet you're so angry with me you can hardly look at me," she said softly, picking at a loose thread on the white blanket.

A gesture he knew about, thanks to peripheral vision, so maybe she had a point. He fixed his full attention on her, saw her shifting on the bed. An IV was taped to one wrist. She wore a hospital gown. Someone must have helped her change for the X-rays.

He'd been a wreck trying to dress her back at his house, scared of hurting her more. Worried that he'd already hurt her somehow when they'd been together earlier.

He rested his hand over hers, careful to stay clear of the IV. "I don't want to argue with you while you're not feeling well. I know stress isn't good for your condition." He used a whole lot of restraint to limit his remarks to just those few words. "I'm not about to add to the tension factor."

"You don't cause me stress." She linked her fingers with his.

Just a few hours ago, her hands had been all

over him, pulling his clothes off. He'd thought it was the start of something special. It'd sure felt that way to him. But while he'd been thinking about getting closer to her, she'd already built walls around herself.

"Of course I do. I'm having the town sheriff investigate your father's political past. Turning the public eye on your family. I've caused a lot of tension for all the Finleys, but you especially." Guilt pounded with every heartbeat, forcing out the fear that had been dogging him all evening. "That could have triggered this episode, you know. The strain and anxiety from that."

"That's not true."

"You don't *know* that." Too frustrated to sit still, he sprang off the bed and stalked around the small space. He grimaced. The walls were painted a bright blue, which was probably supposed to be calming, but it seemed too damn cheery. "For all we know, sex caused it. What if—"

A sharp rap sounded at the closed door a split second before it swung wide.

A woman in a white lab coat entered. She had frizzy dark curls and sharp features, but her smile seemed genuine and—bonus—she wasn't distracted by sports on a handheld device. She carried a clipboard under her arm.

"I'm Dr. Ruiz, the rheumatologist your admitting doctor sent for." Setting down the clipboard, she checked the notes on the IV bag. "Ms. Finley, I've reviewed your X-rays and blood work, along with your past history. Do you mind if I look over your joints? You don't need to get up. I'd just take a peek at your arms and hands."

Heather's eyes strayed toward Zach before she answered.

Dr. Ruiz followed her gaze.

"Unless you prefer privacy?" the doctor asked.

Zach held his breath, wondering if Heather would ask him to step out.

He should at least offer. But he wanted to hear what this doctor had to say. Heather would only keep it secret. So frankly, unless she made him leave, he planned to sit tight. He leaned against one wall, averting his eyes but listening just the same.

Heather must have given her approval because he heard the rustle of the blanket and the quick directives from Dr. Ruiz, including a request that Heather try to make a fist or exert pressure on the other woman's hands.

"Okay. That's fine." Dr. Ruiz stepped back and leaned against a built-in counter. "I'm going to disagree with Dr. Watts that your condition is unrelated to the rheumatic disease. I think the episode you experienced tonight is the direct result of the RA."

"The arthritis?" Zach asked before remembering he wasn't going to say anything.

"Yes." The doctor folded her arms across her lab coat and crossed her clog-covered feet. "Although the condition is poorly named since the arthritis is a symptom of the larger autoimmune disease. I tell you this, Ms. Finley, because you are a new patient and your chart shows you haven't begun aggressive treatment yet. The non-steroidal anti-inflammatory drugs you're taking won't prevent flare-ups like this. You need something stronger, and most likely a range of medications to address multiple facets of the disease."

Zach thought of ten more questions he wanted to ask, including, what exactly had caused *this* flare-up? But he kept them to himself and waited for Heather to speak. When she didn't say anything, he looked up. Found her watching him.

"Zach, would you mind very much if—"

He didn't stick around to hear the rest. He could tell by her worried expression she wanted him gone so she could speak to the doctor privately, after all. Of course he understood.

She cared about him. But he was beginning to realize she didn't care about him as much as he cared about her. And that hurt.

"Text me if you need anything." With a nod, he pushed through the door and strode out of the room, his shoulders as tense as Heather's had been when he'd carried her out of his house hours ago.

Stalking past Lorena's desk, he was tempted to

tell the nurse she'd been right—he didn't belong back there where he wasn't needed. Sure as hell wasn't wanted. He clenched his fists, hating that he couldn't call her brothers, at least. Her sister Erin might be on her honeymoon, but Zach knew Scott's wife, Bethany, and Mack's fiancée, Nina, would want to be with Heather through this.

But what pissed him off more than being shut out—of the irrefutable evidence that she didn't want him any more involved in her life than he'd already become—was knowing that she denied herself support, help and the necessary treatment. From his reading about the disease, he knew that the drugs Dr. Ruiz mentioned weren't strong enough to slow down the effects of RA. Heather must know that, too. How could she put the needs of everyone else in front of hers? To the point that she would let her joints deteriorate so much she'd ended up in the hospital?

Too angry to separate that frustration from his old resentment at the way his teenage sister had concealed her depression, Zach dropped into an uncomfortable waiting room chair and fumed.

Pulling out his phone, he scrolled through his messages, including some new ones from Sam about the investigation. A reminder that he still needed the Finley family's permission to review the former mayor's personal computers. There was also an email from his sister and a reminder in his calendar to follow up on the interview with Megan Bryer.

He'd planned on calling the teen's father and alerting the guy to watch for signs of trouble in Megan's life. For example, did she avoid answering the phone or regularly clear her browser history? Had she been dodging former friends or social gatherings with peers? Things he knew now were red flags for people who were stalked or bullied online.

The signs he'd missed in Ellie. Zach had figured that as long as he and Sam kept her physically safe, she'd be okay. He'd been too young, too stupid and too caught up in his own fury at his father to notice that—emotionally—his sister had fallen apart after being attacked by her stalker.

So Heather wanted to keep Megan's secrets? Zach was going to call bullshit on that one. Heather had the right to hide her own health problems, but she didn't have the right to hide her student's. Zach would call Dan Bryer today.

But first, he planned to dig deeper online to see if he could find any evidence of bullying. If it existed on the internet, it was a matter of public record anyhow, so Zach wasn't worried about breaking confidences or protecting privacy.

Searching on his laptop would be easier, but since he had time and too much frustrated energy now, he used his phone to hit a few social media sites that were popular with the kids. At first, he found nothing. One social media site after the next came up clean for mentions of Megan—at least the negative that he'd been worried about.

Then it occurred to him to check archived pages—a feat that was trickier with social media pages when you didn't know fixed URLs. But there were plenty of tools to view deleted web pages. He started running a few of them, setting new archive searches in motion on various browser pages so he could search multiple platforms at once.

When he got a hit, he clicked it.

And scrambled to turn the screen off his phone before anyone in the waiting room saw what was on the page.

Shit. He cursed that word and a whole lot more, his brain reeling from the images he'd seen. Images that were definitely not Megan Bryer, but pictures digitally altered to look like her. Anyone would know it was the work of malicious slander. But oh *shit*.

Her father would be devastated if he saw that page. Any father would. But most of all, Megan must be humiliated.

Plus, Heather had told him how overprotective Dan Bryer could be when it concerned his daughter. The girl needed adult help. She had a serious cyberbully, and whoever it was didn't settle for just calling her names. The smut on that page— directed at an underage teen—was horrifying. As tough as it might be for Megan's father, it would be worse for Megan. The emotional consequences of that kind of public abuse could drive a teen to desperate acts, a risk Zach would not take.

He'd call Sam and involve law enforcement. Let them handle getting in touch with Megan's father. And no matter how much he didn't want to cause Heather more stress, Zach planned to give her a heads-up. For one thing, he felt as if he owed her that much since she'd asked him to wait until she spoke to Megan.

For another, he refused to keep secrets from her. She'd been hurt that he hadn't divulged the news of the missing town money sooner, and he'd sat on that for all of a day because he'd thought he could fix it. Yet, she'd been keeping her health issues hidden for months, and she must know there was no fix for her condition. How long did she plan to battle the disease by herself? Zach knew firsthand how much that kind of self-imposed emotional exile could be soul-destroying. Ellie had barely survived it.

Heather could choose to walk that lonely path by herself. As an adult, that was her right. But Megan didn't get to make that choice. Not as long as Zach was around to help.

DISCHARGE PAPERS IN HAND, Heather waited on the curb outside the small medical facility as Zach pulled up in his SUV. After her conversation with

Dr. Ruiz, things had moved quickly. She had a prescription for some temporary medications, but the doctor had insisted on follow-up care and had scheduled an appointment for Heather next week.

Her head spun with the new information about her condition, information she'd avoided hearing before tonight since she'd been afraid of what the disease meant for her future. But the doctor had been encouraging. The people who best managed RA were the patients who sought aggressive, regular treatment. Something Heather had planned on down the road. She simply hadn't wanted to start off with that approach immediately. And to be honest, her pride had kept her from doing so because the effects of the drugs might be noticeable.

She breathed deeply. She needed to confront the next phase of her problem: explain to Zach why she hadn't shared her health issue. Dreading that conversation on the long ride home, she allowed the hospital orderly to hand her into the vehicle. Her joints weren't quite as stiff and painful, thanks to a cortisone shot, but she didn't exactly move fluidly. And she still felt drained.

Once the orderly closed the door, she glanced at Zach and tried to find the right words to explain herself. No easy feat when his jaw was set, his cheek muscle working back and forth as if he were chewing over the harsh words he wanted to say.

As he pulled out of the parking lot onto the small county road that would lead back to the highway, he shot her a glance across the console. His amber eyes were serious, his expression grave.

"Are you sure you're feeling well enough to go home?" he asked. "Do you need somebody to stay with you?"

"I'm better now," she assured herself as much as him. "I'll be fine once I get home. I'm just going to catch up on some sleep."

His terse nod acknowledged the answer, but he was a long way from agreeing with it.

"You could call Bethany or Nina. I understand why you're wary of telling your mother about this, but one of them could—"

"I'm not burdening them with that." She pulled the blanket tighter to her chin, grateful for the warmth and wishing she could turn back the clock to when they'd shared the same covers.

This was so not how she had wanted their night together to end.

"Your family would never view it as a burden. You know that."

"I just want them to be happy for me when I leave, okay? I don't want everyone second-guessing my decision and worrying about how long it will be before I give in and come back here."

"You're denying yourself a whole lot of support." He quieted for a long moment, but she had nothing else to say on the subject. She wasn't ready to share this news with her family.

He huffed out a long breath. "Okay. I get it. I disagree with your decision to deny yourself the help and support of a family who loves you, but I understand it's your business and not mine."

"Thank you." Her voice wavered. She cleared it and sat up straighter.

"I discovered a whole other problem while I was in that waiting room." His expression remained grim. "Megan is in more trouble than we first realized."

"What do you mean?" She chewed her lip, hating to think of her student battling more problems.

He picked up his phone where it had been sitting in the cup holder. Passing it to her, he flicked the screen to turn it on. "Take a look at the web browser. And brace yourself."

Instantly, her focus shifted.

Shoving aside the discharge paperwork she'd been carrying, she tapped the button on his phone. The simple touch opened a page on the web.

"Oh, my God." She wanted to tap it closed again, her hands trembling with the urge to throw the phone aside like a poisonous thing. There hadn't been a way to brace herself for what she'd just seen. She scanned the content from a popular social media community. It was set up to look like

Megan's profile, but the short description read as though she was a prostitute.

It related the information in the foulest terms possible, including detailed information about her services. The images on the page were clearly tampered with, the photos of an absurdly proportioned woman with Megan's pretty face copied and pasted onto the shoulders of the mostly naked body.

"The page has already been removed from the site," Zach informed her. "It looks like it was only posted briefly. But I'm not sure if the site took it down because of the violations of their rules, if Megan saw this and reported it, or if the bastard who posted it in the first place thought the better of it and pulled it down himself."

"Or *her*self," Heather replied numbly, her heart broken for the innocent teenager. For Megan's poor father, too. "Girls are not exempt from posting cruel things about each other." She flipped the phone upside down on her lap, needing a break from the images and all the mean, hateful words. "How did you find this if it's not online anymore? How can I be looking at it?"

Zach steered the SUV onto the highway heading south. There weren't many cars on the road, partly because of the hour, but mostly because they were driving into a rural area.

"I searched for live pages first. When nothing

came up, I used archives sites to see what else had been posted in the past."

"I can't believe anyone would post such a thing. She's such a bright, beautiful girl with so much talent." Tears stung her eyes. She needed to turn off the phone. "How could anyone be that cruel?"

"I don't know, but I'm getting Sam involved. Her father needs to be informed that she's being targeted, Heather. If you want to warn her, call her right now because I'm not delaying for even a day." He turned down the heater with a press of a button, his eyes still on the road as they drove past miles of four-rail fences in horse country.

"She's in school. She can't take a call during school hours."

His hands white-knuckled the steering wheel. "This is too important to wait."

"I agree." She chose her words carefully, realizing he was close to exploding. Talk about stress. He'd been put through the wringer in the past twelve hours on more than one level. "This is a vicious attack on her character. For all we know, the person who posted this could take it to the next level and attack her personally."

"You're right. I can't afford to wait on this."

Heather listened silently while Zach phoned Sam. When he'd finished the call, he asked her to use his phone to text Sam the link so the sheriff could begin work.

The tension she heard in his voice helped her

to understand some of the frustration she'd seen in his eyes back at the hospital. This upset him deeply.

"Can I ask you a question?" She flexed her fingers over and over as movement returned slowly to her hands.

Maybe if she stayed in motion, her body wouldn't be able to shut down the way it had the night before.

"I guess. Although the fact that you want to clear it with me first makes me uneasy." Zach rolled his shoulders, as tense as her, but for reasons beyond arthritis. She could tell he took Megan's case personally. Knew it must be because of his sister's experience with a stalker.

"When you were on the phone with Sam, you asked him, 'Do you think it could be the same guy?'" She studied Zach in the bright light of day. Shadows lived under his eyes, rough bristles dotted his jaw. "You don't think that whoever is bullying Megan could be the same person who stalked Gabriella?"

"Sam doesn't think so. He thinks the website sounds like kid stuff—the kind of crap a teen would come up with, not a man who has to be at least as old as me by now."

"Did Gabriella tell the police about her stalker?"

"She reported the early incidents." The frosty answer told her exactly how frustrated he'd been with the authorities. "But she was patronized.

Given advice about how to dress conservatively. So when things got worse, she refused to go back to the police."

"That's awful." She remembered the former police chief, though, and wasn't all that surprised. He'd retired and moved to Florida before her father died.

"I think that's half the reason Sam became a cop. That way, at least *he* knew everything that had happened. He's always kept tabs on her." Zach's jaw flexed as he stared out the windshield. "One day, we'll collar the guy who hurt her."

"I'll call Megan after school to check on her," she said. "If she hasn't heard from Sam by then, I'll give her a warning that he wants to speak to her." She hoped she'd reach the girl first.

He nodded. "I appreciate that."

She licked her lips, needing to cover one more bit of business. "Also, I texted my brothers this morning to make sure they're okay with me turning over Dad's old laptop. They agreed we have nothing to hide, so you can take the equipment when you drop me off."

"Thank you." He hit the turn signal and she was surprised to realize they'd arrived at the Heartache exit. "I'll run some analysis programs as quickly as I can."

His responses had become clipped. Perfunctory. She needed to ease the tension between them.

Even if she wasn't ready to share everything about her health concerns, they had shared an incredible night of amazing sex. To ignore that did them both an injustice.

"I'm sorry how last night turned out. I had such a fun time with you."

"Fun." He repeated the word carefully, the single syllable pulsing with quiet anger. "Is that what you'd call our time together?"

"The karaoke bar was definitely a good time," she hedged, her eyes glued to the windshield as the town of Heartache came into view. The welcome sign remained a relic from the fifties, but by now it ranked as a kitschy small-town classic. "And afterward..."

Her eyes slid toward him as she remembered how that had turned out. Just thinking about the way he'd touched her caused her pulse to speed up. Her skin to heat.

"Afterward might have hurt you, Heather. Have you considered that?"

Gasping, she turned to him quickly. She couldn't let him think that. Not even for an instant. "Actually, I asked the doctor about that very issue when you left. I don't know why I turned into a tongue-tied teenager about sex, but it felt easier to quiz her on things like that without you in the room." It was mostly true. She'd had questions about medications and side effects, too. If she had limited time in Heartache, she didn't want to spend it being loopy and too tired to visit with her family and friends, but Dr. Ruiz thought she'd be fine.

"And?" Zach's hazel eyes swung her way, a heated glance that torched her skin in spite of how tired she felt. How much her joints still ached.

"And we didn't do anything wrong. Flare-ups can happen out of the blue. She said that exercise and movement are critical to maintaining good health." Which had sounded like good news to Heather, but judging by Zach's narrowed gaze, he wasn't as enthused as she. "That's a good thing, by the way. It means we don't need to worry about sex causing problems as long as we don't bring out a trapeze."

Her attempt at humor fell flat. He simply grunted and continued to stare at the road.

Driving through downtown, Heather spotted Last Chance Vintage. Pumpkins surrounded the front door. Up above the street, the town had hung a sign advertising the harvest festival with a special theme this year—Lumberjack Days— to celebrate area woodsmen.

On the surface, small-community charm abounded. Underneath…many darker issues had cropped up lately.

Finally, Zach glanced her way again, making her realize he'd been thinking about what she'd said.

"How can you suggest we 'not worry' about this? It might be too late for that." Zach turned off the main street and headed down the road toward the Finley families' homes. "Sex already created some problems, don't you think?"

At least they were done dancing around the subject. She'd been waiting for this to come up the whole way home.

"I thought it was pretty special," she admitted.

He reached the cul-de-sac with her mother's house and—behind that—her bungalow.

"Really?" He jammed the SUV in Park on the gravel driveway outside her house. "Is that why you were with me, Heather? Because it seems like the only reason you let yourself get close to me was because you knew we came with an expiration date. And once you're done with Heartache, you're going to be done with me, too."

Zach didn't waste any time waiting for an answer, levering his door open to go around and help her out of the vehicle.

His touch seemed mechanical, though. His help only for common courtesy's sake. She hated that she'd hurt him.

"Zach, that's not true." She fished her keys from her purse and let herself in the house, then waved him in so she could retrieve her father's old laptop. "Last night—"

He covered her lips with his fingers. Gently. But firmly. He shook his head wearily.

"Let's wait before we talk about this anymore, okay? I'm tired, and I know you are, too. Frankly, between learning about Megan's problems and this news about you, I'm shredded. If it's just the same to you, I'd like to take the computer and regroup."

She nodded. Because what more could she say? She was shredded, too. She hadn't wanted to end up in the hospital last night. Hadn't wanted their night together to end on this note. So, no matter that her whole body hurt, she dug in a storage closet stuffed with her father's old office items.

She found his heavy, old laptop, and with burning fingers, handed it to Zach. "Here, I hope this helps all of us."

"Are you okay?" he asked, his eyes searching hers.

"I'll be fine. Thank you for the ride." She thought she might collapse if she didn't lie down soon, but she was determined to see him out the door without falling apart.

Again.

Bad enough he'd seen her physically incapacitated. She wasn't going to lose it emotionally, too.

"Feel better, Heather." He laid a chaste kiss on her forehead.

The kind of kiss that felt like an end and not a beginning.

Calling up a half smile, she watched him walk out the door.

And knew she'd screwed things up irreparably with him.

CHAPTER FIFTEEN

SLUMPED OVER HER notes on graphing amplitude, Megan fought sleep. Trigonometry was her last class of the day. She never learned anything from Mrs. Wyman, a teacher who paced back and forth as she lectured, never varying her lecture pitch or speed. Megan had long given up trying to stay awake during the hypnotic pacing spells, learning everything she knew about trig from You-Tube videos.

When the PA system crackled she startled, her notebook falling off her desk as she knocked it with her elbow.

"Mrs. Wyman," the office secretary said over the loudspeaker. "Could you send Megan Bryer to the office?"

Yes! Talk about a "get out of jail free" card.

Straightening, Megan gathered her things, hopeful she could stretch the office visit to the end of the period. She'd been distracted all day between thoughts of what happened with J.D. last night, Wade's unexpected kiss and now the weird note from Bailey. Megan couldn't wait to leave school grounds behind and see Wade at the Owl's Roost.

"Better take your things, Megan," Mrs. Wyman intoned, still pacing in that slow, plodding shuffle. "The homework assignment is online."

"Yes, ma'am." She couldn't pack her patched denim book bag fast enough. She passed Bailey's desk on the way out.

Megan hurried to the office, figuring her dad had brought her an umbrella or something like that. It had started raining an hour ago, and her dad wouldn't want her out in the downpour. Then again, the office wouldn't have called her for one of Dad's visits. He dropped stuff off to her all the time—an extra sweater if it was cold or her lunch if she forgot it. One time, he'd brought her new sneakers when she'd said she wanted to try out for track and her old tennis shoes had a hole in them.

Yes, he was sweetly goofy. Embarrassingly so. But the school clerk didn't mind. Ms. Bartinello seemed to have a crush on him, in fact, always chatting with him long after he was done with his drop-off errand.

Stepping into the office, Megan didn't see any sign of her dad or an umbrella. Ms. Bartinello didn't look up when she entered, either, her expression fixed on what she was reading. Who'd called her down here then?

"Excuse me, Ms. Bartinello."

The school clerk peered up from her reading.

"Oh. Hi, Megan." The woman's guarded smile put Megan on alert. "They want you in the guidance office."

"Okay." She padded down the carpeted hallway connecting the two sets of administrative offices. The assistant at the guidance front desk pressed her intercom when she saw Megan.

"Mrs. Trestle? Megan Bryer is here." The clerk nodded, hanging up the phone. "Hi, Megan. You can go right in."

Curious now, and a little worried, Megan hoped there was nothing wrong with a standardized test score or anything. What if she'd bombed one of the big tests?

When she arrived at her counselor's office, she saw Mrs. Trestle wasn't alone. A woman dressed in gray pants, a black T-shirt and a gray suit jacket sat across from Mrs. T. The stranger's hair was in a tight twist. No makeup. Clipped to her gray pants, just peeking out from the jacket glinted…

A silver police badge.

Megan tried to swallow down the bile at the back of her throat. But all she managed to do was gape at the women through the office door, her mouth hanging open like a gulping fish. Had something happened to her dad?

Or was this about something else? Could she get in trouble for that smutty social media page? Her name was on it. It advertised illegal services.

"Hi, Megan." Mrs. Trestle must have spotted her in the corridor. Normally bubbly and smiling, the counselor's face was pinched and serious. "Come on in. I'd like you to meet Linda Marquette from the sherriff's department."

Oh. My. God.

No.

Megan's feet couldn't work any better than her mouth did. Nervousness made her whole body shake. For a second, she remembered how some people peed themselves when they were terrified. Would that happen to her? It felt like a distinct possibility.

If she didn't pee herself, she'd start retching on the bile in her throat.

"Megan?" Linda Marquette stood and approached her. "Are you okay? I wanted to ask you a few things, but if you'd feel more comfortable with a parent present, we can ask your father to join us. He's teaching today, but we did alert him that we planned to speak with you."

"No." That loosened her tongue. Got her feet working, too. Megan hurried into Mrs. Trestle's office and closed the door. Why had the police spoken to her father? How much did he know? "Please, no. I'm happy to talk to you."

But within thirty minutes, Megan's worst nightmares had come true.

The police knew about the website, thanks to her interview with the mayor. The sheriff's department would investigate, which, on one hand, sounded great. The huge, awful, unfair downside? Her father knew about the harassment and planned to meet with Megan and another police officer at their home once his work commitments were finished for the day. And while Megan's name would be kept out of any official reports made available to the public, thanks to privacy laws, the truth was that the whole town would puzzle out her identity based on whatever facts the cops released.

It was a small town. That's how things worked.

So not only did her dad know, the whole school would see that website even though it had been taken down. Heartache, Tennessee, would probably crash the internet trying to find that page the moment the news of it got out.

"Megan?" the policewoman stared at her, and Megan realized that Linda Marquette had stopped talking about the ways the sheriff's department and the school could protect her.

Ha.

One big fat mirthless LOL to that.

She tried to slow her racing heart and pay attention, but all she wanted to do was go home, hide in her room and kill mutant zombies on her video game for a month straight. She would rid the world of mutant zombies forever right now if she had a controller in her hand.

"Megan?" The cop leaned closer, getting in her

field of vision, her dark knot of twisted hair listing to one side as she did. "I know this is a lot to absorb, but we can't take this lightly. This kind of abuse is not okay."

"Right. But would you want your dad to see something like that about you?"

"When we spoke to your father, his first priority was helping you fix this. He wanted to be here, but he couldn't cancel his class. Your dad sounds like a fighter, Megan. You need that. You need him rooting for you. Helping keep you safe." The cop handed her a box of tissues without comment. "That's what good parents do. They look out for their kids. Not the other way around."

Tears streamed down Megan's face and dripped off her chin to fall on her lap. Well, the tissue box, now. The wet spots grew bigger on the cheap yellow cardboard.

"I can't face him." She yanked two tissues out of the box and mopped her face. "You can meet with him after school, if that's what you want. But I'm not talking about this with him, and I don't want to be there when you do, either."

She stood and the box tumbled off her lap. The chair scraped the floor, a loud screech in the quiet room.

"Megan, we're not quite done yet. Okay? If you want to take a break and get a soda, that's fine. Or if you want a friend to come sit with you—"

"No." As if she had any. "I'll be okay. But

I would like a minute to—" Go scream into a balled-up sweatshirt in a bathroom somewhere? "—grab a drink."

"Sure." The cop pulled out her phone again. "Take five and then we'll finish up as quickly as we can."

Megan grabbed her books, wondering what would happen if she hopped in her car and kept on driving. Sighing, she settled for shoving open the door into the guidance office waiting area.

Where Bailey McCord sat with her pink plaid book bag on her lap.

Megan brushed past her into the hallway outside the office.

"Megan, wait," Bailey's voice called after her.

A voice she *so* did not want to hear.

Fury pumped fresh through her veins. The last bell of the day had rung, so the only kids remaining in school were the ones who had stayed for extracurricular activities or remedial help.

"You know what, Bailey?" She turned slowly and stared down her former friend, keeping a tight rein on her raging emotions. "Now is *not* a good time."

"This is about J.D., isn't it?" Bailey persisted, catching up to her and falling in step as she race-walked for the bathroom.

"Are you on a scouting mission for him?" Megan shoved at the door to the girls' room. She took one look at her face in the mirror and swore. Mascara ran down her cheeks.

"No. Megan, I'm scared of him, and I know you must be, too. Is that why the cop is here?" Bailey twirled the handle on the paper-towel dispenser until a long roll of brown toweling came out. Tearing it off, she thrust it at Megan. "Splash cold water on your face. Want me to hold your stuff?"

Bailey set her backpack on the floor and took a math textbook out of Megan's arms. She placed it on top of her bag.

She hadn't even remembered she'd been holding a book. And she was way too upset to make sense of whatever Bailey said. It was as if she watched her mouth move but couldn't get the words to compute.

"How do you know there's a cop here?" Megan tucked the paper towels under one arm while she bent over a sink.

"The whole school saw the police cruiser out front when the last bell rang. Most kids were guessing Jimmy Rigby got in another fight, but I remembered you got called down to the office and I kind of wondered."

Megan splashed cold water on her face, rubbing at the black marks on her cheeks. "What?" she asked through the barrier of water and hands. "You wondered what?"

How the hell would Bailey know what was

going on unless she'd had something to do with that website?

Megan straightened. Dried off her face.

"I don't know. I got a sick feeling in my gut. J.D. called me late last night after the game, talking all crazy and accusing me of telling you—" Bailey shook her head and covered her face with her palms.

Megan blinked. "What happened to you?" Bailey's hands were covered in bruises.

"Nothing." She shoved her fists in the pockets of her jean jacket. "And I couldn't understand what J.D. was ranting about last night, but I'm scared of him, and I know he's got anger problems or something. I don't know what happened between you two, but if you need me to tell the cops he's a raging maniac, I will. He's just as whacked out as his father. They both creep me out."

Some of the fury in Megan simmered down as she tried to focus on what Bailey was saying. What did J.D.'s dad have to do with anything?

"If you think he's such a raging maniac, why did you go out with him while he and I were still dating?" It was a stupid point that shouldn't matter since Megan now officially hated J.D.

But whereas J.D. was no longer important to her, there was the smallest chance Bailey still could be.

A very, very small chance.

"I never wanted to go out with him. My mom kept shoving me at him for reasons I still don't understand, although I think it has something to do with a business deal she has going on with J.D.'s pervy dad who's always looking at me." Bailey shook her head, perfect blond hair swaying as she moved. "I don't know. Mom says he's harmless, but she's always working an angle. She kept giving me messages to give to J.D. to give to his dad—appointment times for something he was helping her with for the opening of the new store. I told her to email him instead, but she kept insisting good business was built on personal relationships."

Ewww. Megan debated telling Bailey that her mother had probably been trying to hook up with Mr. Covington back then. And she'd obviously succeeded, based on what she and Wade had seen at the ball field.

"So you were talking to J.D. behind my back to help out your mom?" She was not buying it.

But then Megan thought of the bruises on the girl's hands. Bailey might be a liar and a backstabber, but she sure didn't deserve to be frightened of the boy she dated.

Or his pervy father.

Bailey swiped at her eyes. "I didn't mean to do it behind your back. I didn't think much of it. But then J.D. kept flirting with me, and I knew he was trying to make it look like I liked him or something. I figured it was just some dumb act for his friends."

"So why didn't you tell me?" Megan hit the hand dryer, mostly for white noise in case anyone was out in the hallway.

"Because the next thing I knew, J.D. told everyone we were dating. You stopped speaking to me and hung up on me when I called you. My mother told my father I was dating J.D., and started using me as a cover to have an affair with J.D.'s slimeball father." Bailey scraped her hair off her face in impatience, her voice cracking, making Megan realize she knew the score about her mom. "So I hit a point in this whole nightmare where I stopped thinking about *your* feelings. And it was right about the time J.D. started being a power-tripping son of a bitch to me. But I'm past caring what my mom says or what J.D. threatens. If there are cops here asking questions about J. D. Covington, then I want in. Or at the very least, I want to back you up, whether you want my help or not."

Tears trickled down Bailey's cheeks. Megan's understanding of the last few months shifted, the pieces falling into new places that were—impossibly—even more horrible than she'd first thought. J.D. was a bully. Possibly a stalker.

His father was a cheater. And maybe worse, if Bailey's slimeball radar was functioning properly.

Silently, Megan cranked the handle on the

paper-towel dispenser until a long sheet emerged. She ripped it off and pointed to the sink.

"You'd better splash some water on your face, Bailey." She thrust the crinkling brown paper at her. "Then we'll go back in there together."

"I never thought I'd be the kind of girl who would let a guy walk all over her." Bailey didn't move toward the sink. Tears slid down her cheeks faster. "But he got a picture of me. I don't know how. And he said he'd tell everyone that—"

Yeah. Megan knew where this was going.

"It's probably not even you." Unable to hold on to her old grudge anymore, she slid an arm around Bailey's waist. "He Photoshops that stuff."

"Did he do that to you?" Bailey sniffed and blew her nose on the paper towels. "I keep getting creepy notes from him online and then he pretends he didn't send them."

Kind of like his reaction when Megan accused him of posting the site. Something was off here. Really, really off.

"The photos are just the beginning." Megan didn't like seeing Bailey so upset. Another girl who'd been privately going through hell and not letting anyone know.

For some reason—standing outside of herself and being able to see someone else doing what Megan had been doing—made her appreciate how dumb it was to keep silent and let this asshat terrorize them.

And at least Megan's father was going to go ballistic over the crap J.D. was trying to pull. It sounded like Bailey's mother had thrown her to the wolves.

The girls' room door shot open suddenly, startling both of them.

Linda Marquette, with her gray suit and shiny badge, stood in the doorway.

"Megan, we need you back in the guidance office so we can finish up."

"Remember you said I could have a friend sit in the meeting with me?" Megan cleared her throat and gave Bailey a poke in the hip where she still held on to her. "I want Bailey with me."

"Nice." The lady cop smiled warmly and didn't comment on the tearful scene. She dug in her pocket and jingled some change. "I'll grab a third soda and meet you in there."

She backed out of the restroom, leaving Megan and Bailey alone again.

"She seems okay." Bailey splashed cold water on her face.

"She seems like she'll make sure J.D. gets what's coming to him," Megan corrected her.

But a part of her wondered if J.D. was totally to blame for harassing her. If he'd sent the text messages, wouldn't he have admitted it last night?

"My mom is going to kill me for this." Bailey dried off her face.

"It's not her getting bullied, though, is it?"

Megan picked up Bailey's backpack and handed it to her. "Besides, only seven months to graduation and we can ditch this town and everyone in it."

"It's become my daily mantra," Bailey grumbled. "Until then, maybe if we stick together, we can keep J.D. from ruining our lives."

Stick together. The words echoed inside Megan's head as they left the bathroom and headed for the guidance office. She hadn't realized until today how much she needed a friend. Not her dad. Not gamer buddies. Not even Wade. But a true friend.

"If anything," Megan whispered as they walked past the Spanish classrooms. "We can probably keep him from ruining our friendship."

Bailey's cheeks lifted a fraction. The barest hint of a dimple showed on one side.

"That'd be unbelievably cool."

CHAPTER SIXTEEN

"COULD YOU GET any slower, old man?"

Zach ignored Sam's shouted insult as they ran up the hill behind the quarry on the outskirts of Heartache. At six in the morning, there was no traffic out here. The trucks hauling shale wouldn't get under way for at least a couple more hours and the teenage kids who came up here at night to make mischief had long ago found their beds.

The hill's incline was a killer. Sam worked out like this most days, whereas Zach had signed on for only three days a week.

"Just trying to give you a chance to feel good about yourself," Zach said between clenched teeth, hating the endless uphill climb of their usual weekend route.

Five days after he'd taken Heather to the hospital, Zach still didn't have his head on straight about her, the ER visit or anything else in his life. He'd hoped the morning run would distract him as Sam took sadistic pleasure in making the Sunday workout as grueling as possible.

"Kind of you." Sam grinned at him, jogging backward so he could gloat full face and full force. "But I'm not sure I can feel good about this run until you're too worn out to brood over Heather Finley for at least a few hours."

"You're asking for it, Reyes," Zach muttered, sweat dripping into his eyes despite the chill in the air from a cold front that had moved in during the week. "And if you'd do your damn job and clear her old man, Heather would be long gone and out of my head."

Yeah, right. As if he could ever work her out of his system. He was so screwed. But he could make life easier for her. Lessening her stress would help her illness. He knew that much for sure.

Sam snorted as he turned around to sprint the rest of the hill. He might pretend to have an easier time of the run, but while the guy could bench-press his body weight a few times over, Zach's leaner build could track circles around him. Usually. He was only dogging it today because he'd taken last Sunday off for Erin Finley's wedding breakfast.

"I'm not the one who took all week to start analyzing his personal-computer files." Sam kept his eye on the top of the hill, his thicker build starting to slow him.

At last.

"Who knew the former mayor would have a hard drive from the Stone Age. I had to special order a cable to connect my equipment to an adapter." Zach had learned his predecessor was thrifty to the extreme. "The program should finish running tonight."

He felt as if he was wading through peanut butter at this point. And not just to get up the rest of the damn hill. He had no answers on the town's missing funds. He couldn't make the pieces add up in the odd assortment of reported incidents around the deserted roads near the quarry, which brought him no closer to his sister's old stalker. He couldn't move things forward with Heather because she didn't want anything serious—she'd made that clear with all the boundaries she'd put up, starting at the hospital.

Digging deep, Zach found another gear and picked up his pace. He might not control what went on in Heather's head or the choices her old man had made while he was in office, but Zach could damn well beat Sam to the top of the hill.

"Bastard," he heard Sam growl behind him— too close for comfort.

Running harder, Zach kicked up gravel and nearly skidded as he finally hit level surface at the top of Lookout Point. He didn't stop moving, but it felt damn good to slow to a walk. Peeling off his cap, he let the cold wind blow through his hair. The trees up here were changing colors, a few red leaves drying to a crisp on the ground beneath his feet, others floating on the breeze on their way down.

A few hundred yards below them, cornfields, orchards and cow pastures dotted the landscape. In the distance were the pond and the fairgrounds where the harvest festival would take place, along with the new add-on—Lumberjack Days.

Several of Heartache's residents thought this was a scenic spot to have a picnic or to go parking. But for Zach, it would always be the site of Ellie's attack. He knew Sam thought the same thing every time they came here. Hell, remembering the attack was half the reason they had chosen this route for their weekly run.

"Have you talked to your sister lately?" Sam asked, hitting the ground for a round of push-ups at a fast clip.

If not for Sam's promise to help catch Ellie's attacker, he would have gone into the military. He'd never said as much, but he'd talked about it when they were teens and then—after that night—never again. Zach hated that he couldn't have devoted more time or resources to searching for her attacker when it had first happened. But he'd been a kid himself. And he'd needed to devote all his time and energy to getting his sister out of Heartache, away from a mother who paid no attention to her, and to the West Coast where she could start over.

He'd uprooted her, himself and Sam, too, relocating them all. At the time, it had been all he could manage, especially since his sister needed to finish school and Zach wanted to start college. But he'd always regretted not following up on his sister's attacker. And now? Knowing the guy might still be tormenting other girls absolutely gutted him.

"No. I need to get in touch with her." He'd been avoiding his phone the last few days, sick of it showing no messages or missed calls from Heather.

"She's worried that Megan Bryer's stalker could have something to do with the guy who jumped her." Getting to his feet, Sam brushed the stones and dirt off his hands.

"But you told her it was a totally different MO, right? And highly unlikely, given how long it's been." Zach swung on him. "I'm surprised you even talked to her about that."

It didn't matter that Zach shared his sister's fears. He didn't want her worrying about the past anymore.

"She texts me a lot." Sam shrugged. "I figured you'd already told her since the cases could connect."

"Whoever went after my sister is our age or older. Megan's most likely getting hassled by an idiot teenager." Zach had turned things over to the sheriff's department, but he'd figured Sam would damn well keep him apprised if new information surfaced. "Why are you suddenly worrying Ellie because of this?"

"First of all, your sister is a grown woman. Second, she's at least as stubborn as you, so she's not the type of person to let something go when it's on her mind." Sam bent his knees and launched himself up a few feet into the air to grab hold of a tree branch, where he proceeded to do pull-ups with mechanical efficiency. "Third, J.D. says he didn't know that website went up, and I believe him. I think someone else got on his computer and posted the thing."

"Like one of his friends?" Zach knew J.D. had been questioned at the station with his father present, but the meeting had revealed little.

The kid had denied sending Megan text messages or posting the website, although he did admit to creating the site with a bunch of his friends. But he said they designed it for laughs and then deleted it. He'd seemed genuinely baffled about how it got online, and according to Sam, the kid was not a good liar.

"Or anyone else with access to the PC in his house." Sam blew out a hard breath and swung down to the ground.

"His mom's a schoolteacher and his dad is a local businessman who's been on the town board for a long time. Not exactly stalker types."

"Maybe, maybe not. If we're looking for someone who targets teenage girls, that demographic skews toward middle-aged men, and more than half are educated, with above-average intelligence.

But the Covingtons also happen to live right next to the quarry. There are trucks and workers in and out of there all the time. J.D. said the home and business computers are linked."

"So someone who works at the quarry might have seen the page J.D. designed and decided to post it." Zach didn't like the way the hairs on the back of his neck rose, hating to think about a grown man going after an innocent girl. "And the quarry backs up to Lookout Point, where Ellie got attacked. Are you questioning the guys who've worked there for the last decade?"

Sam nodded. "The women, too. But I spoke to Jeremy Covington about it, figuring he'd agree to give me the computers if it would help clear his kid. But he refused. And you know what alternate theory he suggested?"

"I'm listening." Zach ground his teeth together, wondering if they might really be getting close to Ellie's attacker after all this time.

"Turns out he's having an affair with Tiffany McCord." Sam pulled his phone out of his pocket and checked his messages.

Zach swore. "That complicates things."

"No kidding. According to Jeremy, Tiffany and her daughter hate Megan Bryer because she used to date J.D."

"And that kid is such a prize," he scoffed.

"Be that as it may, it introduces a lot of other people to the Covington house and a whole nest of other potential enemies—to the Covingtons, as well as to Megan."

"Does Cole McCord know?" Zach had always liked the decorated war veteran and wondered how he'd ended up with Tiffany.

"Not that he's admitted publicly, but I'm not getting involved with that mess until I check out all the employees from the quarry and see who might have had computer access on the day the webpage went live." Sam continued to scroll through messages on his phone, bracing a foot on a boulder and leaning in to stretch.

A startled bird took flight from the rock. The sun was blazing full force now, the birds amping up their morning songs and flitting overhead.

"That town board is a nest of vipers." Zach shook his head. "I always thought this was a nice town except for the person who went after Ellie. And I always thought the culprit must be somebody from out of town. Not someone who lived here. Someone she knew."

"Statistically, that's rarely the case." Sam's finger paused over his phone. "Ah, crap."

"What?" Zach didn't need more problems. He wanted to go home and call Heather to see what she thought about Sam's theory. Not that he should discuss police business with her.

But he missed her. Worried about her.

Damn it, why hadn't she called him in five freaking days?

"It's your sister." Sam turned the phone toward Zach so he could see a text message. "Ellie says she's on her way home."

"HEATHER FINLEY, WHY isn't your name on this list?" Bethany shouted to her from the registration table for vendors at the Harvest Fest.

They'd arrived at the fairgrounds to help Nina set up a booth for the new restaurant so she could sell food during Lumberjack Days and Harvest Fest.

"What's the list for?" Heather put down the hay bale she'd been loading into the back of Bethany's pickup truck. The festival organizers made it easy for vendors to decorate their stalls with seasonal touches, selling locally grown pumpkins, gourds and Indian corn along with hay bales and chrysanthemums near the check-in desk.

"It's a sign-up sheet for the talent show." Bethany waved the clipboard and motioned her over. "You might as well put your name down just in case you're still around."

Frowning, Heather pulled the clipboard out of her hand while Nina and Bethany looked at the sheet over her shoulder.

"Isn't that sort of like conceding defeat on the *American Voice* audition?" As the time drew near for her tryout, she had debated canceling more than once just to take the pressure off herself.

Her hands seemed better now that she was taking a stronger anti-inflammatory. It still wasn't the full drug regimen that the specialists insisted she start taking, but she'd seen some improvement. Even if her hands were good enough to play later this week in Charlotte, she didn't believe her father's name would be cleared by then. There had been no word from Zach since he'd taken her to the hospital less than a week ago. Not that she'd expected to hear from him after the way they'd left things. But she'd hoped maybe they would at least check in on the investigation. Or maybe touch base about Megan and who was hassling her. The police were looking into it, but so far, the story had been kept out of the papers.

While she didn't expect Zach to speak to her in an official capacity about either of those things, she missed simply talking to him. Being around him. Trying to make him smile. Her heart ached with missing him, all the more when she thought about the fact that she'd hurt him.

"No." Nina shook her head and handed her a pen with the restaurant logo. "If you decide to go to Charlotte, you'll be a no-show on the talent night in Heartache. But if you're around, you can wow us all with a song and win the gift card, right?"

Heather took the pen, but used it to skim down the short list. "I have some students whose names should be on here. There are a lot of very talented people in town."

"Write yours down," Nina reminded her, pointing to a blank spot at the bottom. "I don't understand why you never sing at Finleys'. You know Mack's bar has helped a lot of bands move on to better visibility in Nashville, right? Just last spring one of the bass players who used to play at Finleys' got asked to go on the road for the European leg of Taylor Swift's tour."

"Really?" Heather had declined Mack's offers in the past, not wanting to put him on the spot for helping out a family member.

He owned the bar with a partner. He was in business to make money, not gift slots to people with no performing track record.

"Yes, really. The bar is doing well. We never would have been able to afford to open the restaurant here without it." Nina gave her a sideways glance, her blond highlights catching the sun. "For that matter, you could be packing them in for us at the restaurant if you want to sing there."

"The whole town knows you have a great voice," Bethany added while another truck pulled up to the registration area to check in. "It's a shame we only get to hear it at the occasional ball game when you do the national anthem."

"Well, you know I love to play and sing, but I don't expect you all to turn the restaurant into a nightclub just so I can have a venue. I'll sign up for the talent show, though." She scribbled her name on a blank spot on the list, then pulled her phone out of her back pocket. "I'm going to tell Megan about this, too. She should be showing off her rock 'n' roll style. Her guitar work has really come along."

"Awesome." Bethany patted her shoulder and went to chat with the woman at the registration desk, volunteering to help with the hay bale maze.

"Heather, I'd never ask you to sing at the restaurant just to compliment you." Nina studied her through serious eyes as she ran her credit card through a machine to pay for more chrysanthemums. "You're an incredibly talented musician and vocalist. You must know that or you wouldn't be trying so hard to get to Charlotte."

"Thank you." She finished texting Megan about the talent show, and forwarded the note to two other music students. She jammed the phone back in her pocket. "I appreciate that, and I know you'd be honest with me. I feel weird about relying too much on family and friends, so I try to avoid that situation when I can."

"You've done a lot for everyone in this family by taking care of your mom year in and year out." Nina chose two pots of yellow mums and set them in the back of the pickup. "We owe you favors and help, so you shouldn't think twice about asking for anything." Leaning back against the truck, Nina crossed her red cowboy boots at the ankles and studied her. "However, in this case, *you're* not asking. I'm asking you. Please, please, come sing for our patrons if you ever have a free night."

"Well, when you put it that way." Heather smiled, her heart and muse warming to the idea with a strength that surprised her. "I'll have to see what I can do."

Once they got their paperwork and a few fall items to decorate the booth, they drove out to their site on the fairgrounds lot and began assembling the canopy. Bethany called out instructions and generally directed things, while Nina and Heather followed orders, connecting poles and stretching the canvas top and sides to complete the booth space.

The day had warmed considerably. It was much better than last week's cold front, which Heather realized had probably bothered her joints. She pulled her jacket off as they worked, comfortable in her sweater and long jersey skirt as they stacked hay bales in front of the table. The hay would act as a buffer from the wind to protect the booth, as well as keep people from getting too close until the exhibition opened.

Around them, other local and regional stores and restaurants did the same thing. Some businesses brought tow-behind units and parked them on their space. Finley Building Supply had a huge display nearby with swing sets and backyard play equipment that would be monitored throughout the event. Heather's brother Scott and a few other workers were assembling a sandbox modeled to look like a pirate ship.

"Will you be at the town council meeting tonight, Heather?" Nina asked as they stood back to admire their handiwork on the restaurant booth.

Because Bethany had sold Nina the booth kit, she worked the longest of the three of them to make sure it was just right, busying herself adjusting canvas pieces and staking down a few of the poles for good measure. As the long-time manager of Finley Building Supply, Bethany knew as much about construction as her husband.

"No. How about you?" Heather attended about half the meetings in order to answer questions about the rec department or to keep the council updated on their activities. Nina had gone to a few recently while the town prepped the harvest festival. She and Mack had been on the planning committee the previous year.

"I've got a lot of baking to do to prep for the weekend." Nina pulled a small cooler from the back of the pickup. "In fact, I've got a new cupcake flavor and I need your opinion."

"Yes." Heather clapped her hands in anticipation. Nina's baking skills were legendary, especially where cupcakes were concerned. "You see why I always like helping you with projects? Bethany, come look what Nina made."

"Do not start without me!" Bethany dropped the banner sign she'd been hanging, letting the cream-colored canvas flap in the breeze as she hurried over. "I've been waiting to hear the word *cupcake* ever since I picked her up this morning."

Nina rolled her eyes, her charm bracelets jangling as she opened the lid on the small insulated box.

"You saw me come out of the house carrying the cooler." Nina laughed. "You probably had a good guess what was inside."

"Maybe, but I never take cupcakes for granted these days." Bethany and Heather bumped heads as they jostled to peer inside. "I'm so glad I got my appetite back once I got my marriage on track. I got *all* my appetites back."

Heather winked at her, grateful Bethany looked so much healthier.

"Those look amazing," Heather squealed as she caught sight of white frosting drizzled with caramel and dark chocolate.

"They're mocha coconut frappuccino." Nina produced one for Heather and handed her a napkin. "Mack called it overkill. I call it bliss."

"I'm drooling," Bethany announced, helping herself to a napkin before taking her cupcake.

"Men don't have the right palate for chocolate," Heather insisted, taking her cupcake and settling on one of the hay bales. "Don't listen to him." Peeling off the wrapper, she took her time admiring Nina's creation. As she made eye contact with Bethany—wanting to be sure they were ready for a bite at the same time—it occurred to her how much she was going to miss moments like this. Days like this.

Sisters like this.

Her online friends were no substitute for family.

"Ready?" Bethany asked, taking a seat beside her on the hay.

With a nod, Heather gave the cue so they could try the treat together.

"You won't hurt my feelings if you think it's too sweet," Nina assured them, leaning a hip into the side of the pickup. "I can't decide."

"It's amazing," Bethany mumbled through a mouthful of frosting. "You're a genius."

Heather gave a thumbs-up, unwilling to allow extra air between her taste buds and mocha coconut frappuccino goodness.

"I brought some water." Nina reached into the cooler again, pulling out minibottles for each of them. "And maybe it couldn't hurt if I do another taste test myself." She joined them on the hay bales, settling onto one closer to the ground.

"Chocolate is meant to be consumed with girlfriends." Bethany tucked her feet under her as she ate. "Ally is going to be so jealous when I tell her about this."

"It's my favorite ever," Heather said once she'd finished savoring the first bite. "The coconut is so perfect in there and it keeps the cupcake from being too rich."

"There's no such thing as too rich," Bethany argued around another bite.

Nina licked the frosting, taking the tiniest of nibbles, as if to make it last longer.

"Nina, can I ask you a question?" Heather tested the frosting, too, mimicking the taste-test expert. Yum.

"No, you can't have the recipe. But you can have a free one after you sing at the restaurant." Nina grinned.

Heather rolled her eyes. "I know better than to ask for recipes." A new truck pulled into their row, the trailer painted with the name of a bike repair shop in Franklin. "What I wanted to ask is, what made you decide to open the restaurant instead of another cupcake shop?"

Nina had had a successful boutique business in New York City before she'd returned to Heartache the year before. Cupcake Romance had catered specialty baked goods for weddings and showers, carving out a niche with decadent sweets.

Nina tipped back her water, her lips pursed as she thought about the question.

"It was your dream to have the cupcake bakery, right?" Heather didn't think about how that sounded, as she was genuinely curious about the way dreams and ambitions could morph. "I'm sorry. I didn't mean to suggest—"

"No." Nina waved off her unease. "It *was* my dream. But once I moved to Heartache and got back together with Mack, my dreams changed. Staying here, being near Gram and being with Mack became my highest priorities. I couldn't see a small town supporting a cupcake business, but I did think about maybe opening a catering company where I'd ship them." She shrugged. "But when I saw what Mack was doing at his bar in Nashville, I realized we were both working similar businesses and wouldn't it be fun to see what we could do if we combined our skills."

"So the restaurant was born." Heather remembered how carefully the couple had searched for the right property and how much time they'd spent remodeling it.

"I hope it's got the best of both of us. But even if it doesn't become a runaway success, it's been really cool working on something I'm passionate about with the guy I love. Mack is so smart about business."

"But he doesn't know best when it comes to cupcakes." Bethany pointed to the cooler. "Those are fan-freaking-tastic."

"And you don't feel like you compromised?" Heather's cheeks heated as she asked, knowing she was being too intrusive. But if she couldn't ask them, who would she ever ask?

"I feel like the plan got fine-tuned." Nina gestured at her with her cupcake. "Like the dream was this beautiful but hazy idealized vision until I met Mack, and now it might look a little different, but it's in perfect, sharp focus and I know just how I can obtain it."

Heather took another bite of her cupcake, savoring the advice along with the chocolate-coconut bliss on her tongue. She wasn't ready to change her dreams for a man, though, was she? Sure, she could feel herself getting nostalgic about Heartache. There'd been the rush of pride in her town when Zach had told her she could have been a good mayor. Then there were moments like this when she enjoyed the rituals of small-town life with her family. Even the fishing tournament had felt special and fun, not just because of Zach, but because she wouldn't be running off to cast a line at a moment's notice once she got to Charlotte.

But she didn't want to shortchange her ambitions before she'd given her all to pursuing them. Nina had offered her a nice compromise option of staying in Heartache and singing at the restaurant. Or maybe moving to Nashville and performing at Finleys' bar sometimes. But wouldn't she always know that she'd given up before she'd really tried? At least Nina had the experience of running a shop in Manhattan for a couple of years.

"I think someone's searching for you." Nina

elbowed her as they sat together, the jab to her waist making Heather glance up.

Zach approached them. He strode down the dirt and gravel walkway with that same unflappable air he'd had since high school, as if he could handle anything life tossed his way. His light blue shirtsleeves were turned up to reveal strong forearms, one hand shoved in the pocket of dark gray pants. His shirt was open at the collar, and yes, her eyes ate up every square inch of bare skin. When her gaze met his, she understood why Nina had elbowed her. The way he looked at her told her he wasn't there to see just anyone.

He wanted her.

To talk to, anyway.

Grabbing her water bottle, she took a long drink.

"I'd be guzzling it down, too, if a man was looking at me like that," Nina teased, picking up the napkins and discreetly disappearing with Bethany.

They might have said hi to Zach first. Heather honestly didn't know. Her heart beat so hard she couldn't hear much beyond her harsh breaths and the blood rushing through her veins.

"Can I talk to you for a minute?" He paused a foot from where she sat, his lean, hard body casting a shadow on hers.

She wanted to tell him he could do more than

talk. She'd like it if he tossed her over his shoulder and dragged her into the woods. That's how light-headed he made her feel. And how she knew it had been a mistake to pretend she could put her feelings for him behind her as easily as she drove out of town.

That was no longer a possibility. Pretending otherwise would hurt them both.

"I've missed you." Shooting to her feet, she blurted out the only words in her head.

Whether or not he returned the sentiment, he deserved to hear it.

He studied her for a long moment, their bodies closer than he'd probably intended since she'd risen to her feet.

"Would that be a yes to talking?" he asked finally.

"Definitely." She wondered if it was Zach asking or the mayor. He seemed formal.

Reserved.

No doubt taking his cue from how she'd behaved last week. It hurt to think she'd put that distance between them.

"Let's take a walk then, so we can have some privacy." He gestured at the long gravel path that would fill up with vendors in the next two days. "I'd rather not stir the pot with the town council, and a few of them seem to think the investigation of your father will be corrupted somehow if we spend time together."

"I have no desire to defend myself to Tiffany McCord." She shuddered, falling into step with him as they strode away from the center of the fair. They walked toward the arena where the wood-cutting competition would occur. A two-rail fence had been set up to enclose the space, and a few of the lumberjacks were already on-site, directing trucks with huge logs for carving. Inside the arena, a couple of guys were cleaning chain-saw pieces. A few others stood around the newly delivered wood.

"I don't recognize many locals," Heather observed when Zach remained quiet. She'd forgotten her jacket, but she was still warm in the autumn sunshine, her sweater and long skirt keeping her comfortable.

"It was Quinton Lee who wanted to get the event this year." Zach waved to the owner of Lucky's Grocer as the guy directed a flatbed trailer into the arena. "He started competing a couple of years ago and thought the event would draw some newcomers."

"I'm sure it will." She peered at Zach, more interested in him and why he'd sought her out.

She realized they'd arrived at the Merchants Building, a permanent facility on the fair property where vendors could store their belongings or grab a bite to eat. Zach had a key, and he unlocked the front door to the small structure.

Stepping inside, Heather headed for the chairs in the lounge, but he gestured her toward the office in back. He unlocked another door and sealed them into a small, private room with a desk, an old television mounted on one wall and a wooden bench covered with boxes of flyers for the fair.

Heather couldn't hold back the well of emotion any longer. She couldn't let this conversation be solely about business. "I'm sorry I didn't call you this week. I realized how stubborn I must have seemed about the whole illness thing, but I wasn't sure if you'd want to hear from me after how we parted."

Zach stared back with shocked eyes as he tossed the keys on the desk. "How could you not know?" He moved boxes to clear a spot for her to sit and extended a hand for her to join him. "Heather, it killed me not to pick up the phone this week, but the ball was in your court. You drew the line in the sand, not me."

Hesitating for less than an instant, she took his hand, warm and strong. She sank onto the bench, her back to the wall, her leg pressed to his. Her heart ached. She wanted things to be easy between them, no investigations or chronic illness. Just two people free to explore their feelings unencumbered by baggage.

"I've got a problem taking risks." That was part of the reason she'd never left Heartache to achieve her dreams. Sure, she'd been busy with her family and helping out her mom, but she was also scared. "Remember I told you I've never fallen in love? It helps that I don't put myself on the line."

His muscles bunched beneath his dress shirt.

"Maybe you should work on that before you go halfway across the country for a singing audition." His tawny gaze locked on her. "Take a few smaller risks first."

"I could do that." Her heart beat faster as she took in the hard line of his jaw. The way his hair curled a little bit on one side, as if a greedy lover had pawed a hand through it.

The full, sensual shape of lips that could kiss her like no man ever had before.

"Do you need help coming up with some ideas?" His eyebrow arched, his thumb stroking the inside of her wrist.

"I have several excellent ideas. But I don't want to preempt you since you said you wanted to talk to me. You wanted to ask me a question." With her blood slowly starting to simmer, it took all her powers of concentration to dredge up that detail from her memory.

"Ah." He nodded. "I wanted to ask you why the hell you haven't called."

She laughed. "Because I'm clueless and chicken,

and I kept hoping I was just dreaming how much I liked you."

He reached for her, but only to run two fingers down a strand of her hair. He pulled it taut for a moment before watching it fall back into place with the rest.

"How about now? What are you thinking?"

"I definitely wasn't dreaming how much I liked you." Could she shape her dreams the way Nina had, so that they could include Zach? She definitely felt herself falling harder for him.

Right this very moment.

"That's good to hear. Because I like you a whole lot, too." This time his finger brushed her cheek, and the touch was an electric jolt to her system. "Even if you are clueless and chicken."

She couldn't help a smile. He knew her so well. She might be unsure about many things, but she knew her feelings for this man ran deep. She couldn't bear the thought of passing up the chance to be with him. Now. She'd missed him so much this past week. Denying herself a moment with him seemed like the ultimate foolishness.

"I'm going to fix the chicken part right now," she assured him, pressing her leg hard against his. "By taking one of those risks we talked about."

"Really?" Something flickered in his eyes. A spark of awareness that lit an answering flame in her.

"Really." Her breath came so fast she thought she might hyperventilate, but she didn't let that slow her down. Licking her lips for good measure—just to be sure she had his attention—she reached for the hem of her sweater.

Then pulled it up and over her head.

CHAPTER SEVENTEEN

WHEN ZACH HAD gone looking for Heather at the fairgrounds, he had wanted to ask her a legitimate question. And he had some important things to tell her, too.

But he couldn't remember any of them after she'd said how much she missed him.

The woman had him wrapped around her finger, and that was long before the sweater came off.

Now?

He was putty in her hands. He knew it even as he clamped a palm on either side of her cheeks and held her still for his kiss. A long, slow, thorough meeting of the lips. She tasted like vanilla and promises, like a woman he wanted the right to kiss every day.

Still, he forced himself to ease back, tipping his forehead to hers while they sat together on the bench. His breathing was ragged.

"This isn't the right place. I didn't bring you here for this—honestly."

She pressed kisses along his jaw, her hands

running back and forth across his shoulders, heating his skin through his shirt.

"I think it's a great place," she whispered against his skin, her tongue darting out to tease the spot below his ear. "Especially for a woman who wants to take a risk."

"You should be comfortable." He didn't want her hurting herself. Couldn't let that happen again.

"I'm going to be incredibly comfortable on your lap," she said, her hand finding his thigh and rubbing a slow, torturous path up one leg. "And I'm on different medicine, so I'm not going to worry about my joints. It hurts more now simply wanting to be with you."

It was killing him, too.

Vowing to be careful with her, he pulled her onto his lap, and her long pink skirt fell around his legs like a blanket. She had goose bumps on her chest. He breathed kisses along the tops of her breasts, spanning her shoulders with his palms. The soft sounds she made in the back of her throat urged him on, driving him a little crazy.

Everything else disappeared—the worries he'd had all week about where they'd go from here, the knowledge that she needed to leave here to be happy. This second, none of it mattered. What they were feeling was bigger than any of that. If this was all the time he had with her, he would make sure she remembered every moment.

Peeling the skinny gray bra straps off her shoulders, he tugged them down until the cups stripped away from her curves. The muted sunshine slipping through the blinds burnished her skin to a soft gold, the taut peaks to bronze. Cradling her hips with one arm, he brought her closer to capture one tight crest in his mouth. She arched her back, her fingers locking around his neck to hold on tighter while he stroked and laved and nipped at her. All the while her skin flushed to a deeper rose, her temperature rising right along with his. When he juggled his hold on her to find the other peak, she freed her hands to undo the buttons on his shirt.

She made slow work of the fastenings, her fingers pausing whenever he drew on her nipple, her breath coming faster. His blood surged hot, his body rock hard with want.

He found her bare ankle and circled it, sliding off her shoe. He followed the back of her calf beneath her long skirt, mesmerized by the softness of her skin as he touched the hollow behind her knee. She felt so warm, and each inch that he traveled with his palm only turned hotter. By the time he cupped her satin-covered bottom, she wriggled against him in earnest, yanking his shirt off.

"I want you inside me." She lowered her mouth to his chest and pressed a kiss to one flat pectoral muscle. "Please say you have the necessary accessory to make that happen."

Any other time he would have smiled at the word choice. Right now, he was too busy congratulating himself that he was an optimist and yes, carried a condom.

"Back pocket. But I'm not letting you go, so you're on your own to find it." He toyed with the satin hem of her panties, sliding one finger beneath it and then two, hardly able to tell where satin and silky skin began.

She skimmed a touch up the front of his pants, drawing a groan from him.

"Here?" she asked, teasing a touch back down the length of him.

"Wicked, wicked woman," he breathed in her right ear, then gave the outer rim a gentle nip.

"Eager woman," she corrected, sliding her skirt higher on her thigh.

Higher.

When he spotted a hint of gray satin panties, she shifted to straddle him.

"I might need help," she admitted, rocking her core against him, right where he needed her most.

He was seeing stars behind his eyelids. Every time they touched, it just got better and better.

"Where?" he asked, skimming the back of his knuckles up the front of her underwear. And down again, landing in the hot, damp center of the fabric. "Here?"

Head thrown back, her chest heaved, her nipple right at mouth level. He sucked one into his mouth and slid a finger beneath the soft satin, stroking along the slick folds.

"Yes. There." She lifted herself slightly, her hands on his shoulders to balance herself as she leaned forward. Then back, angling herself right where she wanted him.

He teased the nipple with his tongue. Flicked his thumb back and forth across the taut bud of her sex. When she went still, he touched her harder, a rush of power pumping through him at the thought of giving her pleasure.

She broke apart with a harsh cry, her body stiffening against him for a long, long moment while he sank two fingers inside her. Felt the sweet, gentle pulse of her feminine muscles around him.

He wanted to taste her more than he wanted his next breath, but he knew this wasn't the place. Wasn't sure he could get her comfortable. He reached into his back pocket with one hand, found his wallet and awkwardly dragged out a condom. She sagged against him, her hip resting against his chest while his fingers were still buried deep inside her. Her harsh breathing was sweet music in his ears. He ripped the condom packet with his teeth.

"Oh, let me." Her eyelids fluttered, bright points of blue as she gazed down at him. "I can help."

She unzipped his pants and yanked them down, then took the condom and rolled it onto him with trembling fingers. He gripped her hips to position her right where he needed her. When he looked up at her, she was still wide-eyed and fascinated, her gaze on him. Them.

He would never get tired of looking at her.

Never get tired of wanting her.

It was the only thought in his head as he eased inside her, sinking himself as deep as he could go. She froze, her hands balanced on his chest, her teeth clamped on the soft fullness of her lower lip.

When he began to move, she met him thrust for thrust, each slick stroke taking him higher. Her forehead fell forward, trailing long red hair along the side of his cheek like a curtain unfurling. The silky strands teased his jaw, snagging on the rough edge of his whiskers, casting her face in shadow.

He captured her chin and kissed her hard. Holding her there, he pressed deeper into her. Again. And again.

When she started to move with him, he broke the kiss, the tension so high his chest burned. He reached between them to find the tender bud between her legs and rubbed it slowly, plucking at the swollen dampness.

She hit her peak again seconds before he did, her body slick with sweat, her hair sticking to her neck as she bit his shoulder and cried out against his flesh.

His release went on and on, wringing him out until he twitched with the aftershocks. He slumped on the bench, not sure he remembered his name. Not sure he needed to know it anyhow.

He stroked Heather's shoulder. Her back.

"We should move you," he said. "It's not good for your joints to stay in an awkward position."

"You're right. Thank you for the reminder. For caring." She levered back gently as they disentangled. "It's nice that you know that about me."

He'd like to know so much more about her, but he didn't think now was the moment to press his luck. His time with her might be limited, but he would spend the rest of it making her happy and not pushing for more.

A rap on the outer door made them both go still.

"Zach!" a woman's voice shouted. "Are you in there?"

"Who is that?" Heather asked, already straightening her skirt.

He closed his eyes and pressed a thumb to his temple. Of all the times for his sister to show up. He needed to help her, but God, if he could have had ten more minutes to hold Heather.

He picked up her sweater and passed it to her. "Did I mention my sister is in town?"

"Really?" Heather squeaked, yanking the sweater over her head.

"Unfortunately." He zipped up his pants.

"Why unfortunately?" She tossed his shirt at him. "I thought you two were close."

"We are." He jammed his wallet into his back pocket and slid the shirt on while Heather found her shoes. "But I worry about her being back in town since her stalker has never been caught."

"Zach?" Another shout came through the front door, followed by more banging.

"Then we'd better make sure we keep her safe." Heather opened the office door and hurried toward the main entrance of the Merchants Building.

Zach braced himself as he locked the office behind them.

When he heard the front door open, he heard his sister squeal like a teenager.

"Heather Finley!" she shouted, stepping into the lounge area in a jingle of bracelets and beads. Even her earrings were decorated with tiny crystals. "So good to see you again!"

"Gabriella?" Heather said softly, perhaps confused what name to call her.

Zach nodded as Ellie reached behind her to close the door. Except that Sam barreled in right after her.

"Sorry, Zach," he muttered. "I tried to keep her occupied." Sam closed the outer door so the four of them were inside the Merchants Building alone.

"Too bad he refuses to occupy me the way I'd like to be distracted." Ellie made a pretty pout at Sam, but he hardly noticed.

"Heather, my sister is back in town briefly in case we find out Megan Bryer's stalker is the same guy who attacked Gabriella ten years ago."

Heather's jaw dropped, her expression stunned before she shook her head and refocused.

"And we call her Gabriella?" she clarified.

"Definitely." Sam pulled off his aviator shades now that they were indoors. He prowled around the room, checking the blinds and making sure the windows were locked. "Everyone in this town knows her by her birth name. We'll have a better chance of her stalker contacting her if we all call her Gabriella. Plus, it will keep her West Coast identity more secure."

Zach had several choice words to say about that, since he considered her security well and truly compromised now that she'd come here. He would not debate it with Ellie for the tenth time, though. Not in front of Heather, when he didn't have much time left with her.

"I was under the impression that Megan's ex-boyfriend was hassling her?" Heather combed through her hair with her fingers, making him realize how tousled she looked.

And beautiful.

And how much he wanted her again.

"Did she tell you that?" Zach asked, frustrated with how hard it had been to draw information from Megan.

She'd finally started cooperating with one of

Sam's deputies, but she'd been so embarrassed about the social media page that she had refused to discuss it with her father, slowing down the law enforcement response.

"No." Heather's cheeks changed to a deeper shade of pink, reminding him how she'd looked just a little while ago when he'd been deep inside her. "That's the consensus of the Heartache rumor mill as related at the Tastee-Freez on Saturday night."

"Have you seen her since the news came out?" Ellie asked, sliding a purple crystal pendant back and forth along a silver chain. She settled onto a lopsided futon in the lounge area.

Heather shook her head. "No. But I've heard she's still working her hours at the Owl's Roost and going to school, so she hasn't been hiding."

"That's good." Ellie nodded, but Zach knew his sister well enough to know she didn't think it meant much. "But I head up a bullying victims' support group online, and I've seen a lot of people go through the motions of everyday life while they're growing more and more depressed. It always helps if girls in these situations have friends and mentors checking on them."

"Absolutely," Heather said. "She's told me before that music is therapeutic for her, so that makes it easy. We can play for a while."

While the two of them discussed music as therapy—something his sister had studied for her support group—Zach worked his way over to Sam. The man stood with his back to the wall so he could see all the windows and the entrance.

"Have you told her yet?" Sam asked, folding his arms across his chest.

"I was just about to when Ellie started banging on the door." Zach didn't need to ask Sam what he was talking about—his whole purpose in seeking out Heather had been to tell her that he'd tracked the missing money from the town coffers. Now he remembered!

"You were just about to." Sam didn't smile. But since his usual demeanor tended toward fierceness, Zach could tell he was amused.

No doubt they all needed a break from the real-world problems they'd been tracking.

"I hadn't seen her for a whole week. We had other things to discuss. Not that I owe you an explanation."

"You have a habit of delaying my press conferences," Sam observed. "And I would like to show the town that I can do something right."

Now it was Zach's turn to be amused.

"I had no idea you cared what anyone thought."

"That's me. Full of surprises." Sam returned to his usual scowl. "I'm sleeping at your house as long as she's in town. You know that, right?"

The "she" in that statement was obvious. But then, he and Sam went back so long they didn't require a lot of words. His friend had been Ellie's—

Gabriella's, he reminded himself—self-appointed protector for a long time.

"Of course." Zach nodded. "How's that going to go over with Isabel?" He knew Sam had his eye on the waitress at the Owl's Roost, along with half the rest of the men in town under fifty.

Sam shrugged. "I don't know. But you've got the best security in town. I'm having one of my guys follow us when I bring her home. Make sure you text me before you come in so I don't, you know."

"Shoot me?"

"Better to be safe." Sam grinned for real this time. "Gabriella?" he called. "Are you ready to go?"

"Already?" She looked at Heather. "We were having a great talk."

"I think your brother wants to talk to her more." Sam headed for the door. "'Night, Heather."

Gabriella stood with a sigh, although she leaned back to squeeze Heather's shoulder. "Don't forget what I said."

Heather rose. "Of course. So good to see you again."

They hugged in the way women who hardly knew each other would. But even as he thought as much, he couldn't deny a warmth in his chest to sense an accord between two of the people he cared most about in the world. He'd always admired the closeness of Heather's family, even if she thought it was too much sometimes.

The room quieted in a hurry after Sam and Gabriella left.

"I should probably get back, too." Heather drifted closer to him, peering at him through her lashes. "Bethany and Nina will wonder where I've gone."

"They didn't look terribly concerned about you when I walked up." He remembered the way her sisters-in-law had scattered to the breeze. "Do you want to text them and tell them I'll take you home?"

"I'd really like that." She paused a few inches away from him and he couldn't resist folding her in his arms.

Taking a taste of her neck.

"I should grab my phone, though," she murmured in his ear. "As incredible as that feels."

"Right." He edged away. "Plus, I need to get you out of the Merchants Building. As charming as it might have been in a pinch."

Laughing, Heather keyed in something on her phone.

"There. All yours." She slid the device into her bag and closed the gap between them again.

And as much as he wanted to take her home and bring her to bed, he needed to tell her about the investigation.

"We found the missing money."

She stopped midstride. "Is it bad news?" Her

voice wobbled. "I've never thought my father would do something like that."

He held her hands. Squeezed.

"Your father was a good man." He knew that now more than ever. "It turns out he did take the money, Heather. But he put it back eventually. He just didn't do a good job with the bookkeeping, so it made it tough to track it down."

"He took it?" She half fell, half sat on the futon, their voices echoing in the mostly empty concrete-block structure.

"He borrowed it." Zach had worked on a press release at home so he would get the words right when they met with the media tomorrow. "He used it for an experimental drug for your mom's bipolar disorder. Well, experimental back then. I looked it up and it's widely prescribed now to augment more traditional therapy. He imported a very expensive antipsychotic drug from overseas."

Heather covered her eyes.

"Heather?"

"How are you going to tell that to the papers?" She dragged her hand down her face, tears glinting in her eyes. "People hear 'antipsychotic' and think my mother is…psychotic."

"Intelligent people won't. But you can review the press release I'm writing and we can use the wording that your family prefers."

"You'd let me do that?"

"Of course. Sam won't care. The money is found.

It went back into the recreation department fund when your father restocked the softball league with all new bats, helmets and catchers' equipment."

"I remember when he bought all that stuff." She sniffled. "I can't believe he took money from the town."

"Borrowed. His business was successful, but he needed cash for the purchase and pulled out whatever he could liquidate quickly."

"It was wrong and he would have been the first to say it was wrong. But still, I'm touched he would take such a risk on medicine for my mom." She raked her hair out of her eyes, blinking away tears. "He avoided home so much. I know her illness was hard on him. It makes me glad to think he really was trying to help her in his own way."

"Family first." Zach pulled her closer. Kissed the top of her head, allowing his cheek to rest on all that silky hair. "He really did live it."

"I guess he did."

HEATHER SAVORED THE feel of Zach's kiss. The weight of his arm around her. The thoughtful way he treated her—whether it was being careful of her compromised health or inviting her to weigh in on a press release about the Finley family.

It was more than the residual endorphins of phenomenal lovemaking that caused her heart to swell with emotion. She cared about him. Maybe even loved him.

Maybe?

That was her reflexive "protect yourself" side talking. There was no maybe about it. Leaning against his shoulder, the warmth of him under her cheek and all around her as they sat on a truly crummy futon in a spectacularly utilitarian building, Heather couldn't deny what she felt for Zach.

"I want to be there for the press conference tomorrow." She straightened, needing to be face-to-face with him for the admission that he deserved.

She'd been playing it safe for too long—in life and love both. But that was going to change. Had already started to change when she committed to the audition in Charlotte.

"I think it will be good to see your father's legacy restored as much as possible." He took her hands in his. "Also, you can field any questions from the media and put an end to the whole conversation about the money."

"Right." She needed to share this news with her brothers as soon as possible. Would her mother be touched to know her husband had risked his legacy as the town's longest-serving mayor to buy her medicine that he hoped would make her well? Heather hoped so. "Once that's behind me, I'll be free to leave Heartache with plenty of time to make it to Charlotte for the audition."

"That's good for your dreams and career ambitions," he said carefully.

She took a deep breath. And gambled everything. Her pride and her heart.

"I would love it if you'd make the trip with me." A part of her was so nervous that she wanted to close her eyes, cross her fingers and hope for the best.

But she wasn't a teenager in love for the first time. She was a twenty-eight-year-old woman and the outcome of this talk meant the world to her.

"You're inviting me to go to Charlotte with you?" he clarified, his face giving away nothing. "Tomorrow?"

She caught the note of surprise in his voice. Outside the building, kids ran past laughing. Funny to think they were having such a lighthearted moment a wall away from them when she'd just staked her heart on Zach's answer.

"There was a time you offered to drive me," she teased, but soon realized this was no joking matter. "But seriously, I'd drive. And you could watch that sunrise in the mountains with me." She remembered he'd liked that idea when she'd told him about it the first time. "I know it's spur-of-the-moment, but I want you to know I'm serious about this. About us. And I want you to be a part of my future."

Even as she trotted out the words, she sensed she'd gone about it wrong. But then, maybe she was crippled by the fact she'd never been a spontaneous person. When the moment arose for her to finally live in the moment, she didn't know how.

Something about Zach's expression told her she was making a muck of this.

"You're serious." Again, he repeated her words, making her think he had a hard time believing them.

"Very." She lifted her chin, defensiveness creeping in.

Zach rose from the futon, pacing a few feet away before turning back to face her. The shuttered look in his eyes told her all she needed to know. Her offer wasn't enough.

"My sister just arrived in town. She's here to help me catch a stalker." He nodded. "That's also serious. I've put a lot of time into compiling evidence against her attacker, and I've worked hard with Sam to compare Megan's case to Gabriella's."

She wrapped her arms around herself, preparing for the no that was coming. She'd thought it would make him happy to know she wanted to be with him. It made *her* happy to think of him going with her.

"Heather, I'm the mayor of this town. And while we laugh about that because in some ways it's not some high-paying bigwig job, given this is such a tiny place, but I take my responsibility to this town very seriously."

Guilt pinched at her already sensitive emotions.

"I didn't think about how involved you are in Megan's bullying case."

"It's more than that." He returned to the futon, but didn't sit next to her. He dropped down to sit on the heavy coffee table in front of her so they were eye to eye. "I'm building a life here. I care about a lot of people here. And I didn't work hard to find out what happened to that missing money just because the former mayor is your dad. I wanted to know because his legacy means something to me."

"Zach, you don't have to explain."

"But I want to tell you because it's important to me. Even before I knew you, the Finleys were a family for me when I didn't have one. Family first. I bought into that whole idea when I was a teenager and my dad was the most crooked SOB you can imagine. Your dad inspired me to work my ass off to make my own family with a community. To reach out and care about people around me without waiting to see if they'd help me first."

She remembered how hard he'd worked when his dad was sent to prison. How Zach had practically lived at the local nursing home, helping local residents.

"I'm surprised you'd try to give the mayor's job to me then." She blinked, not wanting to feel tears in her eyes. Had she been too selfish to see what was right in front of her? That Zach needed to stay in Heartache as badly as she needed to leave?

"Maybe I thought a Finley would always do a better job than I could." He shrugged. "I sure as hell wouldn't be handing it over to Tiffany Mc-Cord or half the rest of the town council."

"You do a great job, Zach. My dad would be happy with the way you've run things, and it's clear the town's pleased with you, too."

"If I had my sister's stalker behind bars, maybe it would be easier to walk away. But I can't turn my back on that and the town, too, no matter how much I care about you and want you to be happy."

The words echoed hollowly in the mostly empty room, bouncing off the floor and bare walls to rattle around inside her. He wanted her to be happy. Just not enough to come with her.

Not enough to walk away from what mattered most to him.

"I understand." Her words sounded stilted.

"Do you?" He cupped her chin and lifted her face to look in her eyes. "Because if you're serious about being together, like you said you are, we can figure something out. Leaving Heartache tomorrow doesn't mean you're gone forever."

"I can't think past the audition." And she certainly wasn't ready to think about giving up after the audition and moving back to Heartache for good. She stood abruptly, needing to move. Unable to feel the weight of his rejection on her shoulders. She was supposed to sing her heart out for total strangers in less than forty-eight hours' time. "I mean, I am serious that I care about you and want to be with you. I just want to get through this audition."

"That's understandable." His hazel eyes followed her as she stalked the room like a caged animal. "We're both under a lot of pressure. I hate that I can't be there for you. You should have someone rooting for you in Charlotte."

"I have a friend who might go with me." She said it mostly so he wouldn't worry about her. She hadn't heard much from Sylvia lately, but her former student had told her she'd love to go to Charlotte and cheer her on. "Maybe I'll stop in Nashville tomorrow to pick her up. But you definitely don't need to worry about me. I'll be fine."

Bad enough he'd seen her when her illness had all but incapacitated her. She didn't want to be another responsibility on the list of people he took care of: the nursing home residents, Megan, his sister, the whole town of Heartache…

She paused by the door, needing to leave and half hoping he would try to stop her. But he didn't move. She had gambled with her heart and it hadn't paid off. That's what a gamble meant—the reward was not guaranteed.

And all the rationalization in the world didn't make the ache in her chest hurt less.

"It's not a weakness to need someone, Heather."

Finally, he rose to join her at the door, making her realize she was already fumbling with the knob.

"Sometimes it feels like it." She stepped outside. The sun had lowered on the horizon. The fairgrounds were full of more booths but fewer people than when she'd walked the property earlier.

"Will you still come home with me now?" he asked, sliding an arm around her waist and holding her against him for a long moment while she breathed in his scent. Memorized the feel of him. "I want to hold you tonight. Especially if I won't see you again for a while."

She swallowed hard. Tempted beyond reason.

"If I spend the night with you, I might not have the heart to leave after the press conference tomorrow." She brushed a kiss along his cheek and forced herself to pull away. "And I would never want to look back and feel like I gave up my dream for love."

Even as she said it, she remembered what Nina had told her about modifying a dream to fit a new circumstance. About dreaming new dreams. Together.

But Zach's rejection hurt. And maybe she wasn't ready to give up her dream yet.

Zach locked up behind her and she tried to pretend her heart wasn't breaking. To distract herself, she opened her messaging program and shot a note to Sylvia.

How'd you like to go to Charlotte tomorrow for my American Voice audition?

She'd barely hit Send when she received a reply.

I can't wait! Pick me up at noon? Sylvia included a link to a doughnut place on an interstate exit just outside town for the pickup. It would save her driving all the way into Nashville.

Small consolation, considering what she really wanted. For Zach Chance to return her feelings, make love to her all night long and sit beside her on the way to her audition.

So far, her experience with taking big risks was not a happy one. But she'd be damned if she'd look back at her life and have regrets. She'd put her heart on the line for once. Now all she had to do was figure out how to recover from that trauma. She was pretty sure her new doctor wouldn't have a medicine for that.

CHAPTER EIGHTEEN

"I'M SO BORED, I'm going to lose my mind." Megan spoke into the speakerphone on her cell since she was using her hands to wage battle against mutant zombies online.

But she was grateful that Bailey had called her after the days of boredom with nothing but school and work and police interviews. It was like being grounded at home by the cops instead of her father, although the end result was just as mind-numbing.

She had a new cell phone—a superplain model like the kind drug dealers used when they didn't want anyone to track their calls. The police had recommended it, and no one had the number but her father and Bailey. Her old phone was held captive by the sheriff's department for evidence purposes as they were trying to build a harassment case against J.D.

"I have news that might interest you." Bailey sounded tense. Upset.

"What's wrong?" She muted the sound on the television, but continued playing her game. Like music, it helped relax her, and she'd taken the blisters on her fingers to a whole new level this week.

Playing guitar wasn't an option for a few days.

"My mother admitted she sent you those text messages." Bailey's voice broke in the middle of it, the latter half of the sentence garbled by tears.

"What? You're kidding me." Megan sat up straighter on the floor of her bedroom, watching a mutant zombie explode on contact. "Why would she do that?"

Megan had been so sure J.D. was behind it, or one of his friends. Everything about the harassment felt like something a guy would do. Not a friend's *mother*.

"She wanted you to move out of town so your father would leave the town board or some lame shit like that. I don't know. She's superpolitical and wanted to run the town or something." Bailey hiccuped. Sniffled. "I wouldn't have known except I listened outside the kitchen door when the cops talked to her for a third time. This morning. She kept saying over and over that she used the phone that J.D.'s father gave her. Like that matters? Why didn't she take some responsibility for bullying a kid? And my friend?"

Maybe because Mrs. McCord knew that the phone had done more than simply send a few ugly texts. She was sleeping with J.D.'s father, after all. Maybe Mrs. McCord was worried the phone—and those texts—would show she had created the creepy website and was trying to protect her own ass? Maybe J.D.'s father gave it to her purposely because it had belonged to J.D. or something. Perhaps trying to hide evidence of his evil kid's wrongdoing? It was all very, very messed up.

Megan obliterated the zombie village in a relentless attack, all the while wondering what to say. Maybe she'd watched too many cop dramas. How would she know why Mrs. McCord did anything?

"That's messed up, Bailey. I don't know if this helps or anything, but keep in mind that's her. Not you. My mom is a loser of the first order, right? She adopted me with my dad and then left him because it was too much work. She never calls. She never comes by. And that's a good thing because I don't need that kind of mother, one who walks away. Realizing that helps me love my dad more when he's smothering me with helmets and sunscreen. He cares. And your mom obviously cares about you or she wouldn't have stuck around for eighteen years."

"Maybe. I don't know." Bailey snorted, then sniffled again, her voice small. "How can you defend her? She said you should do us a favor and die, didn't she? She could, like, go to jail."

Megan cocked her head to the side, thinking. She had been so hurt by those texts, but maybe more so because she'd been afraid they'd been from Bailey. A person she'd trusted. Knowing an adult had sent them was a relief in a way. And made her realize how pathetic the texts were.

"Maybe Mr. Covington told her what to say. I don't know. Whatever mistakes she's made, she's going to pay for them. With the cops and with your dad. Maybe she'll realize what she did was wrong and feel bad about it." Megan's game ended and a screen popped up adding points to her overall total. A few online players started gabbing and arranging another round, but she ignored them. "Do you think the cops are any closer to figuring out who posted that webpage?" Had Mrs. McCord done that, too?

The sooner something happened on this case, the quicker Megan would be able to have a life again. She could see Wade outside of work. She wanted to tell him about the bulletin board at the police station with its ad for a program to finish high school and earn freshman college credits, plus a scholarship for cop training. She'd shoved it in her purse, but she didn't want to give it to him at work. She wanted to see him again. For real.

"I don't know. But it sounds like J.D.'s dad turned out to be as much of a prince as his son, because he screamed at my mom when she broke up with him."

Megan sighed. Bailey had gotten a restraining order against J.D. when they'd split since things had gotten physical between them a couple of times. Mostly shoving, Bailey said. The police were keeping an extra eye on Bailey's house.

"How's your dad doing with all this stuff going on?" Megan asked.

"He's moving out. He invited me to go with him if I want to go back to his hometown of Juneau, Alaska."

Hey, Bruiser12?

A chat window opened on the video game screen. Someone obviously wanted to talk to her privately.

Megan typed a question mark back.

"Juneau?" That was like the end of the earth. And cold, too. She felt terrible for Bailey. This whole mess was turning out to be worse for her than it had been for Megan. "I'm sorry."

A response filled the chat window.

It's Sylvia. From guitar. Meeting Ms. Finley for a send-off for her audition and to jam. You're invited! Darcy's Doughnuts on the exit just north of Heartache. Noon tomorrow.

The chat box closed as SweetSylvia signed off.

Megan would kill to have some rehearsal time before the talent show. And it would be really cool to wish Ms. Finley well before her big audition. Sylvia had graduated two years ago and she'd been in Nashville for the last few months. Megan had chatted with her online a few times after Ms. Finley shared some of Sylvia's demo tapes.

"It all sucks." Bailey sniffled again. "Thanks for being cool about my mom. I've been embarrassed to tell you, but I know you're anxious for your confinement to be lifted, and with this new evidence, the cops will probably tell you it's safe to go out, right?"

A bright side for sure.

"Well, I was embarrassed for the world to see I supposedly went to Slutsville Academy and gave blow jobs on the street for bargain prices, but I'm determined to survive it." Thinking about the website—and the fact that her father knew all about it—still made her want to throw up. "It helps having friends who don't judge me, so I'm glad I can be that friend for you, too."

"My mom is calling me." Bailey's voice trembled. "I'm going to that talent show to see you and I'm going to cheer really loud."

"That'd be great. And Bailey? Thanks for telling me the truth."

"That's what real friends are supposed to do, protect each other. I'll see you later."

"Later." Disconnecting the call, Megan clutched the ugly phone for a second and thought about how good it was to have a friend after how horrible things had been at school. But her life was changing now. She had the talent show coming up. And now she had this chance for a jam session with musicians she really respected. That is, if she could sneak out for an hour or two tomorrow.

She didn't know where they could play at a doughnut shop, but maybe there was a back room or the weather would be nice and they could take the guitars outside. Either way, Megan would find a way to escape her house and play the music that had been her lifeline during the nightmare of the last few months.

THE NEXT DAY, Zach reviewed the police records with Sam in the mayor's office, hoping to find enough evidence to make an arrest in Megan's case now that Tiffany McCord had confessed to sending the texts.

Surprised the hell out of him. He'd known she was an ambitious woman who wouldn't mind running the town, but he never would have pegged her for threatening a teenage girl. But she'd denied creating the website she'd referenced in one of the texts she sent. She claimed she merely knew of the website because Jeremy Covington—her secret lover, by the way—had shown it to her. Tiffany claimed not to like Megan because she'd dated Bailey's boyfriend at one time. Tiffany hoped that rattling Megan would hasten Dan Bryer to leave town as a protective measure, and she thought that would be a good thing since she and Dan were frequently at odds on the town council and Tiffany needed a power base for when she ran for mayor.

Meglomaniac much?

Zach found her to be seriously messed up, but he didn't believe she'd posted the website about Megan, and he knew she wasn't the person who'd attacked his sister. And Zach still thought that whoever hassled Megan was the same person who'd hurt Gabriella.

He wanted an arrest that would satisfy his need to throw Gabriella's attacker behind bars. Because something told him there was a commonality there. Even though Megan's ex-boyfriend J.D. couldn't be guilty in both cases, his father was old enough. Could Jeremy Covington have stalked Zach's sister? The guy had been masked. Sam hadn't been able to identify him.

Right now, Zach's sister was in the front office with the town secretary, an old friend from school, since Sam wouldn't let her stay at the house by herself. The press conference had gone as smoothly as could be expected, although a few members of the local media had wanted more details on the drug that the former mayor had purchased for his wife. Thankfully, Dan Bryer had been present and had reminded the townspeople of privacy laws regarding Mrs. Finley's illness, and something about his forceful speech had made the more gung-ho media members wind up their questions. The public in attendance had seemed satisfied with the answers and their former mayor's actions. After the press conference finished, Zach had stayed to work on the case with Sam without outside distractions.

It was better than thinking about Heather leaving town. She'd attended the press conference and kept her goodbye light. Fast.

Superficial.

He didn't mind that she'd left town to pursue her dreams nearly as much as he minded that she wouldn't think about a future that involved him. She'd opened up a door to let him into her life, but if he didn't walk through it on her terms, she didn't have a backup plan that included both their dreams. Nor was she interested in discussing it.

"Damn it." He whipped his pencil across the room, watching it sail end over end until it hit the opposite wall and landed with a bounce on the hardwood.

They'd been working for almost an hour, but he was so tired of looking at bits of evidence that didn't add up.

"You're not the only one pissed off about this," Sam reminded him from his seat at the small conference table. He pointed to the bunch of papers scattered in front of him.

"It's not just the stalker." Shoving back from his desk, Zach pounded a fist on the wall behind him, no closer to real answers or concrete evidence in either case. "Heather left."

"I heard she was going to leave as soon as her father was cleared." Sam used a magnifying glass to check out some old black-and-white photos.

Zach stared at him. "You knew?"

"I get my ice cream at the Tastee-Freez, too." He laid down the magnifying glass. "I know it sucks that she left, but for what it's worth, I don't see her staying away for long. Her sister-in-law is lobbying hard for her to remain in town and play at their new restaurant."

"Really?" Zach frowned, wondering why Heather never mentioned it.

Maybe because she'd known all along she didn't want that kind of small-town gig.

"Yeah. But her brother owns that bar in Nashville. My money is on her coming back and spending half her time in Nashville like Mack does."

"I don't think she likes letting her family give her any help." Zach wondered if she'd said one word to any of them about her health condition.

He hated that she had no support for that.

"Maybe this audition will give her the confidence she needs to see that she's actually helping *them*." Sam waved a sheaf of papers at him. "Take a look at this."

Zach picked up a foam basketball he kept in a

corner of the office and shot it into the hoop over the closet door on his way to the conference table.

"That's fairly astute psychology about Heather's confidence, Samuel." Zach clapped his friend on the shoulder. "I hope to hell you're right."

Not that it meant Heather would suddenly fall into his lap and be his for the rest of his days. Because at this point, Zach knew that's what he wanted.

Heather. Forever.

Sam rubbed his jaw. "I've been looking for commonalities in the incident reports from roads that back up to Jeremy Covington's quarry—everything from traffic mishaps to lost kids and drag races." He slapped a hand on one fat manila folder. "These are from the interstate." He patted another folder. "These are from local reports from the quarry road."

"And?" Zach took a seat at the conference table, his focus shifting to the investigation. "Anything stand out for you? These are a lot of incidents."

"Deserted roads attract more vagrants, illegal campers, dumping, drag racers, that kind of thing. But even after weeding out that stuff, we have a significant volume of reports."

"Several accidents." Zach thumbed through some of them. And frowned. "A lot of young female drivers."

"An inordinate number." Sam leaned back in

his chair and grabbed the foam basketball that Zach had left behind. He pitched it over his head and caught it a few times. "I double-checked the stats on that type of thing."

"The reasons are that the sign was out for that sharp curve. Drivers out of gas. Hitting a large rock." The wording on some of the reports set off warning bells.

"Right." Sam nodded. "Gabriella went up there because she thought she was meeting a friend. She missed the curve because the sign was down, and next thing you know, she's totally vulnerable up there."

Zach's chest hurt. "Thank God you were there."

"She was underage and had no business driving." Sam had followed her that night because he'd been worried but had told Zach he'd been scared to try to make her pull over because he didn't want her to panic and get in an accident.

She'd gotten in an accident anyway, which hadn't been the worst of the ordeal. A masked man had been waiting, as if he knew exactly where that accident would happen. As if he'd taken the sign down.

"Heather ran out of gas on the interstate the night after the wedding," he remembered, his skin going cold. "She hit a rock and told me she was glad to see me because she heard someone in the woods."

"So what if our guy isn't just a stalker, he's also

a scattergun shooter, seeing who ends up alone and vulnerable in a place he knows well. Which puts Covington or anyone who works at the quarry front and center." Sam pointed to a third folder. "I'm starting another file of cases where a girl was sexually assaulted or feared being sexually assaulted by someone she met on the road."

There weren't many, Zach noted. And the MOs were different. It was too dark to describe the guy. Or the guy wore a cartoon mask. Or a hoodie. There were no weapons involved.

"These span over a decade."

"Carefully under the radar. And not necessarily stalker victims."

"That we know of." Zach stood, a bad feeling making his gut sink. "I'm calling Heather. She's on her way out of town right now. Your guys are watching Megan Bryer?"

"I don't have that kind of manpower," Sam admitted with a wince. "But her father was going to keep her close to home other than work and school. You really think Jeremy Covington could be our guy?" Sam paused. "There aren't many people who've worked at the quarry for more than five years besides him. And there was less internet stalking back when your sister received those messages. Yet the quarry was hardwired for service even then."

Sam frowned. "Maybe if we read the messages,

we'd find something to link old cases and new cases. Syntax. Turns of phrase. Something."

But Zach had other concerns as he listened to Heather's cell phone ring and ring before going to voice mail.

"My sixth sense or whatever it is that makes the hair on your neck stand up is tingling like mad." Zach stared at his cell phone and redialed. "She's not answering."

"I'll call Megan." Sam pulled out his phone. Punched in numbers.

And waited.

Zach's sixth sense buzzed louder.

He swore.

"We still don't know who our guy is," Sam pointed out, stabbing numbers on the office phone, obviously trying a different line.

"Doesn't matter. We'll know when we catch his ass, if we have to put cameras all over that quarry. Why the hell isn't she picking up?" Heather's phone went straight to voice mail again.

"You really think someone's after her?" Sam asked. Then he put his head down to speak into the desk phone. "Dan, hello. It's Sam Reyes from the sheriff's— Excuse me? Sir, slow down."

Zach didn't wait to find out what was happening at Megan Bryer's house. He called Bethany Finley's house. When no one answered there, he searched online for a number for Diana Finley. And called.

"Mrs. Finley, it's Zach Chance. I'm worried about Heather and can't reach her, but I remember she talked about stopping in Nashville to pick up her friend Sylvia. Do you know how to reach Sylvia or what her last name might be?" He clicked the call to speaker so Sam could hear what she had to say.

"Sylvia Hauf. I don't have a number or an address, but she was a year ahead of my granddaughter, Ally, in school, and she was one of Heather's best students." She paused. "Mayor, can I tell you something without you thinking I'm a crazy old woman?"

"I know you're not crazy or old, Mrs. Finley. Please do."

"That Jeremy Covington practically salivated on my Heather when she walked by him at Erin's wedding. I know you're looking for a troublemaker at the quarry, and if you ask me, it's that man right there."

Zach wanted to ask her how she'd seen that when she'd hidden in the house all day, but getting ahold of Sylvia Hauf and finding Heather was more important.

"Thank you, ma'am. And if you hear from Heather, please call me."

"Likewise, young man. I'm counting on you to be sure she's safe."

"I won't let you down." He disconnected the call and did a quick internet search for Sylvia

Hauf. "I need a phone and address on this woman," he said to Sam when the sheriff got off the phone with Dan Bryer. He showed Sam his cell so he could see the social media profile of Heather's former student.

"Megan's missing," Sam informed him, feeding the information on Sylvia into a tablet. The all-business cop look on Sam's face was an ominous portent. "Her dad says he realized it a few minutes before I contacted him. He was in the backyard yelling her name while we talked. Her car is gone."

Zach told himself to shut down the emotions making his blood run cold. Heather and Megan needed him to focus right now.

"APB on the car. Helicopter over the quarry?" he suggested.

"Definitely." Sam barked orders into a police radio, then turned the tablet toward Zach while he held his hand over the mouthpiece on his radio. "Turns out Sylvia's in rehab. Her last-known number is this." He indicated the digits on the screen. "I need to get to the station to coordinate this. I'll bring Gabriella with me."

"How long has the woman been in rehab?" The ground gave way beneath his feet. His whole world would topple if anything happened to Heather. "Are you sure this is accurate? Could she be getting released today?"

"Looks like a court-appointed stint for heroin

and she's done two weeks of a four-week bid. No way is she out and using her phone to arrange a meeting with Heather."

Zach swore. "Someone jacked her profile. Did I mention that J.D. is excellent with computers? It's his only good subject in school." He grabbed his keys, trying to make the pieces fit. J.D. was too young to be Gabriella's stalker. But he might be helping his father. "I'm going to the station with you and I'm getting in the fastest squad car you have. You can arrest me for misuse of equipment when I find her."

"Fuck that." Sam scooped up his tablet. "Gabriella can stay here. We'll take your Porsche and I'll put my badge in the window. No one's getting arrested today except a stalker."

CHAPTER NINETEEN

IMPATIENT, HEATHER TAPPED her foot inside the fifties-themed doughnut shop just outside town shortly past noon.

She'd ordered two doughnuts and bought two coffees for the road, but now she needed to get back on the road. Yes, she desperately wanted company for the ride to Charlotte. Needed someone to keep her spirits up and assure her she hadn't made the biggest mistake of her life by walking away from Zach Chance. But Sylvia was a newly minted adult and maybe didn't fully appreciate what a big break this was for Heather. How the hell could she be late when they needed to get on the road? Heather's nerves grew more frayed by the minute, especially since she hadn't received a confirmation note from Sylvia this morning.

Giving up, she headed back outside. She debated hopping in her car and driving away, but first she walked around the back of the restaurant. She'd gotten some food here a long time ago with her family and remembered there were picnic tables in the back. She stopped. Not anymore, but there were a couple of parking spots. There was a plain white service van in one spot, and in the other, a car she could have sworn belonged to Megan Bryer.

Suddenly, a plastic hood was shoved down on her head. Darkness enveloped her. She dropped the coffee and doughnuts, and her hands scrabbled at the hood to tear it off.

She wheeled backward as the plastic was yanked hard. The material sealed to her lips and nose, choking her so that when she inhaled, she pulled the garbage bag-like material into her mouth. She would pass out in a minute between the pressure of the plastic squeezing her windpipe and the bag closing her nose and mouth. She heard a scream, muffled swearing and brakes squealing right before she was kicked in the back.

She fell on top of a body. A body that moved, thank God. The feminine form beneath her squealed but didn't try to shove her off.

The hand that had been holding the bag over her head was gone. She used the freedom to shake her head hard and dislodge the thing from her airway.

Precious, precious oxygen flowed into her lungs before she turned herself to slide off the person she'd landed on. Her shoulder hit cold metal. She tore the bag off her head and found Megan Bryer lying next to her inside the back of a van, her mouth duct-taped. Shock froze Heather for a moment before she lurched forward to help.

"Oh, my God, Megan." She put an arm around the girl and tugged at the tape with her other hand.

Only then did she realize that Megan was staring out the back of the van at the fight in the parking lot. Sam Reyes had a big boot in another person's back. A person who was… J. D. Covington?

Horror had her reaching for Megan's hand. She squeezed it as she watched the teen face down in the gravel. Until Zach stumbled into her line of view, grappling with another man.

Jeremy. She couldn't believe her eyes.

Her mayor punched town council member Jeremy Covington in the face. The gut. The jaw. Heather couldn't believe a long-time member of the town board had done this. With a teenage son as an accomplice, no less. She squeezed Megan tighter to comfort them both.

Zach's last jaw punch knocked Jeremy to the ground. Sam wasted no time tossing a pair of handcuffs at Zach. Heather sat up, dragging Megan to sit with her.

"Are you okay?" Heather pulled her eyes off Zach to check over Megan, scared for what might have happened before she arrived. Looking for signs of trauma, she realized the girl's wrists were taped together behind her back. "Did they hurt you?"

She tore at the tape and freed Megan's wrists.

"No." Her lips trembled. "There was no time. They grabbed me just a minute before they got you. I thought I was supposed to meet you here. I got a message—"

Clapping erupted. A group of diners had gathered to watch Zach and Sam save the day. Zach's Porsche sat in the middle of the action, a red-and-blue light flashing in the windshield.

Jeremy wore handcuffs now, his face pressed against the gravel parking lot and the coffee Heather had spilled. Sam ordered the appreciative crowd to stand back, but a short, curvy woman with pink-and-blue-plaid nursing scrubs ignored him and ran for the van.

"I'm a nurse," she called, waving a stethoscope from her pocket as if it was an ID badge. "Are you all right?"

"I'm fine," Heather insisted, and gestured to Megan. "She might be in shock, though."

Then again, maybe she was, too.

Everything around her seemed to move in slow motion. She should be helping somehow. Calling Megan's father. Reassuring the girl. But she was too stunned and shook up. Where was Sylvia? Was her friend okay?

But no sooner had she remembered her friend than she spotted Zachary Chance sprinting her way. His shirt was torn. His lip cut. Every knuckle on his right hand torn open and bleeding.

He was the most welcome sight ever, and it felt like decades since she'd seen him, instead of hours. She wanted to throw herself at him and weep with gratitude—for this and about a thousand other things.

"Did they hurt you?" Zach's eyes missed nothing as he slowed his step and tipped up her face to examine her. "Are you okay?"

"Never better." The words were true. Her heart was so full it nearly burst her chest open wide.

His relief was palpable. Wiry tension hissed out of him with a deep sigh, and he pulled her into his arms for a hug that was way too fast. Maybe it was because of the crowd around them that he set her aside awkwardly.

"How on earth did you know where to find me?" She couldn't imagine what would have tipped them off to her whereabouts, much less that she was in trouble. "I was supposed to meet my friend, Sylvia. I'm worried they hurt her."

"Sylvia's fine. I spoke with her on the phone on the way here. She never contacted you. We'll get ahold of the Covingtons' computers and we'll find evidence they hacked Sylvia's online credentials to impersonate her."

Heather tried to follow what he was saying, but she was still so rattled. They stayed close to Megan in the back of the van while the timely

Good Samaritan checked her over and spoke to her quietly. Heather wasn't letting the girl out of her sight until she was back with her father.

Zach stroked her hair. "We called for helicopter support when we started putting some pieces together. But Harlan Brady has a CB radio on the farm, and when he heard the call, he fired up the crop duster and started searching on his own."

Heather shook her head. "I believe it. There are some pretty amazing people in Heartache. And it's going to be better now that we've weeded out these two." She frowned, her brain fuzzy. "I don't understand why Jeremy Covington would target me."

"Opportunity, maybe?" Zach shrugged. "Sam will investigate. We'll learn more now that we have enough reason to gather evidence from the quarry and his house. But we're guessing he's been increasing his activity over the years and getting sloppier at it."

"Hey." Megan scooted closer to them, a bit less shaky. Her voice was steadier as she interjected.

"How are you doing?" Heather asked. "Hanging in there?" She scrubbed a comforting hand along the girl's arm.

"I should have known it wasn't Sylvia." Megan angled her shoulders around the nurse who was wrapping a second blanket about the teen's shoulders. "She hardly ever plays mutant zombies, but when a chat window opened after the game, she—well, someone—invited me here. She said we were going to jam for a little while and give you a proper send-off for the audition."

"I would have liked that," Heather admitted, shuddering with how close they'd come to...so much worse. "But from now on, I'm arranging all meetings with human beings I speak to."

Another police siren wailed in the distance, growing louder as it neared them.

"Excuse me, sir," the nurse said. "I can clean up your fingers for you so they don't get infected."

"I'll wrap them at home, but thank you." He pointed to Heather. "Does she look okay to you?"

The nurse studied her, eyes lingering on Heather's forehead. "Looks like she might have a bruise. But other than that, I'd say she's in good shape. I think the girl is okay, too. Lucky for them you were here." She smiled at Zach.

Heather grinned at the flirtatious tone in the woman's voice. Who wouldn't want Heartache's mayor?

"Well, thank you." He nodded politely at the woman and then slid an arm around Heather. "I'd better get her home to her mother. I promised I'd return her in one piece."

"You spoke to my mom?" Heather tipped her head into his shoulder, so grateful to feel the warmth of him close to her.

"I called to see if she knew where you were. She told me Jeremy Covington was drooling on you at Erin's wedding reception."

"My mother doesn't miss much." Heather remembered all that Diana Finley had observed from her window overlooking the reception.

The police car arrived and the cop turned into the driveway. J.D. and Jeremy were read their rights and put into the squad car. In the meantime, a tow truck arrived—one of the Elliotts' vehicles, but it wasn't an Elliott behind the wheel.

Megan seemed to recognize the young man, though, since she threw off the blanket and bounded into his arms. Her father was in the passenger seat, and it took him a bit longer to clamber out of the monstrous truck. By the time he did, Megan broke free from the boy to hug her crying father.

"Dan Bryer sure does love his daughter." Heather swiped a tear from her eye, thinking she hadn't gotten enough hugs from her dad, but she had adored him just the same.

"Wade Sanderson seems pretty fond of Megan, too." Zach laid his cheek on Heather's head, and she wanted to stay like that forever, his one arm around her waist, the warmth of his shoulder right where she could kiss it.

"I hope he's a good boy. She needs a good one after J.D." She lifted her head, her muddled brain clearing a little. "Zach, do you think there's any chance that Jeremy Covington was the one who attacked Gabriella?"

"If there's any evidence of it in a computer, I

guarantee we'll find it. And we've got a statement on file from Sam—something he logged with his old police chief in San Jose. There's a dated record of the brawl he got into to save my sister. He made notes about the types of injury he inflicted on the perp. We might be able to use it to check for scars or doctor visits Covington made around the same time. It would be circumstantial, but it would build the case." His jaw tightened. "My gut says yes, it was him."

Heather hadn't fully understood how invested Zach had been in finding his sister's attacker.

"If he was the one who tried to hurt Gabriella, he'll be sent away for a long time." She had faith in Heartache's sheriff, who seemed to have the crime scene well in hand.

She also had a lot of faith in Mayor Chance. He probably had more training in digital forensics than anyone else in Tennessee. If there was any scrap of digital evidence that Covington had stalked Gabriella online, he'd unearth it.

Zach held out his cell phone. "Do you want to call your mother and tell her you're okay or would you like me to?"

Just then, one of the sheriff's deputies interrupted.

"Excuse me, Ms. Finley? Sheriff Reyes asked me to take your statement, if you're feeling well enough."

She nodded, reluctant to leave Zach but eager

to get this over with so she could be with him. "I am." She touched his arm, gathering strength from him—this man she loved and could have lost today. "Would you mind calling her while I give a statement so we can finish up faster? I might ask you for a ride home, if it's not too much trouble. I'm a little too shaky to drive."

Another clipped nod was her only answer, making her wonder if she was giving him too little, too late. One thing was certain. She wasn't giving up Zach Chance again without a fight. Even before she'd been attacked, she'd been second-guessing her decision.

And now she knew.

Her dream had shifted. And no dream was good enough that didn't include Zach.

ZACH HIT THE horn as he drove past Heather's mom's house that night.

Heather arched an eyebrow at him from the passenger seat.

"You and my mom seem to have a friendly accord," she noted.

The bruise on her forehead had darkened, making him angry to think about how close she'd come to...he didn't know what. Rape? Worse? Federal investigators were going to take a look at the case since some of the crimes around the quarry had taken place along the interstate. That would speed things along and give them additional support to build the case against the Covingtons. Gabriella, he knew, would finally come forward with her own statement. They'd discussed it the night before.

"Your mother was clearheaded and articulate in a crisis." Zach pulled into the short driveway in front of Heather's bungalow and jogged around to her side of the car to help her out. "She played a huge part in helping put me right where I needed to be today. I owe her a debt forever."

"I'm so grateful. To both of you. And Sam, too." She pulled her door keys from her bag and passed them to him, their fingers brushing, her eyes holding his.

He liked opening doors for her. Being with her. Calling her mom on the phone. Yeah, he was really far gone on this woman. Sam would mock him for the rest of his life.

But Zach didn't care. He just wanted to make things right between them.

"Let me get the lights." He slipped past her to flick the switches so she could see where she was going. Wherever she was, he wanted to be there, too—on so many levels. "I won't stay if you want to sleep, but it would make me happy as hell to watch over you tonight. I think I might have nightmares unless I spend twenty-four hours straight just staring at you and knowing you're okay."

"I want you here." She dropped her bag onto a

table and toed the door shut with one foot. "More than anything."

She slid her arms around his neck and he told himself to go slow. Talk through every facet of what was happening between them so they understood what they were getting into. And how tomorrow was going to go. This time, there would be no surprises. No backing away from what they'd started.

Or if they did, they'd be backing away knowing they'd given it their all.

"Heather, I don't want you to miss the audition because of that bastard. If you feel well enough, I can charter a private plane and get you there in two hours. You could still make the audition."

"I don't want to go." She shook her head. Her body sealed to his, making thoughts more difficult.

Still, he persevered.

"I don't blame you if you're tired and stressed. But there's another audition option next month in New Orleans, right?" Gently, he smoothed her hair off her cheek, tilting her chin so the moonlight from a high window shone on her creamy skin.

"I don't need to go then, either." Her lips grazed his cheek. The scent of her shampoo made his knees a little weak.

"Why? You can't turn your back on a dream because of this. You don't want to live with regrets."

"I'll tell you why." Releasing him, she stepped back to slip off her shoes.

She stood in front of him in a filmy white blouse and blue-and-white-gingham capri pants with a dirt smudge on the knee. She looked beautiful, but he couldn't wait to burn the blouse, which had a man's boot print between the shoulder blades.

Zach hadn't recovered from seeing Jeremy kick Heather. It was the first thing his eyes had homed in on when Sam had pulled into the diner's parking lot after receiving a call from Harlan and Ethan Brady saying they'd spotted Heather's car. The old man had flown the ancient crop-dusting plane while his grandson had hung out the side using binoculars to search the area. Zach was seriously considering giving the kid the Porsche for Christmas.

"I've held on to the dream of performing my whole adult life. It's a good dream, and it helped me to hone my music and become a better singer and performer." The words flowed easily from her mouth. "I'll always be grateful that dream gave my talent focus and passion. But I realized today that it wasn't the right dream anymore for where I am in my life."

"Heather, you're incredibly talented."

"I know." She gestured for him to sit on the couch. "Not to brag, but I do know. I could get on that show, and maybe even win. But I don't want a life where the focus is on fame more than the music. I'm a musician. I want to entertain. Play. Sing. But I'm also a good teacher, and I don't want to turn my back on that. Because the only thing better than making good music is helping other people make good music."

Zach felt the rightness of the plan. It protected her health, in addition to helping her use her gifts. But would it be enough for her? He knew it was more than enough for him. Now that Gabriella was finally going to report what had happened to her, and there was a chance they already had her stalker in custody, Zach felt as if he could move forward with his own life. He was more than ready.

"What do you see as the right dream now?" Zach hoped against hope that his name came up often in this next part.

It was killing him not to drag her to bed and adore every inch of her. But he needed to make sure they had a plan. That she could be happy in a future that involved him.

"I'm not entirely sure. But I want you in my life all the time, so I'd like to sit with that idea for a while and figure out how I can have more music in my life and you, too."

Zach opened his mouth to say how much he loved her. How much he wanted her in his life, too. But the day had been too emotional, and he didn't trust himself to speak. The pressure on his chest clogged his throat, making him…

He pulled her into his arms. Covered her face with kisses. Possibly a tear or two, but if she noticed, she was too sweet to say so. He pulled her onto his lap and held her tight, burying his face in her hair.

"I love you so much, Heather Finley." God, what had he ever done to deserve her? He wasn't sure, but he intended to do his best to be worthy of her trust.

"I love you, too, Mayor." She kissed all over his face, happiness pouring out of her. Radiant.

"We're going to come up with the best dreams." He touched her with a reverence he knew he would always feel. "And then we're going to make them all come true."

"I have one that involves my bed," she whispered very irreverently in his ear, her kisses as damp as his.

He liked the sound of that. "I have one that involves getting you naked. See how well those two go together already?"

"We're really good at this." She wound her arms around his neck.

He scooped her off the couch and headed for the stairs leading to her loft, where her bed shone in a moonbeam spotlight.

"It's only going to get better," he promised, a promise he would work every day to keep.

"Have I told you lately you make the best campaign speeches?" She traced his mouth, careful of the cut on his lip.

"Did I tell you how the mayor is assigned absolute power in times of crisis?" He climbed the stairs slowly, savoring every moment of having her all to himself.

Forever.

"You might have mentioned it. But I do love seeing you exert your authority, so why don't you remind me what that entails."

Settling her in the middle of the bed, Zach admired her right where he'd wanted for a long, long time. Yanking off his shirt, he tossed it to the floor.

"How about I show you instead?"

* * * * *

LARGER-PRINT BOOKS!
GET 2 FREE LARGER-PRINT NOVELS PLUS
2 FREE GIFTS!

HARLEQUIN®

Romance

From the Heart, For the Heart

LARGER-PRINT
BOOKS!

HARLEQUIN

Presents

PASSION
GUARANTEED
SEDUCTION

GET 2 FREE LARGER-PRINT
NOVELS PLUS 2 FREE GIFTS!

YES! Please send me 2 FREE LARGER-PRINT Harlequin Presents® novels and my 2 FREE gifts (gifts are worth about $10). After receiving them, if I don't wish to receive any more books, I can return the shipping statement marked "cancel." If I don't cancel, I will receive 6 brand-new novels every month and be billed just $5.30 per book in the U.S. or $5.74 per book in Canada. That's a saving of at least 12% off the cover price! It's quite a bargain! Shipping and handling is just 50¢ per book in the U.S. and 75¢ per book in Canada.* I understand that accepting the 2 free books and gifts places me under no obligation to buy anything. I can always return a shipment and cancel at any time. Even if I never buy another book, the two free books and gifts are mine to keep forever.

176/376 HDN GHVY

Name   (PLEASE PRINT)

Address   Apt. #

City   State/Prov.   Zip/Postal Code

Signature (if under 18, a parent or guardian must sign)

Mail to the **Reader Service:**
IN U.S.A.: P.O. Box 1867, Buffalo, NY 14240-1867
IN CANADA: P.O. Box 609, Fort Erie, Ontario L2A 5X3

Are you a subscriber to Harlequin Presents® books
and want to receive the larger-print edition?
Call 1-800-873-8635 today or visit us at www.ReaderService.com.

* Terms and prices subject to change without notice. Prices do not include applicable taxes. Sales tax applicable in N.Y. Canadian residents will be charged applicable taxes. Offer not valid in Quebec. This offer is limited to one order per household. Not valid for current subscribers to Harlequin Presents Larger-Print books. All orders subject to credit approval. Credit or debit balances in a customer's account(s) may be offset by any other outstanding balance owed by or to the customer. Please allow 4 to 6 weeks for delivery. Offer available while quantities last.

Your Privacy—The Reader Service is committed to protecting your privacy. Our Privacy Policy is available online at www.ReaderService.com or upon request from the Reader Service.

We make a portion of our mailing list available to reputable third parties that offer products we believe may interest you. If you prefer that we not exchange your name with third parties, or if you wish to clarify or modify your communication preferences, please visit us at www.ReaderService.com/consumerchoice or write to us at Reader Service Preference Service, P.O. Box 9062, Buffalo, NY 14240-9062. Include your complete name and address.

READERSERVICE.COM

Manage your account online!

- Review your order history
- Manage your payments
- Update your address

We've designed the Reader Service website just for you.

Enjoy all the features!

- Discover new series available to you, and read excerpts from any series.
- Respond to mailings and special monthly offers.
- Connect with favorite authors at the blog.
- Browse the Bonus Bucks catalog and online-only exculsives.
- Share your feedback.

Visit us at:

ReaderService.com

RS15